S0-AHF-348

"ABOUT LAST NIGHT."

Watchful gray eyes flew to Miles's face. "You promised it would be our secret."

"Aren't you curious?"

It was a moment or two before Alyssa confessed in a husky voice, "Yes, I am."

"Was it the moonlight? Was it the summer night? Or the scent of the roses? Or was it simply us? You and me?"

She licked her lips. "I have wondered."

"As have I." Miles cupped her chin with his hand. Her skin was soft and surprisingly warm. "You understand that I have to know," he insisted.

Her eyes grew huge. "I understand."

He wasn't going to make the same mistake twice. There would be no polite pecks on the cheek. No fleeting brush of his lips across hers. By God, if he was going to kiss the lady, then he was going to do it right!

Miles swooped down and captured Alyssa's mouth with his. It hadn't been the moonlight, or the garden with its exotic fragrances. It had been only Alyssa. Dear God, he would like nothing better than to divest her lovely body of its clothing. He wanted to touch her, taste her, tease her—until she begged him to take her there on the cold stone floor of the grotto.

"Funny, furious, titillating, and tender."
—Stella Cameron,
bestselling author of *Pure Delights*

◆◆ TOPAZ

DANGEROUS DESIRE

☐ **DIAMOND IN THE ROUGH by Suzanne Simmons.** Juliet Jones, New York's richest heiress, could have her pick of suitors. But she was holding out for a treasure of a different kind: a husband who would love her for more than just her money. Lawrence, the eighth Duke of Deakin, needed to wed a wealthy American to save his ancestral estate. Now these two warring opposites are bound together in a marriage of convenience. (403843—$4.99)

☐ **FALLING STARS by Anita Mills.** In a game of danger and desire where the stakes are shockingly high, the key cards are hidden, and love holds the final startling trump, Kate Winstead must choose between a husband she does not trust and a libertine lord who makes her doubt herself. (403657—$4.99)

☐ **SWEET AWAKENING by Marjorie Farrell.** Lord Justin Rainsborough dazzled lovely Lady Clare Dysart with his charm and intoxicated her with his passion. Only when she was bound to him in wedlock did she discover his violent side ... the side of him that led to his violent demise. Lord Giles Whitton, Clare's childhood friend, was the complete opposite of Justin. But it would take a miracle to make her feel anew the sweet heat of desire—a miracle called love. (404920—$4.99)

☐ **LORD HARRY by Catherine Coulter.** When Henrietta Rolland discovers that a notorious rake, Jason Cavander, is responsible for her brother's death at Waterloo, she sets out to avenge her dead brother. Henrietta disguises herself as the fictitious Lord Harry Monteith, hoping to fool Cavander and challenge him to a duel. But the time comes when all pretenses are stripped away, as Henrietta and Jason experience how powerful true love can be. (405919—$5.99)

Prices slightly higher in Canada

Buy them at your local bookstore or use this convenient coupon for ordering.

PENGUIN USA
P.O. Box 999 — Dept. #17109
Bergenfield, New Jersey 07621

Please send me the books I have checked above.
I am enclosing $_____ (please add $2.00 to cover postage and handling). Send check or money order (no cash or C.O.D.'s) or charge by Mastercard or VISA (with a $15.00 minimum). Prices and numbers are subject to change without notice.

Card #_____ Exp. Date _____
Signature_____
Name_____
Address_____
City _____ State _____ Zip Code _____

For faster service when ordering by credit card call **1-800-253-6476**

Allow a minimum of 4-6 weeks for delivery. This offer is subject to change without notice.

Bed
of
Roses

❧

Suzanne Simmons

A TOPAZ BOOK

TOPAZ
Published by the Penguin Group
Penguin Books USA Inc., 375 Hudson Street,
New York, New York 10014, U.S.A.
Penguin Books Ltd, 27 Wrights Lane,
London W8 5TZ, England
Penguin Books Australia Ltd, Ringwood,
Victoria, Australia
Penguin Books Canada Ltd, 10 Alcorn Avenue,
Toronto, Ontario, Canada M4V 3B2
Penguin Books (N.Z.) Ltd, 182–190 Wairau Road,
Auckland 10, New Zealand

Penguin Books Ltd, Registered Offices:
Harmondsworth, Middlesex, England

First published by Topaz, an imprint of Dutton Signet,
a division of Penguin Books USA Inc.

First Printing, August, 1995
10 9 8 7 6 5 4 3 2 1

Copyright © Suzanne Simmons Guntrum, 1995
All rights reserved

Topaz Man photo © Charles William Bush
Cover art by Gregg Gulbronson

 REGISTERED TRADEMARK—MARCA REGISTRADA

Printed in the United States of America

Without limiting the rights under copyright reserved above, no part of this
publication may be reproduced, stored in or introduced into a retrieval sys-
tem, or transmitted, in any form, or by any means (electronic, mechanical,
photocopying, recording, or otherwise), without the prior written permission
of both the copyright owner and the above publisher of this book.

BOOKS ARE AVAILABLE AT QUANTITY DISCOUNTS WHEN USED TO PROMOTE
PRODUCTS OR SERVICES. FOR INFORMATION PLEASE WRITE TO PREMIUM MAR-
KETING DIVISION, PENGUIN BOOKS USA INC., 375 HUDSON STREET, NEW YORK,
NEW YORK 10014.

If you purchased this book without a cover you should be aware that this
book is stolen property. It was reported as "unsold and destroyed" to the
publisher and neither the author nor the publisher has received any payment
for this "stripped book."

This one is for my son,
Steven,
heart of my heart.

Chapter One

"Do you believe in ghosts, my lord?"

"Ghosts?" Miles Mountbank St. Aldford, the fourth Marquess of Cork, turned in the saddle and looked at his companion.

The man riding beside him elaborated. "Specters. Shades. Phantoms. Apparitions. Disembodied spirits. Souls of the dearly departed. Those on the other side."

He felt his mouth twist into a wry smile. "Those on the other side of *what*?"

"This earthly plane, my lord."

Miles brought his Thoroughbred to a halt in the middle of the country lane. He leaned forward, patted the chestnut's neck, and inquired with a certain grim amusement, "Have you, perchance, been reading *Hamlet* again?"

"No, my lord." Then, with theatrical flair, his man flung wide one hand—the other had momentarily dropped the reins of his mount and was pressed to his breast—and recited in a Tennysonian voice: " 'What beck'ning ghost along the moonlight shades invites my steps and points to yonder glade?' "

"There is no moonlight," Miles pointed out. "Indeed, the rising sun is on the horizon."

"As you say, my lord."

Miles indicated a small clearing surrounded by a copse of trees. "However, I do believe that is a glade." To give credit where credit was due.

"It is a glade."

He raised his eyes. "And that does appear to be the moon just above the treetops."

"It is the moon."

Miles St. Aldford tapped his riding crop against the side of a mud-splattered boot; it had been raining when they left the country inn at an hour well before dawn. "But I see no beckoning ghost."

"Perhaps if you tried to use your imagination, my lord."

Miles gave a short, dry laugh instead.

Another suggestion was almost immediately forthcoming. "Perhaps if you squinted, then, my lord."

"Squinted?"

"Glanced. Gazed. Stared. Peered. Observed. Looked askance. Cocked the eye."

Miles arched one dark eyebrow in a sardonic fashion.

There was a sigh of defeat from his fellow horseman. "Perhaps not, my lord."

Miles had to confess his interest was piqued. "Who is the author, by the by?"

"The author?"

"Writer. Composer. Scribbler. *Cacoethes scribendi.*"

"Alexander Pope."

"I should have known," he said. "The phrase is so . . ."

"Popian?"

"Precisely." Miles paused with his gloved hands on the reins, and after a moment, inquired: "A little something you learned in elocution class?"

"Dramatics, my lord."

Miles suddenly recalled a dramatic ditty from his childhood. It was but one of the legacies left behind at Cork House by a Cornish maid before she'd run off with one of the other servants. She had also introduced Miles, however vicariously, to the pleasures of the flesh. He had watched through a crack in the schoolroom door as she'd "dallied" under the under-butler. It had been a most edifying experience.

He cleared his throat and recited, " 'From ghoulies and ghosties and long-leggety beasties—' "

" 'And from things that go bump in the night—' "

" 'Good Lord, deliver us!' "

His valet persisted. "Do you believe in the existence of spectral phenomena?"

"Why do you ask?"

"Idle curiosity."

It was possible, he supposed. Hortense Horatio Blunt was a curious fellow. "Idle curiosity, Blunt?"

"Rumors, then, my lord."

"Rumors?"

"Gossip. Tittle-tattle. Idle chitchat. Babble. Bandied about. Whispered about."

Miles was becoming impatient; he snapped his riding crop against his boot again. "Whispered about by *whom*? Bandied about *when*? What the devil are you talking about?"

A hint of color crept up Blunt's neck and onto his jaw. "I don't usually listen to gossip, as you well know."

"Apparently you did this time," Miles muttered as they continued on their way. Gathering clouds once again threatened rain.

"I felt it was my duty."

A black eyebrow was crooked in the other man's direction. "In what way?"

"I knew you would not wish to go into a campaign blind."

"This is not a campaign. And I'm not going in blind, or in any other way," Miles insisted. Privately he only hoped it wasn't another of Bertie's ill-conceived schemes. He'd had quite enough of those to last him a lifetime. "How did we get on the subject of ghosts?"

Blunt sat up straighter in the saddle. "I was inquiring whether or not you believed in them."

"So you were."

"Do you?"

"Don't be an ass, Blunt."

"I shall endeavor not to be, my lord."

Miles grumbled under his breath. "We will regard this sojourn in the West Country as a . . ."

"Holiday, my lord?"

He scowled. "Hardly a holiday. I am being sent to Devon on the express orders of my sovereign."

"An honor for any soldier."

"Ex-soldier."

"Surely an honor for an ex-soldier."

"Perhaps." Miles had his doubts. "There are times, however, when I wonder if this is more H.R.H.'s doing than the Queen's."

Blunt's forehead accordioned into a frown. "His Royal Highness's doing?"

"It may be an elaborate practical joke," Miles said, advancing his own theory. "Bertie does like to have his fun at the expense of others." In addition, more than one of Miles's acquaintances was on the verge of financial ruin due to the enormous expense of playing host to the Prince of Wales and his traveling entourage. The Marlborough House Set could, quite literally, eat one out of house and home. "H.R.H. has a decidedly eccentric sense of humor."

"The Prince of Wales must have his diversions."

"I suppose so." His mouth curved derisively. "But investigating the strange goings-on at Graystone Abbey seems to me to be nothing more than a bloody fool's errand. The whole lot at court are enthralled with the supernatural, the occult, the very notion of apparitions. Why, it was only last month that Lady D— invited me to a séance." Miles urged the Thoroughbred along at a slightly faster clip. "Good God, what a farce! Ghosts. Spirits. Pale shades of the once-living. An avenging knight of the Crusades, complete with battle horse and drawn sword. What nonsense. What utter rubbish. What damnable drivel."

"Then you, too, have heard that there is a knightly ghost who haunts the once-hallowed halls of Graystone Abbey."

Miles looked askance at the man who had been his constant companion through two campaigns, several small wars, numerous battles, and countless skirmishes. "The rational man believes half of what he reads and even less of what he hears."

"Yes, my lord," Blunt said dutifully. Then he hemmed and hawed. "If I may inquire, my lord, what are your, ah . . . intentions once we reach our destination?"

"I—we—will spend a few days poking about the abbey before we declare it free of any otherworldly inhabitants, and go on our merry way. The sooner, the better."

They rode over the rise in the road and there before them, in the blue mist of a summer's morn, was a lush green valley, the thatched roofs of a picturesque village, a church spire, and in the distance, in all its medieval splendor, overlooking the valley below, was Graystone Abbey.

"Easy, Bulle Rock," Miles murmured in a soothing tone as he pulled back on the reins. The dark reddish brown Thoroughbred, a direct descendant of the original Darley Arabian brought to England in 1730, raised its sleek head and snorted. Miles gazed out over the landscape. "It is just as I remember it."

Blunt's ears perked up. "Just as you remember it, my lord? I didn't know you had been here before."

"In my youth," he said cryptically.

Blunt seemed to find that amusing. "You are scarcely in your dotage now, my lord."

"I was very young the first *and* last time I was at Graystone Abbey. It was fifteen years ago, a lifetime ago," Miles said in a thoughtful tone that trailed off.

"That was before I entered your service, my lord."

"Yes." It was not a time in his life that he spoke of to anyone. His parents had been reported missing in a treacherous storm at sea and were presumed dead. His grandfather, the third Marquess of Cork, was old and infirm. And he—Miles sighed at the recollection of his own youthful folly—he had been darkly handsome, astonishingly precocious when it came to the ladies, and utterly fearless. The absence of fear, however, was more a matter of swaggering, youthful bravado than courage. Courage would come later on the battlefield.

That summer everyone, from his ailing grandfather to his dear old nanny, who was still living in the west wing of Cork House at the time, from the horsemaster to the lowliest housemaid, had been at a loss as to what to do with him.

He had been incorrigible.

"It was June of 1863," he related to Blunt. "Realizing that I would soon inherit his titles and estates, my grandfather decided to send me here to spend the summer with his old friend, the earl." He ruminated for a minute or two, and his valet waited.

"At the age of fifteen I did not care for life at Graystone Abbey. There was no hunting. No gambling. No drinking. No weekend house parties. No pretty girls. No excitement."

"One cannot expect excitement in the country. I understand it's supposed to be dull," Blunt announced with a perfectly straight face.

Miles laughed darkly. "It was. No doubt it still is. Thomas Gray, the Earl of Graystone, was not at all my sort. He was always reading great, dusty books from his library, and sitting around discussing history and philosophy and ideas of all things."

"Good heavens!" exclaimed Blunt.

"When he wasn't reading or discoursing on some lofty subject, Graystone was out in the gardens, down on his hands and knees, digging in the dirt like a common laborer."

"You don't say."

"I do say. The earl had a pretty young wife—some years younger than he—and a child, too. A daughter. She was a tiny thing with fair hair and fairer skin."

"Lady Alyssa."

"I believe that was her name," he said, rubbing his chin.

"It still is, my lord."

That brought Miles' head around. "How did you come by the information?"

"It was easy enough, my lord. Too easy." Blunt exhaled a great sigh. "Not like the old days when we went to great lengths to obtain information for queen and country."

"Subterfuge."

"Living by our wits."

"Do you recall the time we were sent to Bavaria?"

Blunt sighed again. "Who could forget climbing the Alps?"

Miles waxed nostalgic. "Or the mission when we both dressed like Gypsies and crawled through the woods on our bellies?"

"Those were the good old days, my lord."

"Indeed they were, Blunt."

They rode on. Some minutes later Miles glanced

down at his black coat and black riding breeches. He was covered with flecks of brown mud, as was Blunt. Despite the rain—they had endured far more and far worse than a little rain and a little mud in the service of their country—they preferred traveling by horseback to taking the train. A hired wagon with their luggage was following a discreet distance behind. "You don't suppose we will put anyone off if we appear at the abbey as we are."

"We have been camping under the open skies and the stars as God intended soldiers to do. I am quite certain that the ladies ensconced at Graystone Abbey will be delighted to see us, my lord, whatever our appearance."

Miles' hands shifted on the reins of the Thoroughbred; the horse lifted its sleek reddish brown head alertly. "I hope you're right."

Blunt seemed very sure of himself. "Lady Alyssa is a damsel in distress. She will regard you as her savior, her champion, her knight errant, as, no doubt, will all the people of this valley."

Odd, but Miles found the idea of being perceived as the lady's hero strangely attractive. He couldn't imagine why.

"I wonder how old Lady Alyssa is now," he said, thinking out loud.

"Twenty-one, my lord."

He brushed away a pesky fly. "Hmmm . . . twenty-one." That old. He hadn't realized. "She is on the brink of being a spinster."

"She is very young and very beautiful, and has rejected more suitors than we have fingers and toes," he was summarily informed.

"The lady is capricious?"

"The lady is choosy."

"Perhaps she is simply inconstant in character and does not know her own mind," suggested Miles.

Blunt spoke in a knowing fashion. "I don't think that is the case, my lord. She has been in charge of Graystone Abbey since the death of her father, the earl, and the disappearance of her uncle, who was his brother's heir. A formidable task for any man, let alone a young woman who was no more than nineteen at the time."

"You are a veritable font of information, Blunt."

"Thank you, my lord."

"So the lady is beautiful, intelligent, *and* independent," Miles concluded. "A dangerous combination in a female."

"Perhaps, my lord."

"A woman should be married. It keeps her out of mischief."

"She isn't the only one," Blunt announced boldly.

"You will not harp on the subject of marriage," Miles said, fixing his companion with a reproachful glare. He knew himself to be a rational man, but the mere mention of marriage made him at once foul-tempered, irritable, and irrational.

"The subject cannot be avoided forever," Blunt stated, concentrating on the country road that wound before them like a dark velvet ribbon.

"It can."

"Only if you have decided that your family estates and your title will one day go to a stranger."

"You don't mince words, do you?" Miles said.

"I try not to, my lord."

He found himself making excuses. "I will get around to it. One day. Someday."

"You aren't getting any younger, my lord."

"Just moments ago you were assuring me that I wasn't in my dotage. Now you make me sound as if I have one foot in the grave," he said, grimly amused.

"You are thirty years old, my lord."

"I am well aware of my age, Blunt."

"Even your two best friends are married."

"I presume you speak of the Duke of Deakin and his younger brother, Lord Jonathan."

"I do indeed, my lord."

Miles deliberated, his brows drawn together. "They were most fortunate in their choice of wives."

"I don't believe His Grace or Lord Jonathan thought so in the beginning."

"How in the world—"

"One hears things, my lord."

The man would be impertinent if he weren't so useful. "You have big ears, Blunt."

"Thank you, my lord."

Miles sighed and tried his usual stalling tactics. "Perhaps once we have settled this business in the country."

"You must not put it off too long, my lord, or—"

"Or what?"

"Or you will have to marry a girl young enough to be your daughter in order to find someone suitable."

"Someone suitable?"

"A young lady of appropriate rank and breeding and—"

"Yes?"

"She must be of the highest moral character."

"Naturally."

"She must be above reproach."

"Of course."

"She must be unsullied."

Miles frowned. "Unsullied?"

"She must be a virgin, my lord."

Miles choked on his own saliva.

"That, of course, leaves out the women of your acquaintance, my lord."

"Hell and damnation."

Blunt was, apparently, not to be deterred. "Everyone knows the reputation of the women who run with the Prince of Wales and the Marlborough House Set."

"They are all married."

"To put it diplomatically, my lord, yes—" Blunt lifted his chin a notch higher in the cool morning air of Devon and sniffed disapprovingly, "they are all married."

They both knew full well that many—most—of the men and women of the Marlborough House Set took one lover after another from among their social peers. The Prince of Wales, due to his exalted rank, was given first choice of the ladies.

Blunt drew himself up to his full height in the saddle and finished making his point. "That is why we must look elsewhere." He cleared his throat. "There is always Lady Winifred, the eldest daughter of the Duke of B——"

Miles bestowed a look of disgruntlement upon his companion. "Bad teeth."

"There is Miss W——"

"Too old."

"Lady Margaret?"

"She is barely sixteen."

"Too young," Blunt concluded. "Lady Anne?"

"Too tall."

"Her sister?"

"Too short."

Blunt blew out his breath expressively. "We have been together for nearly fifteen years, my lord. The time to speak plainly has come. I . . . we . . . that is, everyone in your employ . . . wish to see a gracious lady installed as mistress of Cork House. These matters cannot be left to chance. You must take a wife and produce the next Marquess of Cork," he lectured, albeit affectionately.

"I will, Blunt."

"It must be soon, my lord."

"After we see to this matter at the abbey, I promise I will give it my full attention."

"And I will endeavor to keep a sharp eye, my lord."

"A sharp eye for what?"

"For suitable females."

Miles made a face. "Egods, no wonder Lawrence found the prospect distasteful, if not daunting."

"I beg your pardon, my lord."

"I was simply thinking that I could have been more sympathetic when the Duke of Deakin was searching for a suitable duchess."

"Perhaps you should have married an American as he did, my lord," Blunt proposed.

"Surely a desperate measure," Miles said in a low, mocking tone.

"These are desperate times, my lord." Then his man fell silent. "You don't suppose the Queen had an ulterior motive in sending you to Graystone Abbey, do you?"

"I don't follow," Miles admitted.

"Lady Alyssa."

"What about her?"

"She is said to be a paragon, my lord."

"A paragon?" Miles repeated with a faint, cynical smile.

"An angel." Then Blunt added, "A saint."

"I do not wish to marry a paragon or an angel or a bloody saint," he said, his lips curling in a growl. Surely that would bring an end to the discussion.

"Lady Alyssa is also highly suitable, my lord. She comes from an old and distinguished family. The Grays can trace their ancestry to the time before the Crusades."

"So her blood is a little blue."

"More than a little blue, my lord."

Miles heaved a sigh. "We will agree that the lady has an impeccable lineage."

"Indeed. Furthermore, the Queen likes to see her subjects happily married, since she was herself."

"I do not, for one moment, believe the Queen is playing cupid."

"Her Majesty is a romantic."

That was true enough.

They rode on. Once they had reached the abbey's outer boundary, Miles pulled up. "I will let you take Bulle Rock and proceed to the front entrance. I have a notion to climb over the garden wall."

"As you wish, my lord."

He shrugged off his mud-splattered coat and handed it to Blunt. "Tell the lady and her household that I will be along directly."

Miles grabbed a fistful of thick vine and stuck the toe of his riding boot into a crevice in the stone wall. He had come and gone from Graystone Abbey by this method many times during that long-ago summer. He grabbed another handful of vine farther up the wall, located another toehold, and climbed.

This blasted business!

He was no ghost hunter. He was Miles St. Aldford, Marquess of Cork. He was a trained soldier, a man of the world, a bon vivant, a wealthy aristocrat, and a confidante to the Prince of Wales.

A self-deprecating smile spread across the handsome and slightly dissipated features. He was also world-weary, had a fairly low opinion of the fair sex, and a decided tendency to drink too much champagne.

Could Blunt possibly be right? Would he be seen as the lady's champion, the leading man, a conquering hero, a knight in shining armor? It certainly wasn't a role he would have chosen for himself. Still, it might prove diverting, perhaps even amusing, Miles decided as he swung his leg over the wall and dropped to the ground.

Chapter Two

Men were not in the least amusing, Alyssa decided as she thrust her trowel into the soft, damp earth and turned it over, looking for the slightest sign of a weed.

At least not the men she knew. The list included the vicar, Mr. Blackmore; the village doctor, Aristotle Symthe; several of the local West Country gentry; her own gardener, Galsworthy; and, of course, Sir Hugh Pureheart.

Sir Hugh was a perfect example. He was fairly tall, fairly good-looking, fairly intelligent, and fairly well-educated. Unfortunately, Hugh lacked two essentials: a sense of humor and an imagination. He viewed life in black and white. There were no shades of gray, let alone the veritable rainbow of colors her beloved mother had painted the world with by her words, her actions, even by the flowers planted in her garden, the very garden where Alyssa now knelt weeding.

Like most men, Hugh Babington Pureheart—Sir Hugh, with the recent demise of his uncle, the baronet—was a literal creature. The word *simpleminded* popped unbidden into Alyssa's head.

No, not simple-minded. *Single-minded.* Hugh wanted to marry her and he was utterly single-minded about it.

Alyssa tugged at the headpiece she had plunked down on her hair as she'd left the abbey: She did so hate hats, bonnets, and the like, but she knew she must protect her skin from the summer elements or she would rapidly take on the appearance of a beet root.

She gave the plain black headdress another tug and drove the small trowel into the dirt around the fuzzy gray foliage of lamb's-ears and the pale yellow blooms of lady's mantle.

The subject of marriage had been raised again when Hugh had arrived, unannounced, for tea yesterday afternoon.

"Just passing by and thought I'd stop and look in on you ladies," had been his lame excuse.

The minute Emma Pibble had gone to see about more scones for the tea table, Hugh had pressed Alyssa for an answer, saying in his own inimitable way, as if it were some kind of selling point: "If you marry me, you'll be getting the most eligible bachelor in the district." Then he had added, "We aren't children any longer, Alyssa. It's time we both accepted the inevitable and settled down."

Hugh was twenty-seven, but he seemed younger. He always had.

She'd opened her mouth to reiterate her standard refusal when she had been saved from having to answer at all by Emma's timely return from the kitchens.

Sir Hugh's proposal of marriage wasn't her first, of course. Her first had come five years ago at the tender age of sixteen. Squire Beebe had been thrice her age—old enough to be her father, if not her grandfather—and a wealthy widower. There had never been any doubt in her mind, or, thankfully, in her parents' minds that she should refuse him: The squire had been summarily sent on his way.

Since then her other suitors had included the handsome but rakish younger son of the Duke of N—, a pompous little Bourbon prince whose name she could never recall, several gentlemen of society who happened to stop at Graystone Abbey to see her father on their way to someplace else, and, of course, Hugh Pureheart.

Alyssa ferreted out one small stubborn encroacher from beneath the lamb's-ears. She pulled the offending weed out of the ground, gave it a shake to remove any excess dirt clinging to its roots, and deposited it in the wooden pail beside her.

Sir Hugh was becoming something of a nuisance. He refused to take no for an answer, although she had graciously declined his offer of marriage several times in the past six months. As a last resort, when he wouldn't listen to reason—indeed, Hugh didn't seem to hear anything of import that she had to say—Alyssa had been forced to resort to schemes and stratagems.

Her plan was a simple one: She would not marry while she was in mourning. And she intended to stay in mourning for as long as it served her purposes.

While it was true her parents had been dead for more than eighteen months, and while it was also true that the official period of mourning was over, losing both her mother and her father to a strange virulent fever within a few short weeks of each other had left Alyssa devastated. The church may have laid Annemarie and Thomas Gray to rest on that cold winter's day in 1877, but she still missed them dreadfully.

No more so than now.

Apparently even the Queen had heard about the ghost who supposedly haunted her ancestral home. Alyssa had received a letter only last week from one of Her Majesty's ladies-in-waiting. An emissary was being dispatched from London to investigate the strange goings-on at Graystone Abbey. The Queen's agent was none other than the Marquess of Cork.

"God's mercy!" Alyssa muttered through her teeth as she forcefully drove the garden tool into the damp earth. The last thing she needed about the place was a London dandy.

She could just picture the marquess: immaculate in his country tweeds—he undoubtedly donned a satin or brocade waistcoat for evening and a formal black silk top hat—not a hair out of place and smelling of Macassar oil, nails perfectly manicured, boots polished to a mirror shine. Pish! The man would be utterly useless!

"Oh, Papa, if only you were here to help me keep the hounds at bay," Alyssa beseeched as hot tears suddenly formed in the corners of her eyes. "Mama, there is so much I don't know, of that I'm uncertain. If only you were here to teach me."

But her parents were dead and buried in the family cemetery behind the Lady Chapel. They couldn't help her with the persistent Sir Hugh, the exhausting management of Graystone Abbey, the rumors of restless spirits and ancient curses that were being whispered about in the valley, the disappearance of her uncle on his way home from India, or the impending arrival of the marquess.

What she needed, Alyssa reflected as she dried her tears, wasn't a boulevardier who nibbled on caviar and ortolan and sipped champagne, but a knight in shining armor.

THUNK!

Mere inches from where she knelt, a huge black-booted foot landed on the ground, unceremoniously crushing the fragile lamb's-ears and lady's mantle.

Alyssa gave a cry of dismay. "Hound of Crete!"

"Hound of what?" repeated a puzzled baritone from above her.

"Look what you've done!"

"Done?"

"You've crushed my plants," she exclaimed.

The villainous knave tried to tiptoe out of the flower bed—an impossible task for a man whose feet were as large as his—mumbling, "I am sorry, miss. My apologies."

He didn't sound sorry, and his apology was not acceptable. Alyssa pointed a dirt-encrusted finger at him—she always started out wearing gloves to garden but soon took them off and worked with her bare hands; it was the feel of the cool earth against her skin that she loved—and said accusingly, "You, sir, are trespassing."

"So I am," he said laconically, and she could almost hear the lazy smile in his voice.

The play of light and shadows through the trees overhead made it impossible for her to see his face clearly. He stepped onto the cobblestone path and stood in front of her, legs planted firmly apart, gloved hands on his hips, as the morning sun emerged from behind a bank of clouds.

She began with his feet. He wore black leather boots: They were caked with mud, but she could see they were crafted of first-rate leather by a first-rate bootmaker.

His riding breeches were also black, mud-splattered and of the finest quality. She had never really noticed before the way a pair of riding breeches could fit the figure of a gentlemen.

Her gaze moved up his legs—they were very long and muscular—and came to the juncture of his thighs. There was something tucked into the man's breeches, something large and bulging and . . . malformed.

Alyssa pictured the classical statues in the abbey's formal garden, the ones her parents had collected on their honeymoon to the Greek isles and had had shipped home at great expense. Gods and goddesses captured for all time in marble and stone: the youngest titan, Cronus, in the act of castrating Uranus—from the severed flesh had sprung giants, Furies, nymphs, and the goddess Aphrodite—the virile Apollo in the prime of his manhood, and Ares, the merciless god of war, with his sword brandished high overhead.

Unlike the gentlemen of her acquaintance, Alyssa possessed an active imagination. She could almost picture the figure in front of her without its clothing. For the love of Hera, he was fashioned very much like a Greek god, down to the smallest detail!

Well, perhaps not so very small, at that.

Alyssa swallowed with difficulty. She could feel the heat rush to her face. Her cheeks were aflame with color.

She was a dunce.

The man was not malformed or deformed. He was simply formed as men were meant to be.

She quickly raised her eyes. The stranger wasn't wearing a coat, only a white shirt that had come partially unbuttoned. In the opening at the neck she caught a glimpse of bronzed skin and bronzed muscles and a smattering of hair on his chest.

She continued up past his neck, the jut of his jaw, the mouth with its thinned lips—his mouth would look entirely different, she warranted, if he were out to enchant a woman—the aristocratic nose with just enough individuality to make his face interesting, nay, fascinating; the slash of black brows, the high forehead, the mass of dark hair—long, curly, slightly damp from all appearances; and finally, when she could avoid it no longer, she met his eyes.

If the eyes were truly a reflection of the soul, then this was a most unusual man. For what Alyssa saw in his eyes was intelligence, humor, strength, fierce determination, curiosity, and danger.

This was a dangerous man.

He was also wickedly, darkly, seductively, devilishly handsome.

A strange thrill coursed through her from the tips of her garden shoes to the top of her hair tucked haphazardly under the antiquated headpiece.

Surely this was the devil himself.

Chapter Three

She was an angel.

Hers was a beauty with a profoundly spiritual quality. There was an inner splendor that shone through: She was at once unbearably vulnerable and deeply sensual.

Her features were delicately sculpted. Her cheekbones were high and pronounced. Her nose was slender and perfectly shaped. The natural arch of her brows—there was a mere hint of color to them—gave her an expression of perpetual surprise, rather like a startled doe.

Her skin was luminous. Her mouth was slightly agape. Her lips were naturally pink; the lower lip was marginally fuller than the upper. She had yet to smile. Nevertheless, Miles caught a glimpse every now and then of small, straight, white teeth.

Her eyes were the soft, velvet-gray color of the lamb's-ears he had inadvertently trampled underfoot. They were large, intelligent, observant, and fringed by long, light brown eyelashes. She was young and fresh, and she put the summer morning to shame.

It was all there in her face.

Indeed, her face was the only thing Miles could see clearly. Deep shadows were stealing across this section of the garden as the sun slipped in and out of the clouds—at least the threat of rain had passed—and a great sprawling tree shaded the very spot where she knelt at his feet, hiding the rest of her from view.

"You, sir," she repeated, "are trespassing."

He was momentarily distracted by a smudge of dirt on her cheek; it drew attention to the translucence of her skin far more effectively than any beauty mark could.

"So I am," he finally conceded.

Her chin came up. "You don't seem concerned."

"I'm not."

She folded her hands in front of her, fingers intertwined, rather like a penitent at prayer. "This is private property."

He lifted his head and glanced at the deserted landscape. "Very private property."

"You oughtn't to be here."

"Possibly not."

Probably not. Although trespassing was the least of Miles's worries at the moment. His primary concern—it was more a matter of masculine curiosity, really—was his fascination with the ethereal creature in front of him.

The girl dug her small, straight white teeth into her bottom lip. "Do you often go where you oughtn't to?" she inquired.

He had to smile. "I must confess that I do."

She cocked her head to one side and looked up at him. She was wearing a dark, threadbare swathe of cloth draped over her head and shoulders. The gown underneath appeared to be well worn, the color between mouse-gray and faded black.

Her shoes were covered with garden mud; there was just a glimpse of a toe and a heel beneath the hem of her dress. Dirt was embedded under her fingernails. Then there was the smear on her cheek where she had brushed her hand across her face.

The evidence led him to an obvious conclusion: She was employed at the abbey as a housemaid or a scullion.

Still, there was something in her manner and speech that gave Miles pause. Her voice was softly modulated and cultured, albeit with a West Country accent. Naturally, if she were going about in London society, she would be regarded as a country bumpkin, but that was neither here nor there.

Perhaps she was a poor relation of the Grays, forced by dire circumstances, circumstances beyond her control, to throw herself upon the charity of the young woman left in charge of Graystone Abbey with the death of the earl and his countess.

No doubt Lady Alyssa—she of the impeccable lineage, she of the sharp mind and the sharper wit, according to Blunt—was far from being a paragon. He could almost picture her in his mind: spoiled, as demanding as she was beautiful, flouncing about the abbey like a princess, her skirts trailing behind her, her nose in the air, rejecting suitors at every turn of her dainty hand.

Egods, he'd had his fill of capricious females!

"Why did you climb over the garden wall?"

Miles's attention reverted to the girl. He was

tempted to answer her with, *to get to the other side*, but he didn't. "Impulse?"

She regarded him with genuine interest. "Are you, by nature, impulsive?"

"Yes." He frowned. "No." He reconsidered. "Sometimes." He heard himself ask: "Are you?"

She crinkled up her forehead. "Impulsive?"

He nodded.

She gave his question due consideration. "I would like to be."

"Meaning that you aren't."

"I can't afford to be impulsive," she said with what sounded very much like regret.

He supposed not. Being the poor relation was a most unfortunate state of affairs for any man or woman.

Miles studied the plants he had unintentionally reduced to a few crushed leaves and broken stems. "I'm sorry about your flowers." He went down on his haunches to make a closer inspection of the damage. "I'll have them replaced."

"It isn't necessary," came the reply.

"I insist," he said, flashing her his best smile.

By nature, Miles St. Aldford was not a conceited man, but he was aware of the effect his smile seemed to have on the average female, whether her age be nine or ninety or somewhere in between. He had been told by any number of society's beauties—sophisticated women who had seen and done just about everything there was to see and do—that his smile was charming, disarming, even seductive. He saw no reason to dispute the fact.

Yet the girl in the garden didn't so much as bat

an eyelash when he smiled at her. She was either dim-witted, farsighted, or far from average, Miles consoled himself as he straightened and looked around for the first time since scaling the stone wall.

The gardens at Graystone Abbey were renowned throughout Devon—throughout the whole of England, for that matter. There were the formal gardens and the classical statuary in the style of the French designer Le Notre; the natural landscapes of Capability Brown with vast plantings of trees and shrubs, numerous lakes, ponds, and waterfalls; the topiary of the Italian Renaissance with hornbeam and yew hedges forming great pillars, pointed pyramids, and even the occasional whimsical farm animal; and the rose garden.

"Milady's Bower," he said, thinking out loud.

Gray eyes blinked once, twice, thrice with astonishment. "How did you know that was the name of the rose garden?"

The answer was simple. "I've been here before."

There was an expression of disbelief on the angelic face. "You have?"

"I was once a guest of Lord and Lady Graystone's."

The girl stirred uneasily. "I don't remember seeing you before."

"Nor I you," he countered.

"It must have been some time ago."

"It was," Miles said. "How long have you lived at the abbey?"

"All of my life," she answered.

That couldn't be more than sixteen or seventeen

years, if his was any guess, Miles speculated. From the looks of her, she was barely out of the schoolroom.

He went on. "This was Lady Graystone's favorite garden."

The girl's eyelids lowered; she seemed to have difficulty in swallowing. "Yes. She loved the rose garden."

Miles took in a deep breath. The fragrance of roses was almost overpowering. To his right was a wide wooden arch buried beneath a cascade of vivid pink blooms. There were bright reds and brilliant yellows and pristine whites; there were pale pinks and two-tones, small and large, double-blooms, bushes and ramblers.

Beside him was a delicate yellow rose. The rosebush was filled with unfurling buds and small, sharp thorns. He leaned over and inhaled. The scent was elusive, subtle, mysterious.

In many ways, Miles thought, raising his head, a woman was like a rose. " 'From fairest creatures we desire increase, that thereby beauty's rose might never die,' " he recited.

"I beg your pardon."

He cleared his throat and quickly offered an explanation for his behavior. After all, a soldier—even an ex-soldier—didn't go about spouting poetry. "Blunt has been quoting Pope and Milton and Shakespeare on this journey. I believe it has to do with his dramatics class. Some of his influence must have rubbed off on me."

"Who is Blunt?"

He would keep his answers as simple, straightforward, and to the point as he could. "My traveling companion."

"Is Blunt an actor?" She seemed intrigued by the notion.

Miles smiled ruefully. What man, especially when it came to women, wasn't an actor? "He certainly is."

"And the verse?"

"From Shakespeare's sonnets."

"I thought as much." The subject was unhurriedly changed. "Where, pray tell, are you headed?"

"To the main house."

She blinked in surprise. "Why?"

"I have business at the abbey," he informed her. The girl's manner bordered on the presumptuous.

Moistening her lips with the tip of her tongue, she implored: "Stay a moment, if you will, sir. As long as you're here in the garden, I have need of you."

One dark brow arched instinctively. "Need of me?"

"I have encountered a stubborn vine that will not be exorcised," she explained.

A flicker of a smile came and went. "I see. Why don't you show me this stubborn vine?"

"This way, if you please," she said politely, starting to rise to her feet.

Miles reached out and offered her his assistance. She hesitated, then placed her smaller hand in his. It was a simple gesture, an everyday courtesy, and yet when their fingertips touched, a frisson shot through Miles.

It was the damnedest thing.

The young woman stood, brushed off her skirt, examined her dirty hands, apparently decided that there was nothing to be done about them, and indicated the far corner of the rose garden. "There. By the Knight's Well."

He didn't recall any Knight's Well.

"Centuries ago, perhaps as much as a thousand years ago, the water from the Knight's Well was said to be a cure for impotency," she told him without a flicker of embarrassment.

Miles covered his astonishment with a cough. Somehow it wasn't seemly for a young, innocent girl to be speaking of such matters, even if she was a rustic.

Unless he had miscalculated. Unless she was no innocent.

There were women who managed to retain the appearance of purity long after they were far from it. Perhaps this angelic creature with the fair skin and the huge eyes and the uncreased brow was more experienced than he'd judged.

Either way, he could almost picture what she would look like in the full light of the sun. She would be tall without being too tall. Lithe. Full-bosomed, he hoped. Long-legged and long-limbed. Slender but not reed thin. Nicely round where a female should be round.

"There were once several hundred holy wells in Cornwall and Devon," she continued, intent, it seemed, upon giving him a history lesson. "According to legend, the early saints—St. Kea, St. Piran and St. Patrick, himself—traveled here from

Ireland. They blessed the local people and healed them with the waters from the wells."

"How quaint."

"Now many of the wells are lost to time and memory. The Knight's Well was accidentally unearthed only last year by Galsworthy and myself."

"Who is Galsworthy?"

"The head gardener."

"Do you work for Galsworthy?"

"I work with him."

With that, the girl stepped out of the shadows and into the sunlight, and Miles St. Aldford saw her clearly for the first time. She was even more lovely, even more desirable, than he had initially thought. She was also wearing a plain black cloth on her head that was strongly reminiscent of a wimple.

By all that was holy, Miles swore silently, the girl in the garden was a nun!

The stranger was looking at her as if she were Hydra and had grown nine heads, Alyssa realized as their eyes met.

"My apologies, Sister," he mumbled as if it were suddenly painful to speak.

Sister? What a very singular thing for him to say. "I beg your pardon—"

"No," he stammered, shaking his head from side to side. "It is I who beg yours."

The man was a mystery. Men, she had found, so often were. Despite a superior classical education under the tutelage of first Miss Emma Pibble and then her own father, there were still a great many things she did not understand about men. There was even more she failed to comprehend about men and women.

Alyssa permitted herself a small sigh. If only she had been taught a little less of the ancient Greeks and a little more about the modern Englishman.

"The vine—" the stranger prompted.

Alyssa drew a blank.

He looked at her, and his expression was enigmatic. "The one you wish to have removed."

"Just here," she said, pointing to a secluded corner. She must concentrate on the business at hand and not on the man's broad shoulders, Alyssa reminded herself. And she must certainly not think about the way his riding breeches clung to his masculine figure.

For several minutes they stood in silence and studied the twisted treelike vine—in places it was as thick as a man's forearm—that grew up alongside the Knight's Well and rambled over a good portion of the garden wall.

"It's large," she said unnecessarily.

"It's very large," he agreed.

"It's dead."

"It's very dead."

Alyssa turned her head. "Well?"

"I would venture to say that it has also been here a very long time."

"It has."

"Conceivably as long as the Knight's Well."

"Conceivably." Alyssa reached out and stroked a contorted bough. She was already having second thoughts about destroying something that may have been a part of Graystone Abbey since the days when the many-married Henry VIII purged the monasteries and sold the property to the first Earl of Graystone. Indeed, the well—and possibly the vine—could have been here when the abbey was originally founded in the days of Edward the Confessor.

"If you want me to remove it, I'll need an ax," the man informed her.

"Can't you pull it out?"

"You mean with my bare hands?"

"Actually, I thought you might prefer to leave your gloves on."

He laughed outright. "You seem to have unlimited faith in my strength, Sister, but I'm not Hercules."

"I knew it!"

"Knew what?"

How could she explain? Sometimes her mind was a convoluted maze of ideas and thoughts, memories and impressions, daydreams and dreams that came with sleep, facts and figures, books she had read. The leap from rose gardens to mythological heroes was short and surprisingly logical to her.

Alyssa took a deep breath and plunged forward. "It was Hercules who slew the nine-headed Hydra, spawned of the monsters Echidna and Typhon."

He appeared confused. "The nine-headed what?"

"Hydra. Some accounts say the venomous creature was nine-headed; some say it had as many as ten thousand snaky heads."

He took a relaxed stance, folded his arms across his chest, and nodded approvingly. "I'm acquainted with another woman who includes references to classical Greek mythology in her everyday conversation."

"You are?" Alyssa had to ask. "Who is she?"

"The wife of my best friend."

"I see." She didn't see, of course.

"The lady is an American."

"I don't believe I've ever actually met an American, although we occasionally get a foreign traveler in the valley."

"The lady *was* an American."

"She isn't now?"

"Now she is the Duchess of Deakin."

He knew a duchess.

"Juliet is intelligent, well-educated, and the best-organized person I have ever known."

He had called the Duchess of Deakin by her first name. Only a personal friend would dare to do that, someone of equal rank and breeding, someone—Alyssa tried to swallow the hard lump that had formed in her throat—like a marquess.

Turning, she stared at the man standing beside her. His broad shoulders and rakish expression only enhanced his jagged handsomeness. Not to mention the dark, deep-set eyes, the wide, firm mouth, and the black hair with thin rivers of gray at the temples. He had, she noted, the self-containment of a worldly man with more than a few life experiences.

Alyssa didn't wish to be rude, but she had to know his identity. "Who are you?"

His eyes narrowed slightly. "I'm Miles St. Aldford."

She took in her breath and held it for a count of

three. By the blessed saints, this man was the Queen's emissary. He was Miles St. Aldford. He was the Marquess of Cork.

"You don't look at all like a marquess," she blurted out.

"You don't look like a nun!" he shot back.

Chapter Four

"I don't look like a nun because I'm not a nun," the girl informed him. "Wherever did you get the idea that I was, my lord?" she asked in amazement.

Miles indicated the wimple covering her hair. "You're wearing the headdress of a Benedictine sister."

A dirt-stained hand flew to her head. Her mouth formed a small O. "Of course, I'd forgotten," she said, laughing. "I detest wearing hats," she added, as if the statement made perfect sense and would explain everything to him, which, of course, it didn't.

The sound of her laughter, however, was delightful, like tinkling bells in the wind, or the light staccato of rain on the roof, or the call of a meadowlark on a perfect summer day.

The young woman tugged at the faded headcloth until it came off in her hands and her hair was set free. It cascaded around her shoulders and down her back: great masses of silky stuff the color of the finest champagne.

It took every bit of willpower Miles possessed not to reach out and run his fingers through the girl's hair. His hands were literally itching to find out if it was as soft and luxuriant as it appeared.

Somewhere deep in his brain he dredged up the memory of another time and another place—no, the *same* place—when he had seen a child with hair this unusual shade of blond: not yellow-gold, not white-gold, but something in between.

Then he knew.

"You are Lady Alyssa Gray," he concluded belatedly.

"Yes, my lord."

So, *this* was the lady of the manor. "You're not what I expected," he admitted.

"You're not what I expected, either," she claimed, clasping the headpiece in her hand.

"We haven't been properly introduced," Miles pointed out. Not that he gave a tinker's damn whether they had or not; he wasn't that much of a stickler for the proprieties. He simply needed a minute or two to get used to the idea that this girl was his hostess.

She looked around the rose garden, deserted but for the two of them. "There seems to be no one about to do the honors, my lord."

He clicked the heels of his boots together, gave a small flourish of his hand, and followed that with a brief but polite nod of his head. "I am Miles St. Aldford, Marquess of Cork."

She lifted her chin and gazed directly into his eyes. "I am, as you have correctly surmised, Lady Alyssa Gray. In the absence of my uncle, I welcome you to Graystone Abbey."

He stared at the dirt under her fingernails, the

smudges on her skirt, the mud on her shoes. "I see you are very much your father's daughter."

"Thank you, my lord." Her brow creased. "I think." Her face brightened. "You mentioned that you had been here before as a guest of my parents."

"I spent a summer at Graystone Abbey some fifteen years ago."

"I don't remember you."

"That isn't surprising. You would have been a baby."

She cast him a sidelong glance. "Not a baby, but a little girl of five or six, perhaps."

Young enough to still take her meals in the nursery, Miles calculated. However precocious, a six-year old wouldn't have been permitted to sit at the dinner table with the adults. Not even in the Graystones' rather eccentric household.

It was past time, he decided, to put this business of mistaken identities behind them. "My apologies, Lady Alyssa, for thinking you were a sister."

"And my apologies, Lord Cork, for assuming you were a trespasser, an interloper, a ruffian, a—"

He brought her up short. "I accept."

"Accept?"

"Your apology," he said smoothly. "Just as I'm certain you accept mine."

"Naturally." She went up on her tiptoes and looked over his shoulder with a puzzled expression on her face. From where they stood, the road was visible through a small opening in the garden wall. "Where is your coach and driver?"

"I didn't come by coach," he explained. "I traveled from London on horseback."

"Then where is your horse?" she inquired. "Your luggage? Your entourage?"

"By now, Bulle Rock has been taken to your stables to be watered and rubbed down. My luggage is being transported by hired wagon. And I have no entourage, only Blunt."

"He's the actor who came with you."

"Blunt is many things, an actor is but one of them."

"What else is Blunt?"

"My companion. My *camarade*. My valet."

She nodded her head. "Miss Pibble is mine."

"Your valet?"

"No. My companion. My friend. The one who looks after me, as I'm sure Blunt looks after you."

At the moment Blunt's idea of looking after him was to find a suitable—and suitably virginal—young woman for him to marry. The very thought sent chills down Miles St. Aldford's spine.

"About your recalcitrant vine, my lady."

"You're quite right, of course."

"I am?"

She nodded her head. "It would be a shame to chop down something that may have been here since the time of the Confessor."

Miles was finding it a challenge to keep up with Lady Alyssa. Her mind seemed to flit from one subject to another like a small bird flitting from flower to flower collecting nectar.

Only she wasn't so very small.

Indeed, the lady was quite tall for a female. The top of her head reached his chin. The fact that she was fine-boned and graceful in her movements gave the impression that she was both smaller and younger than she was.

"Shall we go into the house, my lord? No doubt you would like some refreshment after your journey. And once the transport with your luggage has arrived, you will undoubtedly wish to retire to your rooms to bathe and change."

"Undoubtedly."

"This way, if you will—" The girl gestured toward the far end of the enclosed rose garden. There was an old and elaborate stone door, complete with gargoyles peering down at whoever passed through its portals, warding off evil spirits and human intruders alike, a flagstone path, and the house just beyond.

It was curious, but something had changed in the past few minutes, Miles realized as he walked beside the lady. He was no longer dreading the time he had to spend at Graystone Abbey. Indeed, he was almost looking forward to it.

The blame or the credit lay with Lady Alyssa, of course. It had been a long time—he was loath to admit how long—since a woman had sparked his interest, a woman other than Juliet, now the Duchess of Deakin, that is, and Elizabeth, sister of one friend, the Earl of Stanhope, and wife to another, Lord Jonathan Wicke.

He would be the first to acknowledge that he was jaded when it came to the female of the species. Frankly he had known too many women in his thirty years. A pretty face, a lovely figure, and an empty head had once been enough for him.

No longer.

In addition, he had too much money, and too

much time on his hands. His estates practically ran themselves. His ability to buy the best extended to estate managers, gamekeepers, butlers, and housekeepers. Since leaving Her Majesty's military service, and especially since his return from America, he had been at a loss as to what to do with himself. He was a man without a purpose.

Miles paused by the door that separated the rose garden from the outside world. He thought he'd forgotten most of that summer spent at Graystone Abbey, but as they strolled toward the house it started to come back to him: the long, languid summer days and nights, the sound of a bullfrog calling across a tranquil pond, the splash of a silver fish against a golden sun, the distinctive scent of old roses, the sensation of being watched. . . .

Miles gave his head a good shake. Surely it had been his youthful imagination.

Or dreams.

To sleep: perchance to dream . . . for in that sleep of death what dreams may come . . .

"Men are a different species altogether," declared Miss Emma Pibble as the two women sat in the study of Graystone Abbey, sharing a midmorning cup of coffee.

Her former governess's statement wasn't scientifically sound, but Alyssa agreed with the sentiment. "Lord Cork certainly isn't what I had expected."

Emma Pibble gave a delicate sniff behind her linen handkerchief. "Neither is his companion; the one he calls Blunt."

Alyssa looked up from the stack of papers on her desk. "Frankly, I thought the marquess would arrive in an ostentatious coach with his family crest emblazoned on the side and drawn by a four-in-hand. I imagined him dressed in fancy clothes, carrying a fancy walking stick, flaunting fancy manners, and accompanied by a covey of fancy servants."

"They are not fancy," observed Emma, setting her china cup down on the diminutive Queen Anne table at her elbow. "And they are not grand. They are ruffians."

A tiny furrow appeared on Alyssa's brow. "I thought as much in the beginning. Now I'm inclined to suspect that the marquess and his man may have been soldiers."

The older woman by more than a dozen years leaned forward and confided, "As you know, I'm not one who usually listens to gossip, but I have heard that Lord Cork and Mr. Blunt once engaged in clandestine activities for the Crown."

Alyssa blinked several times in rapid succession. "Clandestine activities?"

Emma Pibble dropped her voice to a stage whisper. "Subterfuge."

"Subterfuge?"

"They were spies."

A shiver rippled down Alyssa's back, from her nape to the small indentation at the base of her spine. "How frightful."

How intriguing.

Her companion went on. "Heaven knows what they were called upon to do in the name of Queen and country."

"Heaven knows." Alyssa held one hand out at arm's length for a moment and studied a bit of dirt she had missed under her thumbnail. "I confess I don't understand gentlemen like Lord Cork."

Emma Pibble nudged her wire-rim eyeglasses up the slant of her nose and smoothed the skirt of her charcoal-gray poplin dress; as long as her dear Alyssa was in mourning, she was in mourning. "I shouldn't wonder if the marquess was at a loss as to what to make of you, as well, my dear."

"Make of *me*?"

There was wisdom as well as keen intelligence in the dark brown eyes behind the spectacles. "You are, undoubtedly, very different from the women of his acquaintance."

"Do you think so?"

"I know so."

Alyssa permitted herself a small sigh. "The ladies of the Marlborough House Set must be pretty and gay, witty and accomplished, beautifully groomed and beautifully gowned." She added with just a touch of envy, "I'm sure they always know the right thing to say and do."

"Perhaps. Then again, perhaps not." Emma gave a telling shrug of her capable shoulders. "But you are—you *were*—my star pupil, Alyssa. You have a fine mind, a genuine appreciation for history, a definite flair for Latin, and the most beautiful penmanship of anyone I have ever taught."

High praise, indeed, coming from a taskmistress like Miss Emma Mary Margaret Pibble.

Of course, she was no longer Alyssa's taskmistress. She hadn't been for some years. Now there was only a deep and abiding affection between the two women who had started out as student and teacher. Through the disappointment of her governess's broken engagement—the young man had run off with a pretty little thing without a serious thought in her head—and the tragic death of Alyssa's parents, they had become friends, allies, and close companions.

Alyssa picked up her pen. "Shall we continue with the business at hand?"

Emma nodded. "Mrs. Fetchett has put the marquess in the Knight's Chambers," she reported.

Alyssa gnawed on her bottom lip. The Knight's Chambers was only two doors from her own suite. "I suppose there's nothing to be done about the close proximity to my rooms."

"Not with Sir Alfred and Lady Chubb and their children arriving the day after tomorrow." Emma gave her a sharp glance. "Surely you don't believe the marquess to be anything but a gentleman."

"Of course not," she quickly retracted. "The marquess will have the Knight's Chambers, and we'll put Sir Alfred and his family in the Cloisters as planned."

Emma Pibble was known for being forthright in expressing her opinions. "I don't like having all these strangers in the house."

Neither did Alyssa. But she had put the Chubbs off twice in recent months and she couldn't do it again without giving offense. "We both know my father issued Sir Alfred Chubb an invitation to use the library here at the abbey for his research. Sir

Alfred is, I understand, a respected amateur historian."

Emma made a disparaging sound. "Amateur, indeed."

She gave her friend a gentle reminder. "For hundreds of years it has been the tradition of Graystone Abbey to extend hospitality to anyone who wishes to stop and take his or her respite here."

Emma clicked her tongue. "I am a great believer in tradition, but the Chubbs can well afford to rent a house in the district. They're simply too cheap to do so." She picked up her china cup, took a sip of coffee, and added for good measure, "They will make a great deal of work for everyone."

That much, unfortunately, was true. "Have we been able to find help in the village?"

Household logistics took center stage. "Two additional girls have been deemed suitable by Mrs. Fetchett. One will do nicely, she claims, in the kitchens, and the other will be trained to do the extra housework that will result with so many guests in residence. We can only hope that Lady Chubb and Miss Chubb bring their personal maids with them."

"I have heard that Lady Chubb is very beautiful and very grand," Alyssa remarked after a time. Not that she was one to listen to tittle-tattle. It was simply that Sir Hugh had mentioned it at tea yesterday afternoon. Apparently he had been introduced to Lady Caroline Chubb on his last visit to London.

Emma did not disguise her disdain. "The Chubbs are social climbers."

"Indeed."

"Before Sir Alfred was knighted, he was in trade."

"Being in trade isn't a sin." Although there were those, of course, who thought it was. "Sir Alfred was simply clever enough to parlay his business of . . ."

"Gentlemen's 'unmentionables,' " supplied the older woman.

"Into a resounding success and a sizable fortune."

"Nonetheless, the Chubbs are upstarts. They made it impossible for you to refuse them an invitation."

Alyssa was about to respond to Emma's latest accusation when a knock sounded on the study door. "That will be Mrs. Fetchett."

It was not the housekeeper, Mrs. Fetchett. It was Galsworthy.

"Beggin' yer pardon, my lady," the head gardener said in preamble.

"Do come in, Galsworthy."

Cap in hand, he took a tentative step into the study and stopped. Never comfortable indoors, Galsworthy gave a respectful nod of his head, anxiously fingered the woolen cap he wore whatever the season of the year, checked the bottom of his work shoes for mud, and shifted his weight from one foot to the other and back again. "It's one o' the lads, my lady," he finally announced.

"Yes," Alyssa prompted.

"Ian McKennitt, it is."

"What about Ian McKennitt?"

Galsworthy fixed his gaze on a spot over her left shoulder. "Not so much somethin' about the lad as somethin' he saw in the woods."

"Which woods?"

"The Old Woods, my lady." He shifted his weight again. "Well, not so much somethin' he saw in the Old Woods as somethin' he saw in the Monk's Cave."

"What did he see in the Monk's Cave?"

"A man." He hesitated, as if turning the information over and over in his head before declaring it aloud. "A stranger to these parts."

Getting a story out of Galsworthy was like pulling teeth. "Did Ian McKennitt speak to the stranger?"

"He did, my lady."

"What did he say?"

"Said the fellow was down on his luck. Said he was dressed in tatters 'n rags like a beggar or a—" Galsworthy searched for the right word, "hermit, but he talked like a gentleman."

"I see." She thought for a moment. "The man isn't doing anyone any harm, is he?"

"No, my lady."

"Well, then, that settles it, doesn't it?"

The outdoorsman reached up and scratched his head. "S'pose so, my lady."

"Thank you, Galsworthy."

"What you be wantin' me to do about the hermit?"

"I want you to do nothing about the hermit." Alyssa reconsidered. "Is Ian McKennitt still about?"

He nodded his head. "The lad be just out back where Mrs. Fetchett can keep an eye on him."

"Please ask Mrs. Fetchett for a clean, serviceable blanket and tell Cook to prepare a basket of food: some bread and cheese, perhaps a meat pie or two, and a bottle of stout. I want Ian McKennitt to deliver the provisions to the Monk's Cave. He is to leave them by the entrance. Do you understand?"

He nodded his head. "I understand, my lady. It'll be done just as you instructed."

"Thank you, Galsworthy."

The head gardener gave another quick nod and made his exit.

"Now, where were we?" Alyssa said, thinking out loud.

"We were discussing the Chubbs."

"So we were. I believe we have the rooms suitably dispensed. Now we should decide on the menu for dinner Friday evening. I dare say Mrs. Fetchett and Cook will both want finalized lists as soon as possible."

"Cook has a lovely new recipe for salmon mousse." Emma Pibble was partial to salmon.

"Then we'll definitely have salmon mousse on the menu."

"I presume Sir Hugh is going to be in attendance for the welcoming dinner."

"Sir Hugh is the only one among us who has actually met Sir Alfred and Lady Chubb," Alyssa pointed out.

"He finds great favor in shrimp paste."

"Shrimp paste, it is." Alyssa wrote down both shrimp and lobster paste, and then said out loud, "I wonder what dishes the marquess prefers."

"I will inquire of his man, if you wish."

"That would be very kind of you. Thank you, Emma." She smiled at her companion. "I'm sure our little dinner party will turn out to be a resounding success. After all, we have the marquess to entertain the Chubbs and impress Sir Hugh."

Alyssa pictured the pair of them: the young, handsome, blond, and single-minded Hugh Pureheart and the dark, foreboding, broad-shouldered Miles St. Aldford. The two men were as different as day and night.

"It could prove to be a most interesting evening," Alyssa said as she put her pen to paper again.

Chapter Five

"Lord Cork, may I present Sir Hugh Pureheart, recently the third baronet?" said the vicar, Mr. Blackmore, upon finding himself in the position of acting as host for the evening.

Miles had already been informed by the clergyman that it wasn't the first time he had assumed the role at the behest of their hostess. As a man of the church and a friend of the family, he had often been invited to Graystone Abbey in its social heyday. He was always willing to be of assistance, especially since Lady Alyssa was now alone in the world. Or so Angus Blackmore had said only moments before the other guests began to arrive.

"It's a pleasure to meet you, Pureheart." Miles was determined to be sociable. Until he knew who was friend and who was foe, it was good policy to remain convivial. A lesson he had learned not in his covert work for the Crown, but in society.

"The pleasure is mine, Lord Cork," responded the handsome young man in the stiff white collar, white dress shirt, and dark evening coat. No sartorial allowances had been made for either the weather or for being in the country.

"I understand from Lady Alyssa," interjected the vicar, "that you were an old friend of her father's, my lord."

"Actually, it was my grandfather who was a great friend of the earl's. I did, however, spend a summer here at the abbey when I was a young man." Miles wondered how much had been said concerning his current visit to Devon. "Lord and Lady Graystone were very kind to me. I always meant to return one day to visit them. I'm only sorry that I stayed away so long. Too long, as it turns out."

Angus Blackmore shook his head slowly from side to side. "Yes. Most unfortunate. Tragic business. Strange fever took them both, you know. Just like that. Then the disappearance of James Gray on his way home from India." He shook his head again and added as an afterthought, "James is Lady Alyssa's uncle, of course."

"He *was* her uncle," Hugh Pureheart spoke up.

"I take it you believe the new Earl of Graystone is deceased," Miles said in a deliberately neutral tone.

"I do. It's been over a year since anyone has seen or heard from James Gray. Frankly, the chances of him being alive are remote." Pureheart's argument was convincing.

The vicar made a sympathetic sound. "I'm very much afraid you're right, Sir Hugh." Then he visibly brightened. "Ah, there is Dr. Symthe. Excuse me, gentlemen, while I bid him welcome."

Miles stood with his back to the unlit fireplace; it was an unusually warm evening for early June. From his vantage point he could see both doors into the room, the entire row of floor-to-ceiling windows opposite and the servant's entrance. He rocked back on his heels. "So, Lady Alyssa is all alone in the world."

The handsome man with the pale eyes, the soft hands, and the weak chin announced, "She won't be for long."

"Why is that?" Miles inquired nonchalantly.

Hugh Pureheart dropped his voice to a confidential level. "Because I have asked Lady Alyssa to marry me."

Miles hid his surprise. "Has she accepted?"

"She is still in mourning."

So, Alyssa *hadn't* accepted him. "Still in mourning? But I understood that Lord and Lady Graystone died nearly two years ago."

The young baronet hastened to correct him. "It was eighteen months ago, but Lady Alyssa took it badly. She was close to her parents." An expression of irritation—nay, it was more than mere irritation; it was resentment—marred the man's features. "Perhaps too close."

Miles made a mental note. Sir Hugh had yet to learn the wisdom of keeping his feelings to himself. "The Grays are—were—something of an unusual family."

"Yes. A most unusual family." Hugh Pureheart reflected for a moment, and then offered an opinion. "A woman should not read too much. It only encourages her to think."

"Ahhh . . . and if she thinks, she might get ideas."

"Exactly. A lady of society should concentrate on style and fashion, on perfecting the social graces and obtaining that certain"—Sir Hugh made a flowery gesture in the air with his hand "—savoir faire, as the French say." He abruptly dropped his arm. "Frankly, Lady Alyssa needs some polish."

"And you believe you're the man to give her polish?" Miles said with studied casualness.

"Actually I was hoping someone like Lady Chubb might agree to take her in hand."

Miles didn't move. "I've not had the pleasure of meeting Lady Chubb."

"Then you're in for a treat, Lord Cork, if you don't mind my saying so. Lady Chubb is an extraordinary woman. She is beautiful, accomplished, witty, articulate, gracious, always at the forefront of fashion, and the perfect hostess," Hugh said, singing her praises. "In short, everything Sir Alfred, or any man, could desire in a wife."

"She sounds too good to be true," Miles muttered dryly.

"She is everything I have said and more. You'll see for yourself when the Chubbs join us in a few minutes. The entire family arrived by liveried coach late this afternoon."

Miles had heard the commotion. Everyone in three counties must have. "And you want Lady Chubb to take your future bride under her wing, to guide her, to tutor her, to act as her mentor, so that she may learn to behave exactly like the other ladies of society?"

Sir Hugh bobbed his head up and down like one of those ingenious mechanical French toys that were all the rage on both sides of the Channel. "It will be imperative," he stated. "After we're married, Lady Alyssa and I will be spending most of our time in London, and very little here in the West Country."

The baronet was a fool. Or, at the very least, an utter prig. Miles realized that he would like nothing better than to give the younger man a thorough trouncing. Surely the lovely Alyssa would never consent to marry a jackass like Hugh Pureheart.

Miles tried to imagine the fop beside him kissing that sweet, alluring mouth, touching that angelic face, running his fingers through her silky hair, caressing her, making love to her.

Hell and damnation! He didn't like it. Not one bit.

Lady Alyssa Gray was what society had once called an Original. And while he had initially thought along the same lines as Sir Hugh when it came to her lack of social polish, he had quickly changed his mind. He preferred the lady as a rustic; it was part of her charm.

"I hope to convince Lady Alyssa that it's time to put sorrow aside and look to the future."

"As your wife?"

"As my wife."

Not if Miles could bloody well prevent it! That was the last thought he had on the subject before they were joined by the other gentlemen.

"This is a most singular room, is it not, my lord?" commented Angus Blackmore.

"Most singular," he agreed.

The four of them—Miles, Sir Hugh, the vicar, and Dr. Aristotle Symthe—were standing in the center of a large formal receiving hall. There was an ornate red and gold carpet on the floor and a smattering of furniture along the perimeter, includ-

ing a Florentine cabinet of *pietre dure*, a set of or-
molu commodes by Chippendale, and a very large
Queen Anne wine cooler.

But the walls and ceiling were the focal point of
the room. Every available space was covered with
an elaborate mural of angels, cherubs, the seraphim,
and other heavenly shapes, figures of Rubenesque
men and women, some naked, some with hands or
arms or clothing draped strategically across their
lush bodies.

"This is the renowned Celestial Room," volunteered the vicar. "I believe it was the fourth Earl of
Graystone . . ." he paused, turned to Aristotle Symthe for confirmation, received it with a nod of the
distinguished doctor's head, and finished, "who had
the paintings commissioned."

Dr. Symthe continued the narrative. "The artist
was an Italian, one Antonio Verrio. After Verrio, his
family and his rather extensive entourage had spent
almost a decade living at Burghley House while he
painted the Heaven Room for Lord Exeter, they
moved lock, stock, and barrel here to Graystone
Abbey. It took Verrio another seven years to paint
the murals for the Celestial Room. He completed
them shortly before his death in 1707. The result,
as you can see for yourself, my lord, is an artistic
triumph."

"An appropriate setting for an angel," murmured
Miles appreciatively.

The vicar put his head back and studied one particularly nubile group of winged ladies on the ceiling. "Of course, as a man of the church, I'm not

certain angels are quite as sensuous or voluptuous as Verrio depicted them."

" 'Our acts our angels are, for good or ill.' "

"I beg your pardon, my lord."

"A little something written in the seventeenth century by a man named John Fletcher," he said offhandedly. "Do you believe in guardian angels, Vicar?"

"Certainly I do."

Hugh Pureheart interposed, his lips twitching in an effort not to smile, "And what of ghosts?"

"I'm afraid I must draw the line at ghosts." Mr. Blackmore clicked his tongue in disapproval. "All this nonsense being whispered about in the valley."

Miles stilled. "What nonsense?"

"Then you haven't heard?" It was Sir Hugh again.

"Heard what?"

"We've had a rash of sightings."

"Now, Sir Hugh, two sightings doesn't constitute a rash," the doctor gently reprimanded. Aristotle Symthe turned to Miles. "One of the stable lads claims to have seen the ghost of a medieval knight dressed in full battle array. Apparently one minute the horse and rider were there on the abbey road directly in front of him, the next they had disappeared."

"What was the other sighting?" Miles asked in a quiet voice.

"It was Mrs. McGillicuddy. She's an elderly woman—retired cook, I believe—who lives with her son in the last cottage on the estate."

Miles wasn't about to add that he had heard the

ghostly knight also roamed the halls of Graystone Abbey.

"Of course," chimed in the vicar, "Mrs. McGillicuddy is nearly eighty and doesn't see as well as she used to."

"Neither would be considered a reliable witness, then," Miles pointed out.

The doctor agreed. "People see what they want to see. It adds excitement to their lives. It makes them feel important. It gives them something to believe in. It gives them a sense of . . ."

"Purpose," Miles supplied.

"Exactly, my lord. It gives them a sense of purpose."

Hugh said, laughing unpleasantly, "Besides, people love to gossip. They overhear half a story and make up the rest themselves."

"May I serve you gentlemen some refreshment?" interrupted a masculine voice from behind them.

It was Blunt with a tray of glasses.

"I didn't know Lady Alyssa had hired a new butler," said the doctor.

"Neither did I," echoed the vicar.

"Are you the new butler?" asked Sir Hugh outright as he helped himself to a flute of champagne.

"No, sir, I am not. I'm Blunt." With a respectful nod toward Miles, he said, "Normally I serve the marquess."

Several minutes passed before Miles managed to draw Blunt aside. "What is this getup?"

His valet glanced down at the frill-fronted shirt and outdated black evening suit. "It was the butler's."

"Where is the butler?"

"Dead and buried. As well as one of the footmen." Blunt spoke out of the side of his mouth. "Surely, my lord, you've noticed the lack of male servants about the place."

Miles thought for a minute. "I hadn't until now."

Blunt lowered his voice. "Graystone Abbey may as well be a nunnery."

Miles frowned. "I thought it was."

"Perhaps in the beginning, my lord. But even then it was a double order."

"A double order?"

"Nuns *and* monks, my lord."

"How in the world did you find out something like that?"

"Miss Pibble, my lord. She is an expert on the subject of the abbey. Anyway, it seems when the old butler passed on—"

"How long ago did he die?"

"It's been five or six years now, my lord."

"Egods."

"Anyway, the earl and countess never bothered to replace him. They simply closed ranks; everyone— upstairs and downstairs—pitched in and they did without."

"How extraordinary." Miles gave his man the once-over. "That doesn't explain what you're doing with a tray of drinks in your hands, standing in the middle of a bucolic setting painted by an Italian nearly two hundred years ago, wearing a long-dead butler's suit of clothing."

"We were shorthanded."

Miles cocked a brow. "Shorthanded?"

"One of the few remaining footmen came down with a fever. Lady Alyssa and Miss Pibble were frantic."

"So you volunteered to help."

"It seemed the thing to do, my lord. After all, you had no need of me this evening."

That was true enough.

"As long as you're here, keep your eyes and ears open," Miles said under his breath.

"I will, my lord."

"We'll confer later."

"Yes, my lord."

"Lest we forget, Blunt, we are here to investigate the strange goings-on at the abbey."

"I will keep it uppermost in my mind, my lord."

Blunt wasn't the only one who needed a reminder, Miles admitted to himself as he took a drink of champagne. He, too, must not forget why he was here.

"We mustn't forget for a moment why we are here, Alfred," Caroline Chubb lectured her husband as she checked her toilette in the full-length mirror.

"Yes, my dear."

She turned to her maid and said, with a dismissive wave of her hand, "You may go to Miss Chubb now, Francesca. I have no further need of you."

"Yes, Lady Chubb." A curtsy later, Francesca was gone.

"As I was saying, Alfred, you see to your historical research in the library, and I will make a complete investigation of Graystone Abbey and its inhabitants. If I learn anything useful . . ." she adjusted the diamond necklace around her neck; it had been a nineteenth wedding anniversary gift from her adoring husband, "I'll share it with you."

Sir Alfred Chubb frowned and, in what was an habitually nervous gesture, pulled at his graying muttonchop whiskers. "You believe I'm doing the right thing, don't you, my dear?"

"I *know* you're doing the right thing. After all, it's only what you're morally and lawfully entitled to," Caroline stated, stepping back from the mirror and admiring the full effect. It was a rare woman who wasn't outshone by a fabulous Worth gown from Paris and a diamond necklace fit for a queen . . . or at the very least, a countess. Even at the age of thirty-seven, she knew herself to be one of those women.

"Of course, it's not as if I were doing it for myself," Alfred said, still struggling with his conscience.

Caroline had no such qualms, herself. She had no conscience. She had found very little use for one.

She caught her husband's eye in the mirror. "Always remember, you are doing this for our son, *your* son."

"I'm doing this for Edward."

"It is his birthright. And yours."

"It's his birthright," Alfred Chubb repeated like a litany. Then he visibly relaxed, and a familiar look appeared in his eyes. He placed his hands on her bare shoulders. "You're looking exceptionally lovely tonight, my dear."

Caroline smiled at his reflection. The smile didn't

reach her eyes. Not that her husband noticed. "Thank you, Alfred."

Leaning over, he nuzzled her neck. The diamonds were cool against her skin in contrast to the warmth of Alfred's mouth and the burning scrape of his beard.

He slipped an arm around her waist and pulled her back against him. Even through the layers of clothing and fine petticoats, she could feel his flesh rising, swelling, hardening. His other hand dove down the front of her dress until he found what he was searching for. He caught her nipple between his thumb and forefinger and pinched.

Caroline schooled her features not to reveal her true feelings. Instead, she let her head fall back against her husband's shoulder and opened her mouth slightly so he could see the tip of her tongue. She sunk her serrated teeth into her bottom lip and pretended to stifle a moan of passion.

It was second nature to her after all these years. Alfred Chubb was convinced that he was a good lover. Nay, she had him convinced that he was a great lover. It made him so much more manageable, malleable, willing to do her bidding. She was, if he only knew, a consummate actress.

Of course, what woman wasn't a consummate actress when it came to the male of the species and his physical appetites?

Her breast was tweaked again. Caroline groaned and whispered breathlessly, "Alfred . . ."

He gave a deep, masculine laugh: half regret, half self-satisfaction. "Too bad, my dear, that we have a long evening ahead of us," he said as he withdrew his hand. "Perhaps I can come to you later."

She adjusted the front of the expensive dress. "Perhaps."

"You may be too tired after our journey."

She knew he wanted her, needed her, to contradict him. "I'm never too tired for you." Indeed, the man had never come close to tapping into her sexual energies.

Alfred stroked his jaw. "I think it's time you had a pair of diamond earrings to go with your diamond necklace."

The smile in the mirror was as bright as the glittering gemstones around her neck. "You're too generous for your own good. You spoil me."

"I enjoy spoiling you." Alfred offered her his arm. "Now we must join the others for dinner, my dear, or they will be wondering what is keeping us."

"The dinner was excellent, Lady Alyssa," Alfred Chubb remarked to her as the company moved into the formal drawing room. It was decorated in the Italianate style, all the *di moda* in the time of the eighth Countess of Graystone, who had seen to the refurbishment herself.

"Thank you, Sir Alfred. I'm glad you enjoyed it," she replied, pleased with the way the evening was going. So far, so good, due in no small part to Miles St. Aldford. He had entertained them at dinner with his witty stories about society and his travels. The marquess had, apparently, been everywhere and done everything.

"A wonderful painting," her guest remarked,

drawing her attention to the huge landscape on the wall in front of them. "An impressive likeness of the abbey."

"It is called *Graystone Abbey: A View of the House, the Gardens and the Park with Deer*. Canaletto painted it in 1748 for the sixth Earl of Graystone," she said.

"The sixth earl would have been your . . ."

Alyssa had to stop and think. Math had never been her forte. "My great-great-great-great-grandfather."

Sir Alfred seemed enthralled. "All the Earls of Graystone who have come before. All the history recorded on the walls of this great and grand house." He heaved a sigh. "I regret not visiting the abbey while your father was still alive. Lady Chubb and I were deeply saddened to hear about his premature demise, and that of your mother. Our belated condolences, Lady Alyssa."

"Thank you, Sir Alfred."

"I often pictured myself sitting in the library discussing the history of this region with Lord Graystone."

"I'm sure my father would have enjoyed the opportunity to speak with you."

"Kind of you to say so. Most kind. I'm only sorry my son, Edward, isn't with us on this visit, after all. He's touring Italy with the youngest son of the Duke of B—"

"I believe Lady Chubb mentioned as much at dinner."

"Quite so." Then Sir Alfred indicated a huge

carved ornamental plaque hanging over the fire-place. "And that is, I presume, the family crest."

"It is, indeed."

"Would you explain it to me?"

"Of course." If Sir Alfred really wanted to know about the crest, she was only too happy to tell him. "The crest is divided into four quadrants. The first pictures a lion similar to that of Richard the Lion-Hearted."

"*Coeur de Lion,*" murmured Sir Alfred.

"Supposedly an early ancestor was one of the no-blemen who followed Richard to the Holy Land dur-ing the Third Crusade in fulfillment of a vow the king had made to recapture Jerusalem."

"Remarkable."

"The second is a white flower, now extinct; the third an ornate cross, and the fourth is our family motto: *Vincit omnia veritas.*"

" 'Truth conquers all things,' " came a lilting fe-male voice from behind them.

They both turned. It was Lady Chubb. Gowned in a fashionable silk dress of deep violet—the color brought out the blue-violet in her eyes and was set off by her lustrous dark brown hair—she was stunning.

Lady Chubb smiled beautifully, yet the smile never seemed to reach her eyes. "Do you believe truth conquers all things, Lady Alyssa?"

"Yes, I do." But Alyssa sensed there was more to the question than simply making casual conversa-tion; she just wasn't clever enough to figure out what it was.

Caroline Chubb slipped an elegant arm through

Sir Alfred's and drew him to her side. "I must borrow my husband for a few minutes. It seems Dr. Symthe has a question of historical importance he would like to ask Sir Alfred."

"Of course," Alyssa said politely.

Upon finding herself alone, she turned and gazed up at the painting over the fireplace. Her favorite Canaletto wasn't here, however, but in the study. It was a view of Venice: the palazzos, the canals, the gondolas and gondoliers, and the people of *Venezia*.

"A pound for your thoughts," said a familiar masculine voice.

Miles St. Aldford was standing beside her, an after-dinner brandy in his hand. "A pound, my lord? I thought it was usually a penny."

"Inflation."

She made an expressive face. "Frankly I don't believe they're worth even a penny."

"I'll be the judge of that."

Alyssa indicated the painting above them. "I was thinking about Canaletto."

"Ah—"

She went on. "Which led me to Goethe."

He frowned. "How did you get from an Italian painter to a German poet?"

Alyssa attempted to explain. "My favorite painting by Canaletto, *Venice: A Palazzo, a Gondola and a View from a Bridge*, hangs in the study opposite my desk. So, you see, I was thinking about Venice, which led me to consider two books of such different temperament by the same author: *Venetian Epigrams* and *Italian Journey* by—"

"Johann Wolfgang von Goethe," he concluded.

She clapped her hands together. "Exactly. Hence, from Canaletto to Goethe."

"I think I'm beginning to understand," the marquess stated in a knowing fashion.

"Beginning to understand what, my lord?"

There was a flash of straight, white teeth. "How your mind works, my lady."

Oh dear!

Without preamble, Alyssa changed the subject. "Thank you for entertaining us with your wonderful stories at dinner."

"You're welcome. It was the least I could do when you had your cook prepare three of my favorite dishes."

"It was the least we could do." She permitted herself a small sigh. "I find I often don't know what to say in social situations."

"You seem very erudite to me."

"If I'm talking about books or history or my garden, yes, I can go on at some length. But I will never be clever and amusing like Lady Chubb." They both regarded the gathering around the Louis Quatorze sofa. Caroline Chubb and her daughter, Charmel, were holding court. The men in attendance were beside themselves to hear every word spoken by the two ladies, so very much alike in appearance: dark hair, classic features, stunning figures, the mother with her violet eyes, the daughter with her emerald green. "Not only is Lady Chubb very clever, but she is very beautiful. She has them all eating out of her hand."

Miles St. Aldford's manner was suddenly quite cool. He swirled the brandy in his glass and raised it to his mouth. "Is that what you want? Gentlemen fawning all over you?"

"No."

He looked over the rim of the crystal snifter into her eyes. "What do you want?"

Alyssa wasn't certain she understood his question. "You mean from gentlemen?"

"Or a particular gentleman?"

She hesitated, not wanting to give a frivolous answer. "I would like a man who can respect my mind," she finally said, making the admission cautiously.

Miles St. Aldford seemed to choke on his brandy.

"Are you all right, my lord?"

"Yes." He cleared his throat. "Go on."

She did. "I would like a man who finds joy in music, literature, nature."

"Gardening?"

"Yes, and gardening, of course."

"There's more . . ." he prompted as if he could actually read her mind.

Should she tell him? Well, why not? It wasn't a secret. "I have always wanted to travel, my lord," Alyssa announced boldly.

"Travel?"

"I want to see the world. I suppose it sounds silly, perhaps even schoolgirlish to you, since you have been everywhere, seen everything, done everything, but I have been nowhere, and I have seen and done nothing," she said unselfconsciously.

It was simply a matter of fact. She had been no farther north than Edinburgh, no farther east than London, no farther south than the Isle of Wight.

Miles put his glass down on the table to one side of the fireplace. "Why didn't you travel with your parents?"

"They had some notion that I should do as they had done," she told him.

"Which was?"

"Although my father had taken the traditional Grand Tour in his youth, my mother—who was several years younger—had not traveled. So they went together after they were married, and through her eyes he saw everything anew." For a moment, Alyssa could almost hear her parents' voices, filled with the abiding love they'd had for each other. Her hand floated to the spot on her black dress that was above her heart. "That's what they wanted for me: to discover the world with the right man, and he would see it as if for the first time."

"Your parents were romantics," Miles stated.

"Yes. They were."

A trill of feminine laughter followed by the guffaws of the gentlemen erupted on the other side of the room. They watched as Sir Hugh bent his head toward the lovely Miss Chubb and said something that she apparently found amusing. Charmel Chubb laughed gaily.

"Sir Hugh hasn't taken his eyes off Miss Chubb for more than two seconds tonight," observed Miles St. Aldford. "Do you think it was wise to seat them next to each other at the dinner table?"

Alyssa splayed her fan and wafted it back and forth in front of her face. Behind its shield she confessed, "It was deliberate."

"You mean you seated them together on purpose?"

"Of course."

"Aren't you jealous of his attentions to her?"

She fanned herself again. "Why in heaven would I be?"

"But I was given to understand that you and Sir Hugh—"

"No."

"No?"

Alyssa shook her head vigorously. The heat of irritation—it was proportionately irritation *and* embarrassment—spread up her neck and onto her cheeks, staining them bright pink. "I have no intentions of marrying Sir Hugh Pureheart."

"Not now. But perhaps once you are out of mourning," her companion suggested.

"No. Not now. Not ever. I have my plans, Lord Cork, and they do not include marriage to Sir Hugh or to anyone, for that matter." She snapped her fan shut. "Enough about such an unpleasant subject. I know you were sent here to the abbey to investigate rumors of a ghost. Have you reached any conclusions?"

"I have," he said. "I think we should meet in private and discuss the matter."

Alyssa nodded. It was a sound suggestion. "Shall we say tomorrow at eleven o'clock in my study?"

"Tomorrow morning it is, my lady."

"When are we leaving, my lord?" Blunt inquired later that evening as he dealt with the dress coat Miles had just removed.

Miles stood at the window of his bedchamber and gazed out into the night. The heavens were filled with thousands of twinkling stars. The full moon—a bright sphere of silver hovering low in a black sky—would soon be on the rise. "We're not," he finally said to the other man, who patiently waited.

"We're not leaving? But I thought we just agreed that the rumors of a ghost are just that—rumors."

Miles lightly tapped a knuckle against the glass pane. The windows in the Knight's Chambers were open wide and the air in his bedroom was filled with scents from the rose garden below. He mulled it over in his mind and then stated, "Something is amiss."

"What is amiss, my lord?"

"I don't know," Miles admitted. "But we're going to stay and find out."

His valet didn't argue the point. Both men knew they were only alive now because of his unerring instincts on several past occasions. He could almost taste trouble, smell it, *feel* it.

" 'I am amazed, methinks,' " Miles muttered to himself as he looked out over the walled garden, " 'and lose my way among the thorns and dangers of this world.' "

Chapter Six

She was in grave danger.

The night was as black as ink. There wasn't a star in the sky, and the sliver of new moon that should have been clearly visible overhead was concealed by a layer of thick clouds. The grass beneath her feet was cold and wet. A cloak was thrown around her shoulders to ward off the unseasonable chill.

Someone was following her.

She looked back over her shoulder and caught a glimpse of a cowled figure. Large. Dark. Looming. Faceless. Frightening. She couldn't tell whether it was male or female. She only sensed it was foe, not friend, and she must get away.

She found herself at the entrance to the maze. She hesitated. She heard footsteps behind her and she quickly entered. The menacing footsteps followed. She suddenly knew beyond a shadow of a doubt that her life was in danger.

She began to walk, faster and faster. Then she started to run. Her heart was pounding. Her lungs were about to burst. Her feet were like blocks of ice. Her arms were stretched out in front of her. She felt *her way. Every now and then a sharp branch snapped, scratching her skin, drawing blood.*

She came to a dead end.

She had to backtrack and try again from the last turn. She must find her way to the center of the labyrinth, for once she reached the heart of the maze she would be safe.

Her cloak snagged on a hedge and fluttered to the ground. She left it where it fell and kept going. A foreboding wind—or was it someone's breath?— stirred the tiny hairs on the back of her neck. Bony fingers seemed to tiptoe up her spine. Then a hand closed on her bare shoulder. She opened her mouth to scream, but no sound came out.

As she tried to escape the clawing hand and reach safety, two words were suddenly imprinted on her brain: Ariadne's Thread.

Alyssa shot straight up in bed.

For a minute or two the only sound she heard was the thunderous drumming of her own heart. She couldn't seem to catch her breath. She gasped for air, trying to fill oxygen-starved lungs. A sheen of perspiration covered her from head to toe. Her nightdress was damp, as were the pillow slips and the bedsheets wrapped around her body.

Trembling, she raised her hand and pushed the wet tendrils of hair back from her face. She had been dreaming. It must have been a dream. A horrible dream. A nightmare.

She reached for the pitcher of water on the bedside table, poured herself a glass—half of the water spilled onto the lace doily—raised it to her lips, and drank thirstily. Then she managed to take in a deep breath and slowly release it. Thankfully, her heart rate was returning to normal, as was her breathing.

Unfortunately, she was wide awake. There would be no more sleep for her tonight.

Alyssa pushed the covers aside, slipped out of the ornately carved sixteenth-century bed—it was reputed to have once stood in the royal chambers of Anne of Denmark, queen to James I—and went across to the window. Through an opening in the draperies, moonlight streamed into the room. Recalling part of her nightmare, she raised her arms to the pale light and made a careful inspection of her skin. There weren't any scratches, and there wasn't a trace of blood.

Her bedroom was warm and stifling: There was no hint of a breeze coming in the open window. The walls were closing in on her. She needed fresh air.

Alyssa reached for her linen wrapper, located her slippers, and opened the door of her boudoir. She peered around the corner: The hallway was deserted. She moved through the night like an apparition, taking the back staircase and skirting the kitchens and the servants' quarters. No candle or lamp was necessary to light the way. Her lifelong familiarity with the abbey, and the bright moonlight, more than sufficed.

Within ten minutes she was outside on the flagstone path—she was fairly skipping by now—that led to the rose garden, her beloved rose garden. *There* she could breathe. *There* she would be free.

* * *

Miles wasn't certain what had roused him. One minute he had been in a deep sleep; the next he was wide awake. Then he knew. He'd had a dream. A nightmare. A *cauchemar*, as the French called it.

He remembered only the vaguest details. Someone—*something*—had been pursuing him: a monster, a fiend, the enemy, and he had been running in circles, trapped in a dark cave or tunnel.

No, not a cave or a tunnel, but a maze. And he'd had to use all of his considerable skills to escape the twists and turns of the complex labyrinth.

"Ariadne's Thread," Miles muttered aloud as he pushed himself up on his elbows.

He was covered with sweat. The sheets were wound tightly around his legs. He worked himself free, threw the covers off, and stood up. His reflection stared back at him from the large, ornate mirror opposite the bed. He saw a naked man, skin glistening with perspiration, dark hair matted to his chest, his body half aroused.

Violence—or the threat of violence—pumped a kind of powerful aphrodisiac into a man's bloodstream. It heightened his awareness, stimulated his senses, whetted his sexual appetite as surely as the presence of a lush and willing woman. He'd learned that much as a soldier and a spy, and as a man.

He'd had his share of life-and-death situations, Miles acknowledged as he plucked a towel from the washstand and proceeded to dry himself off. And his share of women.

He vigorously rubbed his face and neck, his arms and chest, even his legs with the Turkish towel, careful to avoid—more from habit than anything else; the old wound rarely bothered him these days—the long, jagged scar on his left thigh.

The scar was six inches long and the width of a knife blade. It was a souvenir of a deadly ambush that had taken place some five years before in the Arab quarter of Zanzibar, called Stone Town. he should have known better, of course, than to go alone at night. Where was his "unerring" instinct for trouble on that occasion? But, as Blunt was fond of reminding him, the other man had gotten the worst of their encounter. He had ended up floating facedown in the Zanzibar Channel, his own blade embedded in his belly.

It had been a close call.

Even now Miles shuddered to think of it. He had come perilously near to losing strategic parts of his anatomy on that fateful night. There was such a thing as sacrificing too much for queen and country, he reflected with a sardonic smile.

Combing his fingers through the damp curls at his nape, Miles heaved a well-placed sigh. Not that he'd made use of that particular part of his male anatomy lately. His last liaison had ended several months before he had set sail for America the previous fall, and he could muster no enthusiasm for another affair.

He could always marry, of course. After all, it was his duty as the fourth Marquess of Cork to ensure that someday there would be a fifth Marquess of Cork.

The problem was the females of his acquaintance. They were all alike. They looked alike. They acted alike. They thought alike. They shopped in Paris.

They holidayed in Italy. They followed the social season from London, after Easter, to the Derby and Ascot in June, then the sailing at Cowes, the shooting in Scotland, and the late summer retreat to the country until it began again.

But wherever they were, there was talk of little else but fashion, jewels, and the latest juicy tidbit of gossip. In short, the women of Society were predictable and bloody boring.

The answer to his problem seemed obvious. All he had to do was find a woman who was different, a woman who wasn't predictable, a woman who was fascinating and who would never bore him.

"Jesus, Mary, and Joseph!" Miles swore impatiently as he stalked across the room. "Where do you think you're going to find someone like that, Cork?"

He stood in front of the open window—he hadn't bothered with his dressing gown—and looked out at the moonlit night. He absently rubbed one hand back and forth across his bare chest and watched as a small herd of deer grazed at the edge of the park.

Something on the periphery of his vision caught his eye. He froze. There was someone on the path below his window. A figure in white. A woman. No, it was a girl, with hair of silvery gold flowing down her back as she raced toward the door leading to the rose garden.

It was Lady Alyssa.

Miles watched as she opened the stone door and disappeared into Milady's Bower.

What, pray tell, was she doing? It had to be the middle of the night. He retrieved his pocket watch from the bedside table and brought it to the window. Three o'clock.

"The day is for honest men, the night for thieves," according to the ancient Greek dramatist Euripides.

The night was also for lovers, but Miles didn't believe for a moment that Lady Alyssa Gray was on her way to meet a man. For one thing, Sir Hugh would never act so boldly or so rashly. The baronet was a stickler for proper behavior.

"Well, if she isn't meeting that fool Pureheart, then what the devil is she up to?" he muttered out loud, snapping his pocket watch shut.

Before he had time to reconsider, Miles St. Aldford was pulling on a pair of pants and reaching for his boots and a shirt.

The lady had no business being out and about in the middle of the night, and he intended to tell her so as soon as he reached the rose garden.

Chapter Seven

She was free.

Her slippers were soaked all the way through to her feet. The hem of her sheer cotton nightgown and linen wrapper were wet with dew. But she didn't care. She headed across a patch of grass toward her favorite bench in Milady's Bower. With each step she took, Alyssa felt as if the weight of the world were being lifted from her shoulders.

She plunked herself down on the stone bench beneath the rose arbor, kicked off her slippers, and curled her feet up under her. This had always been her favorite spot to be alone. No one could see her, yet she had an unobstructed view of the abbey, the garden door, the surrounding wall, even the heavens above.

It wasn't the first time Alyssa had escaped to the rose garden. Even as a girl—during those restless years between childhood and womanhood—she had frequently awakened in the dead of night and been unable to go back to sleep. The garden had become her refuge.

If the truth be told, she was restless still. She had no name, no words to describe the way she felt.

She'd always thought of it as a fever that came with High Rose Tide because it seemed to peak on a perfect June night when the rose garden was at its zenith.

On a perfect June night like tonight.

Alyssa put her head back and gazed up at the sky. The stars were bright points of light against a midnight-blue backdrop. The moon was huge, full, bright. It cast a silvery hue on everything below. The roses—their colors transformed by the moonlight—were iridescent shades of wine-red, carnelian, damask, pink, and alabaster.

She recited aloud, " 'The moon like a flower in heaven's high bower, with silent delight, sits and smiles on the night.' "

Mr. William Blake was right. The moon did smile down on her; the same moon that smiled down on a thousand, a million other women as they sat in their gardens tonight—the names were poetry on her tongue—in Majorca, Marrakesh, and Mirzapur, Darjeeling, Denizli, Segovia, and São Tiago. What were those women thinking? Feeling? Surely their hopes and their dreams weren't so very different from her own.

What were her hopes? Her dreams?

She wanted . . .

She needed . . .

She desired . . .

What name did she put to that which she knew only as longing?

Her head and her heart told Alyssa that it had to do with the intimate relationship between a man and a woman, yet she knew so little of men and women. Like most females of her age and class in society, she'd been kept ignorant of the details. There was a conspiracy of silence, and it was a silence not to be broken until the wedding night.

Was the act between husband and wife so abhorrent, so repulsive, so repugnant in nature that no one could bear to speak of it?

No.

She didn't believe that to be true. For she remembered the way her mother and father had gazed at each other when they'd thought no one was looking. It had been obvious they couldn't wait to be alone!

Perhaps it was splendid. Perhaps it was joy beyond description. Perhaps it was, indeed, wedded bliss.

What if she never married? What if she had no wedding night? Was she doomed to go to her grave without ever experiencing the passion, the desire, the quickening heartbeat upon seeing a beloved, that the poets spoke of?

Her reverie suddenly ceased.

Someone had entered Milady's Bower.

Alyssa turned. She knew instantly it was Miles St. Aldford. She recognized the sound of his footfall on the flagstone path—there was an assurance, a purpose, to his walk—the tilt of his head, the unusual breadth of his shoulders, his impressive stature: He was measurably taller than any other man she had known.

He strode toward her through the night, and her heart began to race. She couldn't seem to catch her breath; the air was trapped in her lungs. She shivered, despite the warmth of the evening. A sliver of awareness trickled down her spine, and every nerve ending in her body was on alert. She'd never had this reaction to a gentleman before. What was it about Miles St. Aldford that set him apart?

On some instinctive, even primitive level Alyssa knew what it was. This was a man who had the answers, if she only dared to ask the questions.

"Ten pounds for your thoughts, my lady," the marquess said as he approached the stone bench.

"That's a small fortune," she pointed out.

"Yes, it is," he said with a small stoic laugh.

"This is the second time tonight you've made such a generous offer, my lord. Indeed, the price seems to be going up. Why would you pay ten pounds— or one pound, for that matter—to find out what I'm thinking?"

He took a step closer to her. "Your mind fascinates me."

Was he serious? Or was he making a jest? "I don't see why."

"The important thing is I do."

Alyssa decided to act as if it were perfectly normal to be having a conversation with Miles St. Aldford in the middle of the night while dressed in her nightgown. "Would you care to explain, my lord?"

He took in a deep breath and let it out again. "You're different from the women of Society."

She stifled a small sigh and adjusted the hem of her wrapper so that the tips of her toes were covered. "I was afraid of that."

"It isn't something to be afraid of," he said. "Its something to be thankful for."

She wetted her lips with the tip of her tongue. "I don't understand."

In a superior—and thoroughly masculine—tone of voice, he said, "I know you don't."

The gentleman was irksome; gentlemen so often were. "Please, go on, sir."

"The women one meets in Society—"

It was necessary to interrupt him. "Are we speaking of the ladies of the Marlborough House Set, my lord?"

"We are." A black brow was crooked in her direction. "By the by, what have you heard about the women who run with the Prince of Wales?"

"Very little, really," she confessed. "It is rumored that they are beautifully dressed, usually at enormous expense by Mr. Charles Worth of the Rue de la Paix in Paris, that they are clever and witty and accomplished and—"

"Amoral," he finished for her.

Alyssa wrapped her arms around her knees and looked up eagerly. "Are they amoral?"

"Some of them."

"How fascinating."

Apparently that wasn't what Lord Cork had expected her to say. "Do you think so?"

Alyssa nodded her head. "I've never actually met anyone who was outside the range of conventional behavior when it comes to morality. We could always argue, of course, about whether it is worse to be amoral or immoral."

"We could, but we won't."

She gnawed on her bottom lip for a moment.

"And I stand corrected, my lord. I have met someone of dubious moral character."

She felt as if he were staring right through her. "Who?"

"A pompous little Bourbon prince who once visited my father." Alyssa blushed to think of—Philip, yes, that had been his name. "Looking back on the whole affair, I'm certain the problem arose because I was young and naive, and I didn't understand his intentions."

"What were his intentions?" the marquess inquired in a hard, dry voice.

"Marriage, for one." She paused. "At least in the end."

"What were his intentions in the beginning?"

"I believe he wanted to kiss me," she admitted in a husky voice, a tiny frog having lodged itself in her throat.

"You only believe?"

"All right, I know he wanted to kiss me."

"Did you allow him such liberties?"

She was aghast. "Of course not. Not once I comprehended what he was about."

Something flickered behind the man's dark eyes. "What else was he about?"

Alyssa searched for a delicate way of putting it. "You must remember, my lord, that the prince was French."

"He attempted to seduce you."

She was mortified. How had Lord Cork guessed? Of course, he was a man of the world, and men of the world knew about such things. At least it saved her from having to explain any further.

Apparently he wasn't satisfied with her explanation. "Where were your parents while this was going on?"

"In the library."

Alyssa thought she heard him mutter under his breath, "There is something to be said for *not* being an avid reader." He raised one black-booted foot, rested it on the back of the stone bench, leaned toward her, and continued with his interrogation. "Where did this attempt at seduction take place?"

Her face flamed. "Beneath the marble of the well-endowed Apollo." A raised eyebrow drove her to add, "That's what we call one of the statues in the formal garden."

"I take it this particular sculpture of the Greek god is sans clothing," the marquess ascertained.

"It is, my lord."

"Am I also correct in assuming that Apollo is depicted in the prime of his manhood: tall, broad-shouldered, slim-waisted, narrow-hipped, long-legged, and muscular?"

He had described the statue perfectly. "You've seen the well-endowed Apollo?"

"No."

"How did you know, then?"

"Let's just say I have a vivid imagination." Miles St. Aldford rubbed the back of his neck, shook his head from side to side, and made what sounded like an impatient clicking noise. "Madam, we digress. I recall offering you ten pounds for your thoughts, and the next thing I know we're discussing garden statuary. Tell me, what were you thinking about as I approached?"

'Alyssa chose her words with care. "I was thinking that you know a great deal, and I know next to nothing."

He frowned. "That doesn't seem very likely. Blunt tells me that Miss Pibble sings your praises at every opportunity. You were apparently her star pupil, and are considered something of a scholar."

"I understand things. I want to understand people."

"Surely in your studies you delved into the subject of human behavior and motivation."

"I understand people—men and women—on an intellectual level. That isn't what I mean."

"What do you mean?"

He was deliberately being obtuse; it was most annoying. "I am referring to the relationship between men and women," Alyssa stated with candor.

"Ah—"

It was a very telling *ah*.

A sardonic smile touched the edges of his mouth. "Are you, by any chance, my lady, referring to the romantic relationship between a man and a woman?"

"That's it exactly." Alyssa craned to look up at him. "I'm getting a stiff neck, my lord. Would you like to sit while we continue with our conversation?"

"Yes. Thank you." He nodded politely, came around the end of the bench, and sat down.

The man must have dressed in a hurry; he was in a state of dishabille. His shirt was only partially buttoned, she noticed. He wore no collar, and his shirttail was stuffed haphazardly into the back of his breeches. She tried not to stare, but she suspected there was nothing beneath his outer garments. The realization of how near her bare flesh was to Miles St. Aldford's bare flesh did very odd things to Alyssa's sense of equilibrium.

"W-what were we speaking of?" she stammered, her presence of mind having vanished into thin air.

The marquess was oblivious to her discomfort. "You were confessing to a certain curiosity about the romantic relationship between a man and a woman."

That was it! "You know everything, my lord, and I know nothing." It wasn't fair.

Long muscular legs were casually stretched out in front of him. "That is as it should be."

"Why?"

"Because you're a woman."

"That isn't a good reason," she objected.

"Perhaps not in your eyes, my lady, but it is reason enough in the eyes of Society."

"Then Society is wrong. Give me one good reason," she insisted.

Lord Cork crossed his arms, put his head back, and stared up at the stars. "Because you're unmarried."

"So are you."

He turned his face toward her. "I'm a man."

"We're back to gender, then."

"Apparently so," he said dryly.

"Is that what it always comes down to?" Alyssa didn't receive an answer from her *compagnon de nuit*, nor did she expect one. "It seems illogical to me that a man may know about these matters, but a woman must remain ignorant."

"A woman's virtue must be protected."

Alyssa threw her hands up in exasperation. "How will ignorance protect her virtue? How can she know what to do or what not to do if she is unaware of the facts?"

He stroked his jaw. "For the sake of our discussion, may I ask you a personal question?"

"You may."

"Have you allowed Sir Hugh to kiss you?"

"Yes." He registered surprise. "I've known Hugh Babington Pureheart for many years," she said. "He was kind to me after my parents died. On several occasions, Sir Hugh has placed a chaste kiss upon my cheek or brow."

"Ah-huh." Her answer seemed to please him. "Have you allowed any other kind?"

"Well, as I said, the prince tried. When I realized what he intended to do, I turned my head. His kiss landed somewhere in the region of my chin."

"And the attempted seduction?"

She wetted her lips again. "He lunged at me."

"Go on."

"I quickly stepped to one side and the prince ended up with his arms around the statue, his eyes level with—" Alyssa tried to swallow, "a most well-endowed part of the well-endowed Apollo." Nervous laughter escaped her. "You should have seen the expression on Philip's face when he looked up, my lord."

"I wish I'd been there," said Miles St. Aldford.

She was intelligent.
She was naive.

She was maddening.

She was irresistible.

She was also driving him to distraction. Miles wasn't certain if he wanted to throttle her or kiss her.

He had followed Lady Alyssa Gray into the rose garden with the best of intentions: to lecture her on the imprudence of wandering about alone in the middle of the night. Instead, he found himself sitting beside her on a secluded bench, discussing everything under the sun—or under the moon, in this case—from an attempted seduction to a naked statue of Apollo.

It was most extraordinary.

But then, Lady Alyssa Gray was an extraordinary young woman. Indeed, Miles didn't think he had ever met anyone quite like her before.

"Anyway, my lord, to return to the subject under discussion. It is all well and good to be told about things, to read about them, but there is no substitute for experience. Don't you agree?"

Little warning bells went off in Miles's head. He must proceed with caution. "If I agree with you, my lady, then my answer flies in the face of what is considered acceptable behavior for unmarried women by our society. Inexperience in a female, as we both know, is expected and even treasured."

She made a noise that sounded very much like *hmmph.*

He went on. "If I disagree with you, then you will argue that it is not only acceptable behavior for a gentleman to be experienced, it is expected. In fact, it's encouraged from the time he is barely out of the nursery."

"That is it precisely," she said to him. "You see, you do comprehend the way my mind works."

Miles was beginning to. "Caught between the devil and the deep blue sea," he muttered under his breath.

Apparently Alyssa wasn't finished. "And what of the lady of good breeding who has no intentions of marrying and yet would like to know a little, perhaps even more than a little, of what occurs between a man and a woman?"

He could beat around the bush, but he decided not to. "Are you speaking of yourself?"

Her color rose. "I am."

"Have you decided not to marry?"

She nodded her head and stated emphatically, "I will never marry."

What a bloody waste. "May I inquire as to the reason?"

"Reasons. Indeed, they are too numerous to mention." She fingered the lace on the edge of her linen wrapper. "I will put it in a nutshell for you, my lord."

"Please do, my lady."

"Sir Hugh is the kind of gentleman I am expected to marry, and he is the last man I would want to. So I will remain single. This doesn't mean, however, that I don't have wants or needs or desires."

"Of course it doesn't."

"You aren't married."

"No, I'm not."

"Yet you have undoubtedly felt wants and needs and desires, have you not, my lord?"

Warning bells were starting to go off in his head again. "I must confess that I have."

She flung up a defiant chin. "You have eaten of the fruit and drunk of the wine. You haven't allowed yourself to go hungry or thirsty simply because you're single."

"Are we speaking of food now, my lady?"

"I am using food as a metaphor for physical appetites, my lord," she elucidated, a shade haughtily.

"Ah, I see." He stroked his jaw. "For a moment I thought you might be describing a banquet, or a feast, or a mélange, which is all the fashion this season at weekend houseparties."

"Are you making fun of me, my lord?"

"Of course not, my lady."

Egods, the woman was like a stubborn purebred terrier with a tasty bone between its teeth; she had no intentions of letting go until she was good and ready.

"Sir, you haven't answered my original question."

"Madam, I don't remember what your original question was." There had been so many others in the meantime.

"I will be succinct."

"By all means, do be."

"In the interest of intellectual inquiry, I would like to know what it's like to kiss a man. Will you kiss me?"

This was turning out to be a night unlike any other. "Yes."

The lady was taken aback. "Just like that, yes. Don't you want to discuss it first?"

"There has already been ample discussion in this garden tonight. Look up at the moon, my lady." Miles slid nearer to her on the bench. "Take in a deep breath of air permeated with the scent of roses." He moved closer still. "Listen to the song of the night birds and the distant hoot of an owl, the wind stirring through the trees at the edge of the park, the sound of a bullfrog as it dives into the lake. On a night like tonight, all the senses are razor sharp. One can hear more acutely, smell and see more clearly. Taste the night. Feel the night."

"Sir, you speak poetry."

He was just warming up. "Your hair is like silk. Your skin is soft and sweet-smelling. Indeed, 'that which we call a rose by any other name would smell as sweet.' "

"Act two, scene two," the young woman beside him murmured.

"I beg your pardon—"

"*Romeo and Juliet.*" Gray eyes stared intently into his. "Do you have any last-minute instructions, my lord?"

"Instructions?"

"Before you kiss me."

Miles suppressed a smile. "Don't expect too much of yourself at first, my lady. Kissing is an acquired skill."

Alyssa seemed to be taking in every word he said. "In other words, one *learns* to kiss well. It's a skill that comes with experience and practice."

He supposed it did.

Miles leaned toward her, bent his head, inhaled her scent—Lord, she was sweetly seductive—and brought his mouth down to hers. He lightly touched her lips with his, and drew back. "Well?"

"That was . . ." Alyssa appeared to be searching for the right word, "pleasant."

"Pleasant?" His kisses had been called many things by many women, but no one had ever accused them of being pleasant! "Maybe we should try again . . . in the interest of intellectual inquiry."

"Maybe we should."

This time, at his leisure, Miles explored the tastes and textures of Alyssa's mouth. Her kiss was sweet, in the same way a fine wine was sweet: It was subtle, intriguing, heady, and slightly mysterious. The more one discovered about the flavor, the more there was left to discover.

"How was our second attempt?" he inquired as he lifted his head.

She was circumspect. "It was a definite improvement on the first, my lord."

"But?"

"But I cannot imagine that's all there is to it," she said bluntly. "I have read of the incredible lengths to which physical passion has driven men and women throughout human history. Surely there is more."

"Of course there's more." There was much more. "But you are an innocent, a young woman of gentle breeding and good name, my lady."

Alyssa sighed. "And you are my only hope, my lord. You are my last chance."

"I am?"

She nodded. "Without your assistance in this matter, I will go to my grave not knowing passion."

He hadn't thought of it in quite those terms.

"I am truly a damsel in distress, and I have need of a knight in shining armor who will come to my rescue," she added.

Miles felt his resolve weakening. "Well, perhaps for a few minutes, within the privacy of the rose garden . . ."

"We can pretend that the outside world doesn't exist," she suggested. "No one will hear us. No one will see us. No one will ever know. It will be our secret."

It would be their secret.

Miles slipped an arm around Alyssa's waist and drew her slender body to his. Then he lowered his mouth to hers and drank long and deep. With the tip of his tongue, he explored her lips, her teeth, her tongue. He felt a quiver of awareness shoot through her, and he was immensely pleased with himself.

Then he cajoled her lips apart and delved into her mouth, taking his first intimate taste of her. It was a taste that could very quickly become habit-forming, addictive. Miles found that the more he took, the more he wanted, the more he needed.

Frankly Lady Alyssa Gray wasn't what he had expected. He knew her to be an innocent, yet she had a natural ability—even a God-given talent—for kissing that was unlike anything he had ever encountered. Experience, he decided, was highly overrated.

To think that no man had ever kissed this woman

as he was. To think that no man had ever wrapped his arms around her lovely and lush body and pulled her against his. He was the first one. He was the only one. It was a seductive thought.

He could feel her nipples through her nightdress. He could envision the material wet from his mouth, his kisses, her breasts revealed beneath the fine veil of material, their pink tips visible to his eyes, accessible to his teeth, his lips, his tongue. He could almost imagine sliding his hand along her silky thigh to that pale golden treasure trove, damp for the first time because of his kiss, his caress.

Miles was surprised to find that kissing Alyssa, pressing Alyssa to his chest, feeling the subtle pressure of her breasts against his shirt, had ignited a fire inside him.

Bloody hell, he was as hot as a poker! He was as hard as a rock. He was about to burst his skin. He hadn't reacted like this in years. If the truth be told, he couldn't ever remember reacting to a woman's kiss in quite this way. He felt like his body was too small to contain him: It was great pleasure and great pain.

He was sorely tempted to forget who the lady was, who he was, where they were, everything but making love to her in a beautiful rose garden beneath a silver moon.

Miles raised his head and, looking down at her lovely face, confessed, "I have always wanted to kiss an angel."

Alyssa gazed up into his eyes. "I am no angel, my lord."

Chapter Eight

The sin of omission.

Someone should have told her, *warned* her, how it would be, that a man's kiss could turn the world upside down and change everything in the space of a heartbeat.

She wanted . . .

She needed . . .

She desired . . .

Miles St. Aldford!

The realization stunned Alyssa. Her heart was drumming—rat-a-tat-tat, rat-a-tat-tat—like the timpani she had once heard at a seaside band concert. Her breath was coming in small, quick gulps. Her hands and feet were ice-cold, yet she seemed to be burning up with fever.

Miles's heart was pounding as well. She could feel its rhythmic beat beneath her fingertips. Heat emanated from his body, right through the material of his shirt, warming her.

Alyssa should have been shocked by her own behavior. She wasn't. She should have been mortified to find herself in the marquess's arms, her breasts flattened against him. She wasn't. She should pull back. She had no intentions of doing so.

One minute she was a wide-eyed, innocent girl; the next she was a woman. She suddenly knew what the poet was speaking of when he wrote that passion was "a fever in the mind." This was her first taste of sexual passion, and it was very much to her liking. Even as it frightened her, it attracted her.

In a million years she would never have imagined that an intimate, physical relationship could be like this. The reality of kissing Miles St. Aldford—and being kissed by him—was so much better than any fantasy she might conjure up in her head.

Was it always like this between a man and a woman?

Alyssa didn't think so. Women would be shouting it from the rooftops if intimacy were proven to be this sweet, hot opiate in the veins, this pain that was pleasure arrowing from the tips of the breasts— hers were sensitive to the slightest movement of her nightgown, curling up into tight buds, itching so desperately that she wished she could rub them back and forth along Miles's muscular chest—down to her belly, to that most vulnerable place between her thighs.

Her instincts had been right. He did have the answers, if she only had the courage to ask the questions.

Miles was right, too, of course. Her senses were suddenly more acutely attuned to the world around her. She could hear the night birds singing in the treetops at the edge of the Old Woods. She could smell the roses, not just those overhead—although the scent of the ramblers was heavy and exotic on the night air—but individual fragrances from every corner of Milady's Bower: the slightly fruity essence of the bright crimson Chinas, the delicate perfume of the pale pinks, the mere hint of a fragrance emanating from the fairy roses, the heavy perfume of the deep scarlet blooms, and, possibly her favorite, the milk-white Damasks that cascaded over the garden wall.

Everything was clearly visible, from the individual petals of the roses to the moon high in the star-filled sky. Alyssa opened her eyes while Miles was kissing her, and she could see his long, sooty eyelashes, the surprisingly fine texture to his skin, an errant curl that fell onto his forehead, the attractive curve of his ear.

She didn't know if she could taste the night, feel the night, but she could certainly taste and feel him. His flavor was dark, smoky, intriguing. She alternately grasped his arms, his chest, his shoulders. He was rock solid.

A wanton urge to run her hands down the length of Miles's body, to verify that he was, indeed, fashioned in the likeness of the Greek gods in the garden, coursed through Alyssa. In truth, he was more well-endowed than the well-endowed Apollo. She could feel that particular part of him pressing against her leg, and she was quite certain it was much larger than the corresponding appendage on the marble statue.

Indeed, the marquess appeared to be even larger than when he had first sat down beside her on the bench. She tried not to stare—that would, naturally, be most discourteous—but was she the cause of the amazing alteration in his body?

Alyssa swayed. She was light-headed, as if she had been sipping champagne. She was disoriented and a little muddled. She felt all tingly, from the tips of her bare toes to the top of her head.

A low, masculine groan was emitted as Miles tightened his arms around her and delved into her mouth with his tongue. Her body was instantly covered with gooseflesh. She hadn't known that humans kissed in this incredibly carnal fashion: mouths agape, tongues intertwined, sharing the same breath. She would be revolted if it were anyone but Miles St. Aldford.

He opened his eyes, and for a moment she felt as if she were gazing into the man's soul and he was looking right through to the very heart of her.

Alyssa gave her head an imperceptible shake.

Miles lifted his and murmured, " 'Where the virgins are soft as the roses they twine.' "

She blinked several times in astonishment, but managed no reply beyond a mumbled, "My lord?"

There was a bemused expression on the man's face as he admitted to her: "I once read in a book on horticulture—I was in the library of your abbey at the time—that the bud of a rose is charming, but as the flower gradually expands into full bloom, that is when its true beauty is revealed."

Why would he want to discuss roses now?

"I realize the book was right," he said, gently cupping her face in his hands.

Alyssa racked her brain for something to say. "In Greek mythology, it is Aphrodite, goddess of love, who is thought to be the creator of the rose. The rose is supposed to be a mixture of her tears and the blood of her wounded lover, Adonis."

He was staring at her mouth. "You kiss beautifully."

She blushed and returned the compliment. "As do you." Then she boldly added, "Your taste is very much to my liking."

"And yours to mine. Furthermore, you fit perfectly in my arms," he said.

She did. "You seem to fit me perfectly as well." Alyssa wondered aloud. "Is it always like this?"

A smile formed on his lips. "No."

"Is it often like this?"

"No."

"Is it sometimes like this?"

"It is *rarely* like this," Miles informed her, his expression clearly one of puzzlement.

"You don't understand it any more than I do," she said, fingering the front of his shirt.

Miles shook his head from side to side. "I must confess that I don't have a clue."

Then, before they could explore the subject of their mutual and inexplicable attraction, he froze.

"What is it?"

"Don't move."

She dropped her voice to just above a whisper. "Is someone there?"

His eyes narrowed to slits. "Not someone. Some*thing*."

Alyssa shivered. Miles slowly released her. She could sense the tension in him. She could feel his body—seemingly all hard, sinewy muscle—poised to strike on an instant's notice.

"How many gargoyles?" he mouthed.

She frowned. "Gargoyles?"

A muscle in his jaw started to twitch. "How many gargoyles are there on the stone wall above the garden door?"

That was simple enough. "Two."

"Now there are three."

"Three?" She began to turn around.

"Hold still!" he ordered.

"There can't be three," she insisted, only loud enough for him to hear. "You must be seeing things."

"What I'm seeing is a pair of bright yellow eyes watching every move we make. There is a creature lurking in the shadows by the entrance to the rose garden."

"What type of creature?"

"I don't know what type." Miles swore softly under his breath. "I should have a weapon with me: a knife or a sword or a revolver," he said self-reprovingly.

Alyssa was momentarily distracted. "Were you a soldier?"

"Yes, I was."

"Did you fight many enemies?" she asked in an inquisitive tone.

His eyes were squinted in concentration. "A few."

"In hand-to-hand combat?"

Miles nodded.

She took in a trembling breath and held it. "Have you ever killed a man?"

"Sometimes it's kill or be killed," he said, deftly avoiding a direct answer to her question.

Dear God, Alyssa realized, this man had faced life-and-death situations firsthand. He had looked his enemy squarely in the eyes and had known that only one of them would survive.

"The creature has jumped down from the wall," he announced.

Then they heard a noise: It was part yowl, part hiss; part complaint and part greeting.

Alyssa relaxed and exhaled. "It's only Tom."

"And who, pray tell, is Tom?"

"My guardian angel."

He cast her a skeptical look. "Your what?"

"My cat."

As if on cue, the biggest domestic cat Miles St. Aldford had ever seen sashayed across the rose garden toward them, flicking its tail from side to side.

Swish.

Swish, swish.

The huge male cat—the creature must weigh almost two stone—flicked its tail again, rubbed up against Alyssa, and then performed a ritual dance around her legs.

She leaned over and murmured in an affectionate manner, "Sweet Tom, where have you been?"

Miles could have sworn the animal understood every word she was saying. The ginger-colored tomcat made a chortling sound in the back of its throat, jumped up onto the bench, settled itself in the space between them, confidently turned its back to Alyssa, and—as if it were, indeed, guarding her—sat staring at him.

He decided to take a diplomatic tack. "That is the largest cat I've ever seen."

"Thank you."

It wasn't meant as a compliment; it was more of an observation. "How old is . . ."

"Tom." Alyssa reached out and began to scratch the monstrous feline behind its left ear. "He was a stray, so I'm not altogether certain. Probably twelve or thirteen years old, anyway."

"How long have you had him?"

"Since I was a little girl." A sheepish look appeared on her face. "I should have guessed our mystery creature was Tom. He follows me wherever I go, especially at night. You must have closed the garden door behind you, so he had to find another way into Milady's Bower."

That explained why she'd left the door ajar. It was Alyssa's habit so her "guardian angel" could shadow her.

With a flick of his tail, Tom turned around several times before draping himself over Alyssa's lap. Miles could almost read the creature's thoughts. It was warning him off. It was telling him that this was *his* territory and Alyssa was *his* mistress.

Alyssa brushed the hair back from her face and asked him, "By the by, how did you know where to find me when you entered the rose garden tonight?"

"I saw you."

"But this bench isn't visible from the path."

He shrugged. "Maybe I heard you."

"I made no sound."

Miles lifted his shoulders and dropped them. "I don't know, then. I just knew you were here." He blew out his breath and was relieved to feel his body returning to normal. It was no small matter for a mature man to find himself in a state of painful arousal—indeed, he had nearly popped his cork—as a result of a stolen kiss or two. "What made you leave the abbey in the middle of the night?"

"Impulse."

"I thought you said you couldn't afford to be impulsive," he reminded her.

"I awoke. I looked out my bedroom window. The next thing I knew, I was on my way here to the garden."

Miles was starting to get *that* feeling again. He concentrated on his hands. "What awakened you?"

"I had a dream. A nightmare." The girl shuddered. "It seemed so real."

His brows congealed into a scowl. " 'I had a dream which was not all a dream'—Lord Byron."

"That's what it was like."

"I know."

Alyssa made a quick, seemingly involuntary movement of her hands. "How do you know?"

"I, too, was awakened by a dream."

Her gray eyes widened. "You were?"

His tone was devoid of humor. "I was being pursued through a labyrinth, a maze."

She shivered. "Ariadne's Thread."

He went very still. "How did you guess?"

"I didn't guess. Those were the words in my head when I woke up from my nightmare."

He stared at her, unblinking. "I came out of a sound sleep, sat up in bed, and said aloud: Ariadne's Thread."

For a minute or two, neither of them uttered a word.

Alyssa swallowed. "What do you think it means?"

"Damned if I know," he confessed.

"Did we have the same dream?"

"Maybe."

"Is it a coincidence?"

"I hope so." But his gut instincts—the same instincts that had saved his life more times in the past than he cared to count—told Miles St. Aldford that there was more to it than mere coincidence. "I think we should sleep on it. We can discuss the subject further in the clear light of day."

They left Milady's Bower with Tom trotting along at their heels, made their way back to the abbey, tiptoed through the great house, and didn't speak again until they were standing outside Alyssa's suite of rooms.

"Good night," she whispered.

"It's nearly four o'clock," he said, consulting the clock at the end of the hallway.

"Good morning, then."

"Try to get some rest," he instructed. She appeared almost ghostly in the pale light of dawn.

"I will." Alyssa gave him a shy smile. "Pleasant dreams to you, my lord."

"And to you, my lady."

Much to his surprise, Miles slept soundly—his dreams filled with the scent of roses and Lady Alyssa Gray—until Blunt awakened him for his morning appointment.

Chapter Nine

"Refresh my memory, if you will. Exactly what is Ariadne's Thread?" Miles St. Aldford asked her the next morning as they convened in the study at eleven o'clock as planned.

Alyssa was determined to keep their conversation on an impersonal footing, and keep her distance from the marquess. He was entirely too attractive for *her* own good.

Putting the width of the huge seventeenth-century mahogany desk between them, she said: "In Greek mythology, Ariadne was the daughter of King Minos of Crete. She fell in love with Theseus, son of the King of Athens. According to legend, her father kept the Minotaur—"

"A creature who had the body of a man and the head of a bull," Miles interjected.

"You obviously recall some of your mythology." Alyssa took a seat and indicated that he should do the same.

"Some," he said, sitting down opposite her.

"Then you may remember that the Minotaur was kept beneath King Minos's palace in a labyrinth."

"Which, I suspect, had such intricate passageways

that one who entered it never found his way out again."

Alyssa nodded and clasped her hands together on her lap. "In revenge for the murder of his son by the Athenians, King Minos demanded a yearly tribute of seven young men and seven young women, who were then sacrificed to the Minotaur. The creature tracked down and devoured each of its victims one by one."

With an open palm, Miles St. Aldford lightly thumped the arm of his chair. "Now I remember. Theseus was supposed to be one of those sacrificed."

"Instead, Ariadne gave him a magic sword, with which to kill the Minotaur, and one end of a skein of thread. Theseus made his way to the center of the maze, slew the monster, and used the thread as a guide to find his way back out again."

"Ariadne's Thread was the key," the marquess concluded, stroking his chin.

"Yes," she said.

"Fascinating." He gazed out the window behind her at the formal gardens. "Do you have a maze here at the abbey?"

"Not now. Although Miss Pibble and I have found references in the history books to a medieval turf maze. It was no more than a raised grassy mound."

"What happened to it?"

"We don't know. We assume it wasn't maintained and became overgrown. It disappeared centuries ago." Alyssa felt she had to ask the obvious question. "Why do you think we both dreamt about a labyrinth and Ariadne's Thread?"

Miles flashed her a crooked smile. "Something we ate?"

Alyssa found she wasn't in the mood for jollity. She was quite serious when she suggested to him, "Perhaps we both feel lost in some way."

"Or trapped," he said, without elaborating.

"In mythology and literature a maze is often used symbolically to represent man's quest for truth and enlightenment." Something niggled at Alyssa, something Lady Chubb had said only last night. " '*Vincit omnia veritas.*' "

" 'Truth conquers all things,' " the marquess translated from the Latin. "Isn't that your family motto?"

"Yes, it is." Somehow she knew the two were connected—the maze and the Grays' heraldic motto—she just wasn't sure how. She would have to give the matter further consideration once she was alone. Needing something to do with her hands, Alyssa picked up an earthernware vase from the desk on the pretext of examining the piece of pottery. "About last night, my lord."

"Under the circumstances, I think we can dispense with the formalities when it's just the two of us. You may call me Miles. I certainly have every intention of calling you Alyssa."

He was right. "About last night, Miles."

He leaned toward her. "Yes, Alyssa."

"I don't know what to say."

"Say nothing. The rose garden is a private place separate from the rest of the world. We agreed that whatever happened in Milady's Bower is our secret."

"Thank you, my lord."

"Miles."

"Thank you, Miles."

"What's that in your hand?"

"It's an elephant vase." Alyssa held it out to him. "Fifteenth-century Swankalok pottery from—"

"Siam."

Of course he would know; Miles St. Aldford was, after all, a man of the world.

"Many of the Earls of Graystone have had private collections or pet projects," she told him. "The fourth and the sixth earls were avid art collectors. The latter commissioned the Canalettos." She indicated her favorite painting opposite the desk. "The seventh earl, like my father, was both a scholar and a world traveler who brought back many interesting artifacts: pottery—like the piece in your hand—paintings, sculptures of every size and description. Then there was the eleventh earl, my grandfather." Alyssa came out from behind the massive desk and approached a shelf of leatherbound books. "Grandfather collected legends and stories about the abbey. His specialty was ghost stories." She selected the appropriate volume and, turning to him, inquired, "Do you believe in ghosts?"

Miles set the elephant vase on the desk, gave the arm of the chair another whack, and sprang to his feet. "Why does everyone ask me that question?"

"Do they?"

"Yes."

She cast him a sidelong glance. "Do you?"

"No," he stated emphatically.

Alyssa was relieved. "Neither do I." She opened

to the page she had marked before he'd entered the room. "But you have heard the rumors?"

"I have heard the rumors."

"What do you make of them?"

Miles began to pace back and forth in front of her. "Initially, I thought they were no more than gossip."

She arched a brow. "And now?"

Miles came to a dead stop. "Now I don't know," he admitted. Drawing in a deep breath, he slowly released it. "Someone may be deliberately spreading the rumors."

Alyssa had reached the same conclusion, but she failed to see any motivation behind it. "To what end?"

"Again, I don't know. At least not yet. But I intend to find out." Dark eyes glinted curiously. "What do you have there?" He indicated the book in her hand.

"When talk of a ghost—most often described as a medieval knight on horseback—surfaced in the valley, I began to research the stories that had been compiled by my grandfather."

"I assume you found something."

"I did, only this morning."

He became attentive. "What did you discover?"

Alyssa read aloud from the hand-tooled leather book: " 'In nearly every generation there have been reported sightings of a ghostly knight. He is easily distinguished by the Crusader's cross on his tunic. Usually dressed in full battle array, the knight sits astride a great steed and carries a mighty sword.' "

"Is there any other kind?" Miles said out of the side of his mouth.

"Grandfather went on to write: 'Legend has it, the knight is one Robert the Bold, known to have left his lady behind at Graystone Abbey—some say unmarried and in disgrace because she was with child, his child—to follow Richard the Lion-Hearted to the Holy Lands during the Third Crusade.' " She looked up for a moment. "There's a footnote to the text that states: 'Refer to the genealogy of the Gray family for additional information on Robert the bold.' "

"An early ancestor of yours?"

"Yes."

"The Third Crusade was a very long time ago."

"I looked up the exact date. At the behest of the pope, Gregory VIII, King Richard and his knights set sail from England in 1189." Alyssa continued reading: " 'Letters and papers in the abbey's archives mention the Crusader's cross numerous times. An elaborate version later became part of the family crest.' " She turned the book around and showed him an artist's rendering of the cross and the crest.

"Sir Alfred was asking about your family crest, wasn't he? It hangs above the fireplace in the formal drawing room."

"That's a copy, actually. There are dozens of them throughout the abbey. The original hangs in the Old Hall between the Norman Tower and the Lady Chapel." Alyssa closed the book and put it back on the shelf. "Anyway, there are several more pages about Robert the Bold. One version of the story claims that he returned from the Crusades, only to find that his lady had died in childbirth. Another relates that he returned from Jerusalem with a great treasure, married the lady, and the following year a son was born."

"In the latter version, I presume they lived happily ever after?" His mouth curved derisively.

Alyssa knew herself to be an avowed romantic, but she wanted to believe that the knight had returned home, wed his lady love, and they had, indeed, lived happily ever after. "I presume so."

"Who else might be familiar with Robert the Bold?"

"My grandfather had copies of the book printed and presented as gifts to all of his friends."

Miles gave a mirthless laugh and rubbed his hand back and forth along his nape in frustration. "That should narrow our list of suspects to one or two hundred."

"Do we have a list of suspects?"

"*I* do."

Alyssa dropped her voice to a surreptitious whisper. "Who's on your list?"

"No one by name. Not yet, anyway. But certainly anyone interested in making mischief."

Tapping a finger against her bottom lip, Alyssa said, "Yes, of course, mischief makers. Who else?"

"Those who have something to gain."

"What could anyone hope to gain by perpetuating rumors of a ghost?" she asked, now deeply interested.

"I don't know. But, as I said, I'm going to find out." His mouth was set in an obstinate line. "There is an old saying: 'You can sit on a horse and let it lead you, or you can take the reins.'"

"You intend to take the reins."

"I always have."

"May I ask you a question?"

"You may."

Unsteadily her heart began to pick up speed. "Is it true you were once a spy for Her Majesty, the Queen?"

"It's true."

She looked at him intently. "Then you're the right man for the job."

"Naturally, I'm gratified you feel that way."

Thank goodness he wasn't the sort of utterly useless gentleman of Society she had at first feared he would be. Miles St. Aldford was clever, broadshouldered, brave by all accounts, highly skilled, she assumed, in the employment of any number and variety of deadly weapons. And he was willing to help her. It was most propitious. Under the circumstances, he could supply the muscle and she, the brains.

"We'll form a partnership," Alyssa announced.

The marquess appeared to choke on his own saliva. "I beg your pardon."

"I will be your partner in this investigation."

He silently mouthed the word *partner*.

"Surely, my lord," she went on with an indignant sniff, "you don't expect me to miss out on the most exciting occurrence to take place at the abbey in my lifetime."

Miles spoke quickly, almost harshly, to her. "I certainly do."

"Then you are very much mistaken." Alyssa put her shoulders back and lifted her chin stubbornly.

"This is *my* home, *my* land, and *my* ghost. Besides, you need me."

There was an eloquent pause. "I need you?"

"I can be of invaluable assistance to you. I know the abbey better than anyone."

Miles folded his arms across his chest and regarded her with something akin to amusement. "In that case, where do you think we should begin our investigation?"

"First, we'll take a tour of the estate cottages and the abbey road. You should see for yourself where Mrs. McGillicuddy and the stable lad each claim to have spotted the ghost."

"It's only logical to start with the scene of the crime," Miles muttered, more to himself than to her.

"I've taken the liberty of having our horses saddled and brought around to the front. Bulle Rock and Beauty are champing at the bit even as we speak."

"It would seem, my lady, that you've thought of everything."

"I try, my lord."

"Shall we begin, then?"

There was an old proverb, translated from the ancient Sanskrit, that stated the only way a man knew what was beautiful was to find something he could define as ugly.

Miles had seen his share of the world's ugliness. Perhaps that was the reason he recognized, on a perfect June morning, that Lady Alyssa Gray, eyes bright with excitement, dressed in a fitted riding habit that clung rather nicely to her breasts, and seated upon a prancing mare, was beautiful.

"Easy, Bulle Rock," Miles admonished as he put his foot in the stirrup and swung his leg over the Thoroughbred.

"We will begin by traveling the abbey road, if that suits you," she suggested.

"It suits me well enough," he replied.

They had not gone far—they were just opposite the formal gardens, replete with classical Greek statues—when an estate worker approached, cap in hand.

The man nodded and greeted them with all due respect. "Good day to you, my lady." Sun-squinted eyes darted from Alyssa to Miles. "Good day, my lord."

"Good day, Galsworthy," Alyssa called out to him cheerfully. "How are you on this fine summer morning?"

"Perplex'd, my lady."

"Perplexed?"

"Yes, my lady." Galsworthy scratched behind one ear with his free hand—the other was clasping a woolen cap—and shifted his weight from left foot to right. "Puzzled, that's what I am."

"What are you puzzled about?" she inquired. "It isn't Ian McKennitt again, is it?"

"No, my lady."

"Is there any trouble with the hermit?"

Galsworthy shook his bare head. "We haven't had a bit o' trouble out of him."

"Were the provisions delivered to the Monk's Cave as you and I discussed?"

"They were."

Apparently Beauty was as eager to get started on their morning ride as he was, Miles observed. The mare danced in nervous circles, raised her head, snorted several times, and then concluded her performance with an anxious whinny.

Alyssa leaned forward, patted the sleek gray neck, and whispered a soothing word or two in the animal's ear before she turned her attention back to the man Miles now recognized as the head gardener. "What is it, then?"

"Somethin' I saw in the garden, my lady."

"Which garden?"

"The rose garden."

"What did you see in the rose garden?"

"Somethin' I don't understand, my lady."

"Perhaps if you told me what it was, Galsworthy, I could help you to understand."

He fingered his cap and shuffled his feet again. "I be doubtin' it, my lady, clever as you are about these things."

Alyssa had the patience of a saint, Miles decided. That's what it took to get a story out of Galsworthy.

"What did you see in Milady's Bower?" she asked.

"A flower."

"Go on," she encouraged him.

"The vine, it is."

"The dead vine?"

"Not so dead as it turns out, my lady."

"Of course it's dead."

The man shook his head. "We were in the garden replacing the lady's mantle and the lamb's-ears that his lordship"—he glanced at Miles—"had accidentally trampled underfoot, when one o' the lads ups and gives a shout."

"Yes?"

"Sure as I'm standin' here talking to you, my lady, there was a flower growing out o' the dead vine."

"What kind of flower?"

"A white rose with what 'pears to be teardrops on the petals." The head gardener blew out his breath expressively. "Never seen anything like it afore, I can tell you."

"Thank you, Galsworthy. You were right to bring the flower to my attention. The marquess and I will have a look at it once we return from our morning ride."

He nodded and took two steps back. "As you wish, my lady."

"Until then, you might keep the lads out of the rose garden."

"Yes, my lady."

Alyssa urged her horse along with a click of her tongue and a nudge of her boot. "Let's go, Beauty."

After they had ridden for some time in silence, Miles offered, "A penny for your thoughts."

"Only a penny? Last night the price was ten pounds, if I remember correctly." Alyssa adjusted the skirt of her riding habit. "I'll tell you for nothing."

Miles waited.

"I was asking myself if it was merely coincidence, or if it was something else altogether," she said with a sigh."

"If *what* was?"

"In less than a day's time, something to do with

all four parts of my family crest seems to have miraculously materialized."

Miles wanted to hear more. "Please go on."

"The first quadrant, as I explained to Sir Alfred last night, is a standing lion similar to that of Richard the Lion-Hearted."

"Possibly the heraldic symbol of a loyal knight who followed his king to the Holy Lands."

"Possibly." Alyssa slowed the mare's pace to a comfortable walk; he did the same with the Thoroughbred. "The second quadrant is a white flower, thought to be extinct."

"Lo and behold, one of Galsworthy's lads discovers a white rose growing out of a dead vine; a vine that may be hundreds of years old, that may even date to the time of the Crusades."

"The third part of the crest is the ornate cross mentioned in my grandfather's book, and the fourth is our family motto: *Vincit omnia veritas*."

"Merely coincidence or something else altogether," Miles repeated.

"It's a mystery."

"So much seems to be these days."

Alyssa gave her head a shake. "But I'm forgetting our purpose. Here we are on the abbey road, and that is the spot, I'm told, where the stable boy claims to have seen the knight."

Miles made a thorough inspection of the site, particularly the trees on either side of the road. They provided a natural—and immediate—cover for a horse and rider. He dismounted, went down on his haunches, and examined the ground. It was soft. There had been rain recently. And plenty of it.

Whatever evidence may have once existed, it was gone now, washed away.

He straightened. "Is there a bridle path through these woods?"

"Yes."

"More than one?"

She nodded. "There are literally dozens, and in all directions."

"A quick and effective means of escape is available, then." His eyes narrowed. "Where is the McGillicuddy cottage?"

"Just over the rise in the road."

Miles swung up into the saddle and announced, "That's our next destination."

There he found the same to be true. There were trees all around the cottage, with a number of trails cutting through the woods. If someone was intent on making an appearance and then quickly vanishing again, this would be the perfect setting.

Miles mulled the possibilities over in his mind as they rode along an *allée* of lime trees. In the distance there was a garden folly—rendered as a columned Greek temple—the park, the caves, and, beyond, the woods.

"You may recall the Old Woods," Alyssa said, raising her arm and indicating the thick forest of towering trees.

He did. "Just before that is the Monk's Cave, isn't it?"

"It is. You have an excellent memory."

"Yes, I do." The Old Woods and the Monk's Cave were two of the places he had often explored during that long-ago summer. "I see campfire smoke by the entrance to the cave. It must be your resident hermit."

"It must be."

They continued to exchange pleasantries as they rode. Alyssa pointed out to him the various sights of interest: the hunting lodge used by the first three Georges during their successive reigns—the Prince Regent was not granted that favor by the disapproving Graystones—the natural-appearing ponds created by Capability Brown, a vast lake, a waterfall, and, at last, the Grotto.

"The Grotto was built at the request of the tenth Countess of Graystone. She was particularly fond of picking up seashells on the beach. Would you like to see it?" Alyssa asked.

"Yes, I would."

They dismounted, tied the reins of Bulle Rock and Beauty around elaborately carved posts that most closely resembled tenacles of seaweed, and proceeded inside the peculiar building.

"I didn't know my great-grandmother; she died the year before I was born," Alyssa told him. "But I understand she loved the sea. So she had it brought here to Graystone Abbey." She pulled on a handle molded in the shape of a dolphin. "If you would hold the door for me, I'll try to find a candle."

They stepped inside—Miles propped the door open with his back—and the temperature dropped markedly. Alyssa located a candle and struck the last remaining match. She soon had half a dozen candles lit along the perimeter of the Grotto; their flickering light lent an eerie feeling to the cavernous room.

The walls of the Grotto shimmered with iridescent shells, semiprecious stones, and mother-of-pearl. There were great fishes, writhing sea monsters, and all manner of creatures depicted. Poseidon, Greek god of the sea, worshiped by fishermen and mariners alike, was sculpted with a crown on his head and a trident in his hand. He was seated majestically in a chariot drawn by giant horses whose flowing manes were reminiscent of ocean waves. Fountains of every size and description trickled water; the sound echoed off the stone ramparts.

"Most impressive," exclaimed Miles.

"It's very cool and pleasant on a hot summer day, but, of course, no one comes here otherwise."

He could see why. The Grotto was spectacular, but bone-chilling in more than temperature.

Alyssa shivered.

"You're cold," Miles said, quickly removing his riding coat. "This will help." He draped the jacket, still warm with his own body heat, around her shoulders.

"Thank you," she murmured, burrowing down into its warmth.

Miles took a step nearer. He suddenly realized he was going to kiss her again. In fact, the desire, the need, to do so had been gnawing at him since last night.

He lowered his voice to a whisper—even then his words echoed in the cavernlike room. "About last night?"

Watchful gray eyes flew to his face. "You promised it would be our secret."

"It is our secret. It will always remain so."

Alyssa relaxed and pulled his jacket closer.

Miles reached out and straightened the collar. "Aren't you curious?"

"About what?"

"About us."

It was a moment or two before she confessed in a husky voice, "Yes, I am."

He leaned toward her. "You've asked yourself, then?"

Alyssa swallowed hard. "Asked myself?"

"Was it the moonlight? Was it the summer night? Or the scent of the roses? Or was it simply us? You and me?"

She licked her lips. "I have wondered."

"As have I." Miles placed one hand on the wall behind her; it was cool to the touch. He cupped her chin with the other. Her skin was soft and surprisingly warm. "You understand that I have to know," he insisted.

Her eyes grew huge. "I understand."

He wasn't going to make the same mistake twice. There would be no polite pecks on the cheek. No fleeting brush of his lips across hers. No insipid busses. By God, if he was going to kiss the lady, then he was going to do it right!

Miles swooped down and captured Alyssa's mouth with his, filling his lungs with her breath, his nostrils with her scent, his hands with the sweetness of her.

It hadn't been the moonlight, or the garden with its exotic fragrances. It hadn't been the hour of the day, or the season of the year. It had been only

Alyssa. It was only Alyssa now. She was like the finest champagne: She went straight to his head.

One moment Miles was kissing the lady, his hands at her waist. The next, he was pushing the jacket he had loaned her aside and was caressing her through layer upon layer of clothes. He felt, as much as heard, a feminine gasp of surprise. It didn't deter him. He fussed with the buttons down the front of her riding habit until an opening was created. Then he slipped his hand inside her bodice and found her nipple.

Dear God, he would like nothing better than to divest her lovely body of its clothing. He wanted to rip the flimsy chemise asunder and bury his face between those milk-white breasts. He wanted to touch her, taste her, tease her with his lips and teeth and tongue until she begged him to take her there on the cold stone floor of the Grotto.

There was a moan of masculine arousal. It registered on the edge of Miles's consciousness: It was his own.

There was another sound. He listened. It was feminine protest. He reluctantly withdrew his hand and lifted his head.

Alyssa clutched at her gaping bodice and gasped for air. "My lord, we forget ourselves."

They had, indeed.

"At least we have our answer," he said throatily.

Her cheeks were ablaze with color. "It might be best if we continued our tour another time."

"It might be."

"You may ride on ahead, my lord. I would like

a few minutes to gather my wits and put myself to rights."

Miles frowned. "I'll wait."

She was adamant. "I wish to be alone."

He stood his ground. "I insist on waiting for you, Alyssa."

"I've ridden this far—farther, in fact—by myself many times. I will be quite all right."

"I don't like it," he protested.

"I know." Alyssa reached out and gently touched his arm. "Please, Miles."

Her gentleness was his undoing.

"As you wish." He hesitated by the door to the Grotto and glanced back over his shoulder. "Don't be long, my lady."

"I won't, my lord," she promised.

Then Miles turned and left.

Alyssa breathed a sigh of relief as he rode away. Then she picked up his forgotten coat from the floor of the Grotto. Her hands were trembling; her fingers were like ice. She raised them to her face. Her cheeks were burning up.

How could she have permitted Miles St. Aldford to take such liberties? Why had she behaved in such a thoroughly disgraceful and wanton fashion?

The man was dangerous.

He unleashed something inside her: something sensual, something wild and hot and animallike. She loved the feel of his mouth on hers, his hands on her body. Indeed, she would have liked more of his lovemaking, not less.

The truth left Alyssa stunned.

She groaned and sank down on a marble bench beneath a relief of frolicking water nymphs.

What must Miles think of her?

She couldn't bear to contemplate the answer. In the future, she would have to keep a constant vigil: She was too weak to resist him, too easily tempted by what he offered, too readily *and* eagerly led astray. She wasn't to be trusted when it came to the marquess.

It was a great pity . . . for he was very much to her liking.

Alyssa heaved a long-suffering sigh and went about the business of tidying her hair, fastening her bodice, and straightening her riding habit. Then she doused the candles until only one remained lit. That candle she intended to use to find her way to the door of the Grotto.

Thump.

Was someone there?

Thump. Thump.

Were those footsteps she heard?

"Miles, is that you? Have you come back for me?" she called out, and then felt a little silly for having done so.

There was no reply. And there was no warning. Alyssa was only a step or two from the entrance to the Grotto when the door slammed shut in her face. The force of its closing snuffed out her candle. She groped in the dark and finally found the handle. She turned it. Nothing happened. She tried again. And again nothing.

She called out. "Hello!"

Silence greeted her.

She raised her voice. "Hello! Is anyone there? Could you help me? The door seems to be jammed."

Dead silence.

That was when dread began to creep into Alyssa's heart as surely as the chill air of the Grotto was creeping into every bone and muscle of her body. Even her blood was like ice in her veins.

She was locked in a cold, dark cavern, and there was no way out.

Chapter Ten

He was called the Hermit.

At least that's what the boy had called him, the one who had stood at the entrance to the cave four days ago, cupped his hands around his mouth and shouted in a high-pitched, young voice: "Ian McKennitt, it is, sir. My mistress up at the abbey told Galsworthy who told Mrs. Fetchett who told me I was to bring a basket of food and a clean blanket to the Monk's Cave and leave it outside for the Hermit."

He'd hurried to the front of the cave to thank Ian McKennitt, but the boy had already fled.

The basket had been filled with wondrous things: fresh baked bread, a thick wedge of cheese, meat pies fit for a king's supper table, even a bottle of stout. That night, for the first night in ... he couldn't remember how long, he had gone to bed with a full stomach. That night he'd started to think of himself as the Hermit.

The woman had called him something else altogether.

He'd been walking along the abbey road—it had been a particularly fine day for walking—when a fancy coach had come barreling down on him with a gentleman and two beautiful, dark-haired ladies inside. The driver had slowed the team of horses.

The younger lady had peered out of the window at him as if he were an oddity in the circus, and had said loudly enough for him to hear, "Look, Mother, it's a Gypsy."

An elegant hand had pushed the carriage draperies aside for a glimpse of him. "He's not a Gypsy."

The young lady had appeared disappointed, as if by *not* being a Gypsy he had somehow spoiled her fun. An apology was even on the tip of his tongue when she said insistently: "Is he a vagrant, then? Do have another look, Mother. He must at least be a vagrant. Why, he might even be a gentleman down on his luck."

The beautiful woman with eyes the color of blue wisteria on a summer morning, had glared at him and then disdainfully dismissed him with, "He's nothing more than a filthy animal Charmel." She had pressed a pristine linen handkerchief to her nose. "Come away from the window this minute."

The gentleman accompanying them, red-faced and mutton-chopped, had simply sworn at him and ordered the driver to go on. They had left him in a spray of mud from the carriage wheels.

Hermit.

Gypsy.

Vagrant.

A gentleman down on his luck.

A filthy animal.

For a long time, he'd had no name for himself, only a picture in his mind of a place. Now he called himself the Hermit, and he knew that the place was Graystone Abbey.

The Hermit raised his hand and rubbed the back of his head. He could still feel the raised lump. It was a permanent reminder that some people and some places were best avoided. Then he noticed his hands. There was dirt embedded under his fingernails, and they needed trimming. His clothes could use a washing, as well as the rest of him.

Not far from the cave where he had taken shelter, there was a pond. He needed a bath, and it would do nicely. The mistress of the abbey wouldn't mind. He had seen her that morning riding with a gentleman in the direction of the Grotto. They hadn't seen him, of course. The lady was all sweetness and light, with the voice of an angel. The man was dark and exuded danger.

The Hermit reached the water's edge and went down on his knees. He would like to have had a towel and a bar of soap, perhaps even a razor with which to shave, but he'd have to make do with a handful of small pebbles and the fading sunlight.

He dipped his hand in for a drink. That's when he spotted the horse. A gray mare. A real beauty. She was grazing under a stand of trees. There was a saddle on her back; it was made of fine leather and oiled to a sheen. The reins hung down, dragging along in the sweet grass as she nibbled daintily. He recognized the horse. It was the one the lady from the abbey had been riding earlier that day.

He straightened, searched the trees, the grass, and the area around the pond. There was no sign of the lady, or the gentleman, or his huge reddish brown Thoroughbred. Keeping downwind, he circled around behind the mare. His plan was a simple one: to get close enough to grab the reins before the horse spotted him.

His plan failed.

He was still some twenty feet away, and still downwind, when a branch snapped under his foot. The sleek gray head shot up. The sensitive nostrils flared. And the skittish mare took off at a full gallop.

"By the thousand and one names of Shiva!" the Hermit swore under his breath, disgusted with his own ineptness.

There was nothing to be done about it. The mare was no doubt halfway back to the stables by now. He returned to the pond, removed his shirt, and plunged it into the clear water. Temptation called to him. He quickly removed the rest of his clothes and did a shallow dive into the water.

It was heaven.

The pond was crystal clear, not too cold and not too deep. He stood on the bottom, mud oozing between his toes, the water reaching only to his chin. He splashed about, diving and resurfacing, frolicking like a carefree young boy. Then he came up for air one last time and stood facing the Grotto.

The moment was an echo in his mind.

He had swum in a pond, *this* pond before. He had stood, soft mud seeping around his feet, facing the Grotto. He tried to remember when, how, why, who ... but the harder he tried, the farther his mind pushed the memory away.

With a howl of frustration, the Hermit brought

his fist down, fingers clenched, on the surface of the water. There was a great splash.

He immediately went still.

Had he heard something? Something other than his own futile outpouring of emotion, that is? He listened and he watched as a heron cried out and took wing across the pond. There was a splash at water's edge, a bullfrog or a large fish. Something swam between his legs, brushing against him.

Then he heard it again. A sound. A human sound. It came from the vicinity of the Grotto. He swam toward the opposite bank and peered through the rushes. There was no lock on the outside of the peculiar-looking building, but someone had deliberately stuck a thick, sturdy branch through the handle, barricading the door shut. He could detect a soft thumping, like someone was inside and pounding on the door.

His heart began to beat double-time. Was that someone the lady with the voice of an angel? The one who had sent him the basket of food and the blanket? Who would want to lock her inside the Grotto? And why?

The Hermit started to climb out of the water, then remembered that he was as naked as the day he was born, and hesitated. But not for long. He had learned to improvise. He reached down, grabbed a handful of turf and held it strategically in front of his body. Then he made his way out of the pond and approached the Grotto.

There was no mistake about it. Someone was locked inside, and there was a thick tree limb, the circumference of a man's arm, wedged in the door. He cocked his head and listened.

"Hello," called out a muffled female voice. "Please, is someone, anyone, there?"

The Hermit jumped back. He couldn't remove the barricade and have the lady rush out and discover a naked man standing there. At the very least, the officials would come and take him away from this place. And he could not allow that to happen. Not now. Not yet.

Nevertheless, it would take too long to swim back across the pond, put his clothes on and return to the Grotto. He was already losing the last light of day.

He had to act. He quickly explored the brush on each side of the building. There were bushes thick enough to conceal a man if he were determined not to move or make a sound. He knew how to keep still and he knew how to keep quiet. Indeed, he was quite certain those skills had saved his life on at least one occasion.

Returning to the door of the Grotto, he studied the barricade. One good push in the right direction and the thing would topple. The door would be unblocked and the lady would be free.

The Hermit took a deep breath, gave the branch a shove and ran for cover.

Chapter Eleven

Miles was about to change for dinner that evening when a knock sounded on the door of the Knight's Chambers, and Blunt opened it to reveal Miss Emma Pibble standing outside in the hallway.

"Miss Pibble, my lord," his valet announced.

There was a short pause.

The woman poised in the doorway, her back ramrod straight, stated: "I must speak with you, Lord Cork."

"Come in, won't you, Miss Pibble?"

Emma Pibble took two measured steps—no more, no less—into the sitting room and stopped. "I am not an alarmist by nature, sir," she said in preamble.

Miles would have to take her word for it. "Yes, madam."

"I will come directly to the point."

"Please do," he said, nonchalantly crossing his arms and leaning back against a massive secretary filled with pens and inkwells, every manner of writing paper, and slightly top-heavy with books: the complete collection of Mr. William Shakespeare's plays.

"She has come up missing, Lord Cork."

His voice was perfectly level. "Who has, Miss Pibble?"

"Lady Alyssa, my lord."

He dropped his arms and slid noiselessly to his feet. "What do you mean she has come up missing?"

"I mean just that." Emma Pibble sniffed several times, took a linen handkerchief from somewhere on her person—he did not see exactly where—and dabbed at her nose. Her voice was full. In fact, she seemed to be on the verge of tears. "No one has seen her since you two went riding this morning."

Miles cautioned himself not to jump to conclusions. "Have you checked her rooms?"

"That was the first place I looked for her, my lord."

"Milady's Bower?"

"That was the second." She dabbed at the corner of one eye and then the other. "I knew she would be curious to see the flower brought to her attention by Galsworthy this morning."

The flower. The white rose supposedly growing out of the dead vine. He'd forgotten about it.

"I have been to all of her favorite places." Emma Pibble began to list them aloud for his benefit, checking them off on her fingertips as she went. "The study, the gardens, the walkway, the Lady Chapel, the cemetery behind it—"

"The cemetery behind the Lady Chapel?" he questioned.

"That is where her parents are buried, my lord."

"I see." Miles stroked his jaw thoughtfully. "Did she have any appointments scheduled for this afternoon?"

"Only informally with myself and certain members of the household staff. It is something of a burden for us to have all these strangers—guests in the house."

"I expect it makes a great deal of extra work for everyone," he commiserated. "But I'm certain your efforts do not go unappreciated."

She smiled tremulously. "Thank you, Lord Cork."

"Would Lady Alyssa have gone to visit a friend or someone in the village without telling you?"

Emma Pibble vigorously shook her head. "She knows I would worry, and she is always so thoughtful about my feelings. Besides," she added, "the last place I checked was the stables. Just as I arrived there, Beauty returned without her rider."

There might yet be an innocent explanation, Miles reminded himself. "Perhaps she was thrown from her horse."

"That doesn't seem very likely to me," argued Emma Pibble. "Lady Alyssa is a superb horsewoman."

"And you've checked the house from top to bottom."

"From top to bottom. I didn't wish to raise a general alarm and possibly embarrass her, so I made my inquiries discreetly. She didn't take any luncheon. She wasn't here for tea." Intelligent brown eyes studied him from behind wire-rimmed spectacles. "As far as I can ascertain, the last person to see her, my lord, was you."

The skin around Miles's mouth grew taut. "I left Alyssa at the Grotto."

"That is not one of her favorite places," the diminutive woman pointed out.

"The lady and I had a minor contretemps, which

is of no consequence now," he stated, clearing his throat. He had no intentions of telling anyone, and that included Emma Pibble, what had transpired between them inside the Grotto. "Lady Alyssa asked—nay, she insisted—that I return to the house ahead of her, as she wished to spend some time there alone."

"Most unusual."

"I should never have left her," he said fervently. "My gut instincts told me not to listen to her and I chose to ignore them."

"Your gut instincts, my lord?"

"Here!" He drove a fist into his own belly. "I feel it here when something isn't right. I should have known."

He had known. But he'd been too preoccupied with his own state of sexual arousal, with what he wanted, with what he needed, with what he desired, to pay heed to any warning. He should have thought of Alyssa. He should never have touched her. Then there would have been no reason for her to stay behind to gather her wits and tidy her clothing.

"Blunt!" he bellowed.

Blunt appeared instantly from the adjoining room. "Yes, my lord."

"I will be succinct," Miles said as he began to dig in the bottom drawer of the bureau for his weapons. "Lady Alyssa has not returned to the abbey. Miss Pibble fears something may have happened to her." He located his revolver and slipped it down the back of his belt. The sharp stiletto went into his boot. "As do I."

"Do you suspect misadventure, my lord?"

"It's not out of the question. Or she may have been thrown from her horse and suffered a sprained ankle or some other minor injury." Miles hoped, prayed, it was that simple.

"When was Lady Alyssa last seen, my lord?"

"*I* was the last person to see her, apparently. We were out riding and stopped to tour the Grotto."

"The Grotto is not one her favorite places," piped up Miss Pibble.

"Nevertheless, that is where I left the lady at her request."

Blunt stood at attention. "What do you wish me to do, my lord?"

"See to it that Bulle Rock is saddled and brought around to the front of the house. You may inform anyone who asks that I occasionally enjoy a short ride just before my evening meal."

Blunt frowned. "That would seem unlikely, my lord. You would return for dinner smelling of horses."

"Then make something up," he suggested.

"A fabrication?"

"Yes, Blunt, a fabrication, a story, an excuse. And you, Miss Pibble, will act as if nothing is out of the ordinary until I inform you otherwise. Send Lady Alyssa's regrets for dinner. Tell those assembled that she has a headache."

"Alyssa never has headaches."

"Then make something up, as well." Miles looked from one to the other. "Blunt is an accomplished actor, and you, madam, are educated in the classical plays. Put your talents to use."

Miles was out of the house and in the saddle in

record time. As soon as the abbey was behind him, he urged Bulle Rock into a gallop and headed straight for the Grotto.

A sense of urgency drove him. It was possible that the matter was no longer one of lost and found; it might well have become one of life and death.

He slapped his riding crop against his boot and muttered under his breath, "Damn. Damn. Damn." If anything had happened to Alyssa, it would be on his conscience.

His heart was pounding, but his mind was clear. His senses were razor sharp. His hands were steady. He had always been this way in times of danger. It was one reason he'd been such a bloody good soldier, and an even better spy. Back at headquarters, they used to say that he had ice water in his veins. They were right.

If this incident had anything to do with the strange goings-on at the abbey, he would get to the bottom of it if it was the last thing he did, Miles vowed.

And if even one hair had been harmed on Alyssa's lovely head, he would make someone pay . . . and pay dearly.

Chapter Twelve

Alyssa's throat was raw. Her arms and shoulders ached with fatigue. She had been calling out for help and intermittently pounding on the door since first finding herself trapped in the Grotto.

It was to no avail.

There weren't any windows in the cavern and there wasn't any light: The last match had been used by her earlier that day to light the candles. As a consequence, in the dark, she had lost track of time.

She was cold and tired and hungry. But, thankfully, she wasn't thirsty. There was an abundance of water available; she had only to feel her way along the shell-encrusted walls of the room until she came to one of its many fountains.

Alyssa recalled reading somewhere—it was one of the benefits of an eclectic education—that a human being could survive for days, even weeks, without food as long as water was plentiful. Surely someone would come to her rescue before then. Surely Mrs. Fetchett or dear Emma or one of her houseguests would realize by dinnertime that she hadn't returned to the abbey.

Alyssa pulled the man's riding jacket more closely around her. She could still smell Miles St. Aldford's scent on the material: It was a comforting blend of man and horse, leather and the outdoors.

She permitted herself a small sigh. Just one. Under the circumstances, there wasn't room for self-pity. Self-pity accomplished nothing. Besides, Miles would come for her. she believed that with every ounce of her being.

Alyssa froze. Had she heard something? Or was her imagination playing tricks on her? She cocked her head and listened intently with her ear to the door. Then she rattled the handle and called out, "Hello! Please, is someone, anyone, there?"

There was no answer. A minute or two later there was a thud, like the sound of a solid object hitting the ground. Adrenaline shot into her bloodstream. Her heart began to beat faster. Her hand was shaking as she reached out and turned the knob again.

This time the door opened.

She was free.

Alyssa staggered out of the Grotto, arms and legs stiff with cold. It took a while for her eyes to adjust to the pale light; then she looked around. It was evening. The setting sun was behind the trees, and a blue mist was forming over the nearby pond and the park beyond. There was no one about. Not a soul. No Miles. No Beauty. No one. She had never felt more alone in the world.

"You are a silly goose, Alyssa Gray," she lectured herself aloud. "It's not the first time you've found yourself alone, and I'll warrant it won't be the last."

Somehow the sound of her own voice cheered

Alyssa. She rubbed her arms and hobbled about, stomping her feet. The evening was warm, but she was thoroughly chilled to the bone. Why shouldn't she be? She had been locked in a cold, damp cavern for hours.

Had someone deliberately barricaded her inside the building? Or had the door merely become jammed? If so, how, in the end, had it become unjammed?

She glanced down. There was a large branch by the steps leading into the Grotto. She supposed it could have been used as a lever to prevent her from opening the door.

It didn't matter. Nothing mattered except the fact that she was free. Since it was a considerable distance back to the abbey, she'd better be on her way. It would be dark before she reached home.

Alyssa had gone perhaps a mile when she heard the familiar sound of hoofbeats. She peered into the gray mist ahead. Suddenly—there!—at the edge of the Old Woods, was a horse and rider. She raised her hand and was about to call out when something stopped her. She was hesitant, she realized, to bring attention to herself.

She waited and watched. The steed was a huge, dark, muscular beast. The man riding on its back— if it was a man—brandished a great sword in the air. She couldn't see his face, but there was something on the front of the rider's tunic, something that appeared to be a . . . Crusader's cross.

Perhaps if she hadn't spent all day trapped in the Grotto, thinking about her fears, facing the possibility of her life in peril, Alyssa would have been more afraid. As it was, she squeezed her eyes tightly shut and intoned a heartfelt prayer. She opened her eyes. The evening mist was thicker still, but the horse and rider had vanished. Breathing a sigh of relief, she quickly continued on her way.

She hadn't gone far when she heard it again. Hoofbeats. This time directly ahead of her on the trail. He came riding out of the mist: her knight in shining armor.

"Easy, Bulle Rock." In one fluid motion, Miles St. Aldford pulled back on the reins, brought the Thoroughbred to a halt, and swung down from the saddle. "My lady."

She moved her lips. "My lord."

He ran his eyes over her. "Alyssa."

She tried to smile and found she couldn't quite manage it. "Miles." Then, to her utter mortification, she fainted in his arms.

When Alyssa opened her eyes only moments later, Miles was holding on to her for dear life. She was caught up in his embrace, her head resting on his shoulder, her hands around his neck.

"I don't know what came over me," she mumbled apologetically.

"Dear God, woman, you're like ice." He sounded almost savage.

"The Grotto was cold," she said in a hoarse whisper.

Miles reached behind him with one hand and snagged a pouch hanging from his saddle. He removed a small silver flask, unscrewed the top, and held it to her lips. "Take a drink of this."

Alyssa eyed the flask. "What is it?"

"Brandy."

She took a sip. It burned all the way down to her stomach, but it took away the chill.

"Another," Miles insisted.

This time she obeyed without question.

"And another," he repeated.

Again, she obeyed him.

She'd never had a taste—or, for that matter, a head—for ardent spirits. A glass of champagne to mark a special occasion was the most she allowed herself. But the brandy that Miles was pouring down her throat was warming her rather nicely.

"Do you think you can ride?"

Alyssa pushed his arm aside, stood on her own two feet, if a little unsteadily, gave the long skirt of her riding habit a swipe with the back of her hand—there were twigs and bits of mud clinging to her costume—and headed for Bulle Rock. "Of course I can ride," she declared. "I'm a superb horsewoman."

"Perhaps when you're not under the weather," her rescuer observed dryly. "We'll both ride Bulle Rock," he said, settling her on the Thoroughbred and swinging up into the saddle behind her.

"Sir, you have your arms wrapped around me like the muscular tentacles of an octopod," Alyssa felt it necessary to point out. "It is most inappropriate."

"Madam, I have my arms around you so I can hold on to the reins," Miles explained.

Her mind went blank. "Oh." she attempted to keep her back ramrod straight, but the effort proved to be too much for her. Alyssa relaxed, leaned back against him, and confided, "I knew you would come."

"Did you?"

She nodded her head. "It was just a matter of time." She pondered the subject of time for a moment, then inquired, "Why did it take you so long, my lord?"

"I only realized you were missing when it was brought to my attention at the dinner hour by Miss Pibble," he admitted with what sounded like chagrin. "She'd been searching for you everywhere, and was just checking the stables when Beauty returned without her rider. Naturally Miss Pibble was concerned."

"Naturally."

"She was worried sick."

"I would be in her shoes."

"She was on the verge of tears."

Alyssa clicked her tongue sympathetically and nestled closer to his warmth. "Poor Emma." Her eyes were growing heavy; she didn't think she could keep them open much longer.

"Were you thrown?"

She tried to sit up straight. "What, my lord?"

"Did the mare throw you?"

What a suggestion! "Beauty would never do such a thing," she informed him.

"What happened, then?"

Alyssa frowned. "I'm not altogether certain. I think I was locked in the Grotto. At least I believe the door was locked, although it may have been barricaded shut."

She could feel the muscles in his forearms tense. His hands were fists on the reins. His thighs were like a vise on either side of the leather saddle.

"The important thing is you're safe now," Miles said in a deceptively mild tone.

"I'm safe now."

"I should never have left you." His voice was heavy with self-reproach.

He wasn't to blame. She was the one who had insisted on staying behind to attend to her toilette. "Good heavens, it's not your fault, my lord."

His tone was grim. "You need a keeper."

She did not need a keeper. She was perfectly capable of taking care of herself. She had been on her own, after all, for nearly two years.

Nevertheless, Alyssa found she didn't have the energy to argue with the man. In fact, once they reached the abbey, she allowed him to carry her upstairs to her rooms. There, Emma Pibble took command of the situation: fussing over her, helping her into a nightgown, tucking her into bed, even ladling a little of Mrs. Fetchett's special medicinal soup—she was certain that one of the secret ingredients was more brandy—into her.

As she was drifting off to sleep, Alyssa suddenly remembered she hadn't thanked Miles St. Aldford for rescuing her.

Turning her head on the pillow, she murmured drowsily, "Emma, I forgot."

Emma Pibble moved in the chair she had pulled up beside the bed and reached out to clasp Alyssa's hand in hers. "What did you forget, my dear?"

A furrow formed between her eyes. "I forgot to thank the marquess for coming to my rescue."

The older woman patted the back of her hand reassuringly. "I'm sure he knows."

After a pause, Alyssa inhaled deeply and whispered, "I knew Miles would come."

Emma didn't contradict her. "Did you?"

She nodded and slowly let her eyes close. "He is a knight in shining armor."

"You're up early this morning, my lord," Blunt remarked as Miles stalked into the Knight's Chambers and slapped his gloves and riding crop down on the table.

"I was out," he said succinctly.

Hortense Horatio Blunt was well trained as a gentleman's gentleman. If he was needed, Miles made certain he was aware of it. Otherwise, he was to afford his master a certain degree of freedom.

Blunt continued with his task of brushing the lint from the black evening coat.

Miles strode across the room to the large silver breakfast tray, apparently brought while he was gone, and poured himself a cup of coffee. He lifted a lid here and a lid there, then slammed them down again without making a selection. "I am a dunce."

Blunt kept brushing.

"I am an idiot."

Blunt examined a loose button.

"I am a jackass." Miles paused, coffee in hand. "You might at least say something."

" 'They also serve who only stand and wait,' " Blunt quoted under his breath.

Miles made a gesture in the air. "Which one?"

"Milton, my lord."

Miles knew it had to be one of the three classical English writers—Pope, Milton, or Shakespeare—

that his valet had been quoting on this trip. "I have been to the Grotto."

His companion paused and looked up from his sartorial duties. "Ahhh."

"I wanted to be there at first light before the scene could be contaminated."

Blunt took a needle and thread from his sewing kit and went about the business of securing the loose button. "Did you find anything?"

Miles held up his hands, examined the palms, then lowered his hands. "It rained in the night."

"Most regrettable," his man said.

Miles crossed to the window and gazed out over the rose garden and beyond to the Old Woods. The morning mist was beginning to lift. It would be a fine summer day, an exemplary summer day, by midmorning. "There were several bushes to either side of the Grotto door with fresh marks on them: a broken branch, a bent twig or two."

"Animal?"

"Possibly."

"Deer?"

"Probably." Miles fell silent, musing. "It could have been a man crouching."

"To what purpose?" Blunt challenged, playing *advocatus diaboli*, devil's advocate.

"I don't know," he confessed, driving his fingers through his hair as he was wont to do when working out a problem or a sticky bit of strategy. "I also found a large stick."

"Hm."

"There was a clump of grass that appeared to have been pulled from the edge of the pond."

Blunt finished his task and returned the coat to the wardrobe. "What is on the other side of the pond?"

"First," Miles said, holding up his index finger, "a meadow of sweet grass where a horse might well be tempted to stop and graze."

"Regrettably the rain wiped out any evidence of tracks?"

"Regrettably." Miles propped up one boot on the edge of a blanket chest. "However, I had a talk with the stable boy who feeds and grooms Lady Alyssa's mare. He said Beauty wasn't interested in her usual bucket of grain when she returned last night. He even tried to cajole her with a special treat. She turned up her nose."

"The mare's belly was full of sweet grass," concluded Blunt.

Miles nodded. "Second," he said, holding up another finger, "not far from the pond and the meadow is the Monk's Cave."

"Where there is a hermit camping."

"Exactly."

"Did you speak with him?"

"He wasn't at home." Miles took a gulp of the coffee.

"What did Lady Alyssa say last night?"

His eyes narrowed. "She said she was cold and hungry and had been locked inside the Grotto since soon after I'd left her. That would be some eight hours, by my estimate."

Blunt shook his head and made sympathetic noises. "That is most distressful, my lord."

"There is no lock on the building."

That got the other man's immediate attention. "No lock, did you say?"

"No lock."

Blunt's brow creased. "Would it be possible to barricade the door shut?"

"It would."

"The large stick," they said in unison.

Miles knew his eyes were shimmering fiercely. "If that is the case, then someone deliberately blocked the door of the Grotto with Lady Alyssa inside." He slapped his thigh and lowered his boot to the carpet. "Why?"

"Why?"

"What is the motivation behind such an act?"

Blunt thought for a moment. "To frighten her?"

"Why try to frighten her?"

Blunt shrugged. "To do her bodily harm?"

"If a villain were intent on harming the lady, there would be countless better ways of doing so."

His valet hesitated, then said, "To be mean."

Miles's features grew stern. "That is a possibility."

"I can't imagine, my lord, who would wish to play a mean joke on an angel like Lady Alyssa."

"Neither can I." Frustrated fingers combed through his hair. "The whole bloody business doesn't make any sense." Miles blew out his breath in exasperated spurts. "Maybe I'm seeing duplicity where none exists."

"Maybe."

"The door could have jammed on its own."

"It could have."

Miles returned to the silver breakfast tray, lifted a silver lid, plucked a large, luscious, ripe strawberry from the plate underneath, and popped it into his mouth. One by one, a bunch of dark purple grapes followed, and then several slices of succulent melon. His appetite was returning. "There is only one thing for me to do, Blunt," he announced to his valet as he poured himself a second cup of coffee.

"What is that, my lord?"

The china cup hovered in midair. "In the future I must stick to the lady like glue."

Later that afternoon Miles was strolling alone in the formal gardens, Miss Emma Pibble having assured him, on at least three separate occasions since luncheon, that Lady Alyssa was resting comfortably and there were no ill effects from her confinement beyond a certain exhaustion.

In other words, the marquess was not to inquire again after the lady until evening.

Miles was attempting to walk off some of his pent-up energy in the gardens when a boy approached him, cap in hand.

"Beggin' yer pardon, my lord."

"Yes, lad. Who are you?"

"Ian McKennitt, it is, my lord."

"What is it, Ian McKennitt?"

The boy stood tall and straight and didn't squirm under his scrutiny. Miles liked that.

"A man gave me somethin' to give to you, yer lordship."

"A man? What man?"

Ian McKennitt's young forehead creased a moment perplexedly. "The man said if you was to ask, I was to tell you that he is a true friend."

"A true friend, huh?" Miles repeated, a touch of cynicism lighting his eyes.

"That's what he said, my lord."

"What are you supposed to give me?"

Ian McKennitt dug around in his pants pocket and carefully brought out what appeared to be a piece of tree bark wrapped in a large broadleaf. "The man had to make do on account he didn't have any writing paper." The boy approached and dropped the piece of bark in Miles's outstretched palm. "All right if I get back to work now, yer lordship?"

"Yes." Miles drove into his own pocket for a coin. "Thank you for delivering the message, Ian."

The boy's face lit up when he saw the coin. "Thank you, my lord."

Once he was alone again, Miles carefully unwrapped the piece of bark. There was something etched on the inside of the wood where it was smooth. He held it up to the sunlight. He could just make out the words: NO ACCIDENT. PROTECT LADY. SIGNED, A TRUE FRIEND.

Miles read the message again, hoping it was wrong, hoping that whoever had written it was wrong, but he knew the man who called himself a true friend was right.

It had been no accident. Alyssa *had* been deliberately locked in the Grotto.

Somehow, some way, Miles vowed, someone would pay.

Chapter Thirteen

"You're up early," Caroline Chubb remarked to her husband as he strolled into her bedroom.

It was just after eight o'clock in the morning, but Alfred had never quite gotten out of the habit of rising early to go to the office. On the other hand, even here in the country, she rarely made an appearance before luncheon.

"I have been thinking, my dear," he said, first tugging at his side-whiskers and then stuffing his hands into the pockets of his silk dressing gown.

Thinking was a dangerous pastime for Alfred. Caroline had always thought it best if he left important matters in more capable hands: *her* hands.

She sat up in the elaborately carved canopy bed—there was a small, brass plaque affixed to the wall beside the headboard that read "Elizabeth R slept here, 12 September in the year of our Lord, 1578"—and plumped the pillows behind her back. It was a task usually reserved for Francesca, but she'd already sent her maid off on an important errand. "What have you been thinking about, Alfred?"

He stood at the windows opposite and looked out

over the formal gardens and beyond to the park, with its herd of grazing sheep. "How many menials would you estimate it takes?"

"To do what?"

"To tend to all of this," Alfred said, making a grand, sweeping gesture with one arm.

She wasn't certain what he was getting at. "By 'all of this,' I assume you mean the abbey, the gardens, the stables, and the various other outbuildings—"

He cut her off without apology. "Yes. Yes. I mean the whole kit and caboodle."

Caroline chose to ignore her husband's lapse in good manners. "It takes a small army."

"At no small expense," he stated, pivoting on a slippered foot. "If my calculations are correct"—Alfred's calculations, as they both knew, were always correct—"the upkeep of Graystone Abbey costs nearly ten thousand pounds per annum."

"It requires a great many servants to maintain a great country house. Just as a certain number of employees are no doubt needed to successfully operate Chubb Enterprises," Caroline reasoned, tucking the bedcovers around her waist. Her hand-embroidered nightdress slid off one shoulder, creating a picture of unintentional seduction. Nothing she did, however, was unintentional. "Indeed, I imagine running a country estate must be very much like managing a business."

Alfred wagged a finger at her. "That is precisely my point. But I see no reason why the owner of a great country house should bear all the expense. Therefore, I have been thinking . . ."

"Yes?"

"Why not open the gardens of Graystone Abbey to the public and charge each visitor a shilling? We might even offer guided tours of the house . . . at an additional fee, of course. Perhaps there should be a shop." Sir Alfred's eyes narrowed in speculation. "Yes, a tea shop where people can sit and enjoy a cup, and then purchase mementos of their visit."

Caroline managed to conceal her horror. Leave it to her husband to find a way to turn a profit. The man could wring blood from a turnip. Unfortunately, he had no notion of class. He was common from the tips of his toes to the Macassar-oiled hair on his head.

Still, money was power in today's world, and Alfred did have a genuine talent—some said a genius—for making money. He had taken a modest garment factory, founded by his great-grandfather at the turn of the century, and turned it into a worldwide industry. Theirs was a household name from one end of the British Empire to the other. Chubb had become synonymous with men's underwear. In particular, men's pink silk stockinette drawers.

"Wash out my chubbs." "Fetch my chubbs." "Don't forget to pack my chubbs," was heard from India to the Crimea, from Sydney to Edinburgh.

Caroline sighed and leaned her head back against the pillows. Marriage to Alfred Chubb was both a blessing and a curse. It gave her the financial backing she needed to put her plans into action. At the same time, she was always conscious of the social chasm that existed between those who were in trade and those who were not, between a woman like herself and a lady like Alyssa Gray.

"How is your research progressing, Alfred?" she inquired. There was no sense, after all, in putting the cart before the horse. Graystone Abbey wasn't theirs yet.

He shook his head, gazed out the window again—there was a row of stained-glass panes, depicting the twelve apostles and dating from the fourteenth century, above beveled glass from the later Elizabethan period—and whined, "Sometimes I feel like I'm looking for a needle in a haystack."

"You mustn't give up. It will be worth it in the end," she reminded him.

"I know. I know." He rubbed a hand across his eyes. "It's simply that I've been poring over genealogy charts and old maps of the abbey until I'm quite exhausted." He looked out at her from between his fingers. "You don't happen to know what Ariadne's Thread is, do you, Caroline?"

A deep furrow appeared momentarily between her eyes. "No. Is it important?"

Her husband shrugged his noticeably rounded shoulders, the result of years spent behind a desk, bent over accounting books and shipping schedules. "I don't know yet. I happened upon several references to it yesterday." He turned his full attention on her. "What have you found out, my dear?"

"It has been a most lucrative week when it comes to gossip, Alfred," she bragged. "Everyone—everyone but Lady Alyssa, that is—believes that James Gray died on the journey home from India. They're convinced he will never return to England or to Graystone Abbey."

"Poor blighter."

She scoffed and took no pains to hide her lack of sympathy for the missing gentleman. "One man's misfortune is another man's opportunity. James Gray's disappearance has turned out to be a bit of luck for us," she pointed out.

He reflected on this. "A bit of luck?"

"It's one less obstacle to overcome. In a manner of speaking, the position of Earl of Graystone is available."

"I see what you mean." Alfred grew cautious. He lowered his voice. "You don't think anyone suspects, do you?"

She shook her head. "They haven't any idea."

"What about the marquess? I've heard that he was sent here by the Queen herself."

"He was."

"To what end?"

"To investigate a ghost."

"Bosh!" A florid color washed across Alfred Chubb's coarse features. "Ghosts! Poppycock!"

"I know that. You know that. And I'm sure the marquess knows that."

Alfred pulled on one ear. His ears were markedly larger than they should have been for his head, and his chin was too small. Hence his reason for growing muttonchop whiskers, in her opinion. "Well, I wouldn't want Lord Cork to get wind of what we're up to until I'm good and ready to present my case."

"Don't you worry about Miles St. Aldford. I've

taken care of him," she said, pursing her lips with satisfaction.

"What have you done?"

"I have created a diversion for the marquess. He will be kept busy. Very busy."

"Doing what?"

"Chasing after shadows," Caroline related with relish.

Alfred frowned. "I don't understand."

It wasn't necessary for her husband to understand. Indeed, it was preferable that he didn't know everything she was up to. "Don't worry about it. You have your work cut out for you, and I have mine." She noticed that certain look in Alfred Chubb's eyes and patted the mattress beside her.

He trotted over and plunked himself down. "Yes, my dear?"

"What are you thinking about now, Alfie?" She rarely used his nickname from the old days; only on special occasions. This was one of them.

Alfred licked his thick lips. "I was thinking how lovely you look this morning." He reached out and grasped the bare shoulder where her nightdress had slipped off. His hands were large and he was clumsy, but she never let him know that.

"Your skin is like a girl's," he said gutturally.

Caroline worked very hard for that effect. But as far as he knew, it was effortless. "I feel like a girl with you, Alfie."

He glanced furtively toward the door of her boudoir. "Where is Francesca?"

"I've sent her off to do some errands for me in the village. She won't return until luncheon."

"And Charmel?"

"Charmel has gone riding with Sir Hugh this morning."

Alfred was momentarily distracted by the news of their daughter's social engagement. "Sir Hugh and Charmel seem to have taken to each other."

"It is a harmless flirtation that will come to nothing in the end," Caroline assured him.

He gave a little grunt that may have been a laugh. "How do you know that?"

"I will make certain of it," she stated without reservation. "Our daughter is beautiful, clever, witty, and charming, and she will have a season next year in London. I dare say, Charmel can *and* will make a better match than a mere baronet."

"If you say so, my dear. I leave these things in your very capable hands," he said, taking hers and placing them on him.

She pretended to be surprised by what she felt under his dressing gown and nightshirt. "Why, Alfie, you naughty boy, whatever do you have there?"

"A surprise for you, my girl."

Caroline laughed in the back of her throat; she did love playing the game of seduction. . . . If only the outcome were more to her liking.

"A surprise for me?" she exclaimed, feigning delight as she snaked her way under his clothing. A button undone here and a sash there, and his hot, ready flesh sprang into her waiting hands. "Alfie, how very big you are!"

"All the better to poke you with," he said crudely, laughing through his nostrils and pushing her back into the mound of pillows.

It was only through her considerable skill and experience that Caroline was able to untangle the bedcovers, divest her husband of his dressing gown and nightshirt, and still give the impression of eager anticipation when he pulled at her bodice.

She heard a small ripping sound. He had torn the exquisitely embroidered gown. It didn't really matter, she thought with a sigh. Alfred had paid for it, and he would pay for another. Indeed, he would buy her a dozen such nightgowns if she so desired. For Caroline Chubb had learned a valuable lesson long ago: The one thing that wielded even more power in this world than money was sex.

Alfred pawed at her bare breasts, kneading them between his palms like so much bread dough. Then he lowered his head, clamped onto one nipple with his teeth, and bit down hard. The resulting pain shot through her, raising her chest—her entire torso—off the bed and driving her vulnerable flesh even farther into his mouth.

He snickered. "Like that, did you?"

All she managed through clenched teeth was his name: "Alfred!"

He reached down and stuck a finger roughly inside her. She was as dry as a bone. Caroline closed her eyes and imagined another time, another place, another man, and her body responded as she had taught it to do. She was soon wet and ready.

"Here's one for you, girlie," Alfred gasped as he huffed and puffed and drove his hard shaft into her, right up to the hilt.

He pounded away—she raked her nails down his back, knowing that he felt it somehow marked him a man—then went rigid, thrust again, and emptied himself inside her.

As was his custom, her husband rolled off her and, without a word, turned his back to her. Within several minutes she could hear his soft snores. He had fallen asleep.

Caroline waited another five minutes. Then she slipped out of bed, clutching the remnants of her nightgown around her, and padded into the adjoining dressing room. She quietly closed the door behind her and crossed to the full-length mirror.

She dropped the ruined gown—it floated to the floor and pooled around her feet—and scrutinized her reflection. Her nipples were red and slightly swollen, not from passion but rough handling. There was a scratch on her shoulder from Alfred's teeth, a scrape on her breast, and another lower on her belly from his beard, but all in all she had emerged relatively unscathed this time.

"No harm done," Caroline murmured under her breath.

Since Francesca had yet to return from the errand her mistress had sent her on, she would draw her own bath. She was not one of those totally useless ladies who couldn't do for themselves in a pinch. Indeed, the household in which she had grown up had had no bathrooms and no servants.

Thank God the Graystones believed in modern plumbing, Caroline thought as she poured her favorite perfumed oils into the bathwater and stepped into the huge copper tub.

"Ahhh . . ." She leaned her head back on the terry pillow and breathed a sigh of relief.

Alfred was a clumsy ox, but he was necessary for her plans. For a woman to succeed in Society—and attract the attention of the Prince of Wales—she must be pretty, clever, rich, if at all possible, and married. She must definitely be married.

And to an obliging husband.

Caroline suspected that Alfred would *not* be obliging, but he could be deceived.

"One step at a time, Lady Chubb," she admonished herself as she sank lower into the warm, fragrant water.

For, once she was accepted into the Marlborough House Set, Caroline intended to make her way, discreetly and cleverly, toward her ultimate goal: to become the mistress of His Royal Highness, the Prince of Wales. Bertie, to his friends.

Caroline's eyes fluttered shut. She entered the dream world she had created for herself: one of power, of class, of royal balls and royal yachts, of all the things money could *not* buy.

Her talents wouldn't be wasted on the Prince. He would appreciate her beauty, her wit, her skills in the boudoir, skills that were wasted on an uncouth man like Alfred Chubb.

Caroline reached for the handled sponge on the table beside the tub. Eyes still closed, she began to wash her body, lingering over her breasts, her sensitive nipples, down her rib cage to her belly, then lower to that wicked, prurient place between her thighs. Tingling now as she had not been when Alfie had driven his rigid manhood into her, she tipped her hips forward slightly and began to touch herself. With the face of the Prince pictured in her mind—no, today it wasn't Bertie, but the darkly sensual, aristocratic features of the Marquess of Cork that she saw—Caroline eased the smooth handle of the sponge into her body. She sought her own satisfaction and when the hot, liquid feeling washed over her, she suddenly knew what the next step in her plans would be.

Miles St. Aldford.

She smiled to herself. There was no rest for the wicked.

Chapter Fourteen

"No rest for the wicked, eh, Sir Alfred?" Miles said amiably as he strolled into the abbey's library bright and early the next morning.

Alfred Chubb looked up from the book he was reading—there was an assortment of papers and leatherbound volumes spread over the entire surface of the library table at which he was seated—covered the page in front of him, the one he had been intently studying when Miles walked into the room, and blinked several times in rapid succession. "I beg your pardon, my lord."

The man had no sense of humor, Miles decided. Sir Alfred was deadly serious *and* deadly dull. After spending one week in the company of the Chubbs—surely it had been longer than a week; it seemed more like a month—he still didn't understand what they were about.

Sir Alfred Chubb had been a successful business-man with a genius for making money; that was a well-documented fact. Now he was an amateur historian of noted reputation, or so Miles had been informed by Lady Alyssa. The gentleman was solid, unimaginative, and socially inept. He also played a rather tedious second-rate game of baccarat, or "baccy," as he called it, yet he insisted upon challenging Miles to a few hands of cards each evening after dinner.

He invariably lost.

Indeed, after last night's tally, Sir Alfred owed Miles nearly twenty pounds.

Lady Caroline Chubb, on the other hand, was clever, witty, in full possession of the social graces, and could speak intelligently, if superficially, on any number of topics. She gave every appearance of being a professional beauty, and would, no doubt, in time end up in the ranks of Lady Randolph Churchill, née Jennie Jerome, originally of New York and later of Paris; or the Duchess of Manchester, who once accompanied Bertie to a music hall where it was rumored she danced a cancan; or the newest entrant into the Prince of Wales' circle of friends and acquaintances, the lovely Lillie Langtry.

There was something about Lady Chubb, Miles mused as he stood in the center of the vast library, that reminded him of the women of the Marlborough House Set.

He knew only what he had been told, of course, about the absent Mr. Edward Chubb—close friend and traveling companion to the youngest son of the Duke of B—, but Charmel Chubb was her mother's daughter. He predicted that Miss Chubb would have a stellar season next year in Society and, between her beauty and her father's money, make a most advantageous match. Miles was willing to lay odds on her marrying at least a baron, possibly even a viscount.

"Can I do something for you, my lord?" Sir Alfred inquired, removing his reading glasses and pinching the bridge of his nose between the thumb and forefinger of his left hand. He had apparently already been at his task for some time.

"I'm looking for a book," Miles replied.

"On any particular subject, sir?"

He nodded his head. "Horticulture."

"Horticulture?" Sir Alfred repeated, lifting one bushy eyebrow in a questioning arch.

"Specifically roses."

"Didn't take you for a gardener, Cork," Alfred Chubb commented as he put his spectacles down, pushed the heavy library chair back, and lumbered to his feet.

"It's a recent interest," he said by way of an explanation.

"Bit frilly for a soldier, roses."

"Ex-soldier."

Sir Alfred wiped away this last consideration with a wave of his hand. "Once a soldier, always a soldier."

Miles merely smiled and changed the subject. "I understand you're an historian."

"I dabble in history," the man said modestly. "When I retired from business a few years ago, my dear wife felt I needed a hobby to keep me occupied." Alfred Chubb made a noncommittal gesture. "So I became a student of West Country history."

Miles leaned back against a carved wooden banister—there was a staircase behind him that led to the second floor of the library—and folded his arms nonchalantly across his chest. "Why West Country history, if I may inquire?"

As he circled the room, Sir Alfred tossed over his shoulder, "My people came from here originally. Always thought it would be interesting to look up the Chubb ancestry." He paused and studied the shelf of books in front of him. "Horticulture, hmm?"

Miles glanced at the stack of thick tomes piled on the library table. Their titles were sobering: *A Complete and All-Encompassing History of the West Country*; *Legends, Lore and Landscapes of Devon*; *The Holy Wells of Cornwall and Devon*; *The Western Peninsula and the Legacy of the Irish Saints.*

Lying open, partially concealed by a scrap of paper, was the book Alfred Chubb had been deeply engrossed in when Miles had interrupted him. Painstakingly, for the page was upside down to him, Miles deciphered the title: *The Family History and Genealogy of the* . . .

Blast! He couldn't make out the rest.

Moving closer, and quickly lifting the edge of the paper just for a moment while the other man's back was still to him, Miles read the missing words: . . . *Earls of Graystone.*

Why would Alfred Chubb be studying a book on Alyssa's family? Perhaps even more curious, why try to hide the fact? Why not simply confess that he was being a bit of a snoop?

"The section on agriculture, botany, and horticulture extends from this marker to the corner of the room," Sir Alfred said, drawing Miles's attention to the other side of the library.

"Well done. Thank you, Chubb. You've saved me

a great deal of time and trouble," Miles said agreeably. "I'll find what I need and be on my way."

"Glad to be of assistance." The man returned to his work, mumbling, "Peace and quiet: That's what it takes to do the kind of research I'm involved in."

Miles ran his hand along the row of leatherbound spines, looking for the book on roses he had read as a young man, wondering if he would recognize it after all these years.

It was here, in this library, in this very room, thanks to his host Thomas Gray, that Miles had learned he never had to be lonely simply because he was alone. For the first time in his life, he had read because he'd wanted to.

Well, maybe not in the beginning.

He'd been impatient, after all, blustery and full of himself when he had arrived at Graystone Abbey on that initial visit. But as the days and weeks had passed, he'd begun to retreat to the library to read. First, out of sheer boredom, there had been little to do at the abbey if one didn't read or converse or garden. Then because he'd discovered that books could be his friends. They had opened up a whole new world to him; an infinite number of worlds.

Before that summer, Miles had been, at best, an indifferent student. Afterward, when the time came, he had gone on to Oxford, much to his grandfather's delight, earned a reputation as a scholar—he had excelled in both classical and modern languages— and become fast friends with Lawrence Grenfell Wicke, then the Viscount Lindsay, now the Duke of Deakin.

All thanks to the kindness, the generosity, the patience of Lord and Lady Graystone.

Miles selected a familiar small red book from the bottom shelf. He opened it to the title page and read with a feeling of immense satisfaction: *A History of Old Roses, Specifically Those Grown and Cultivated at Graystone Abbey*. The author was given as Thomas Gray, twelfth Earl of Graystone.

"This is it!"

Alfred Chubb looked up, peering over his eyeglasses and failing to conceal his relief at the announcement. "Gratified to know that you found what you were looking for, Cork."

Miles tucked the book under his arm. "Thank you for your assistance, Chubb. I'll leave you in peace now."

It was obvious the gentleman couldn't wait to be rid of him. Miles considered several possible reasons for Sir Alfred's attitude as he strode across the Great Hall toward the study. Was Alfred Chubb truly a serious scholar? Or was the man merely up to no good?

He knocked on the door of the study and entered. Alyssa wasn't behind her desk. Miss Emma Pibble was.

"Ah, Miss Pibble," he said, with a decisive nod of his head. "A word, if I may?"

The woman put aside her paperwork. "Yes, my lord."

"Where is Lady Alyssa?"

Emma Pibble frowned. "You haven't lost her again, have you, Lord Cork?"

"No, Miss Pibble, I haven't lost her again." He

hadn't even found her yet today. "I have something I want to show her," he said, indicating the book under his arm.

"She mentioned a meeting with Galsworthy. I believe you'll find them in the rose garden, my lord."

"Thank you, Miss Pibble." He backed out of the study. "Your information, as always, is invaluable."

If he was right—and he had a strong hunch that he was—then Alyssa was going to find *his* information even more invaluable, Miles thought as he headed toward Milady's Bower.

"Good morning, my lord," Alyssa said when she looked up from her gardening and found Miles hovering over her. In a mere three days it was astounding how far the weeds had gotten ahead of her.

"Good morning, my lady," he greeted her in return. "Quite recovered from your ordeal, are you?"

"Quite recovered, my lord."

"Weeding, are we?"

"We are." She quickly corrected herself. "I am."

"Where is your wimple, my lady?"

Alyssa put her head back and laughed. Unlike the other men of her acquaintance, Miles St. Aldford really was most amusing. "I don't have my wimple on me, sir, but what is that you have with you?" she inquired.

"A book on Old Roses," came the surprising answer.

The marquess seemed to have the singular ability to render her momentarily speechless. "I didn't realize you were interested in Old Roses," she finally said.

"It's a recent interest of mine." There was a mysterious smile on his handsome face. "Or perhaps I should say an old interest recently renewed." He took the small red book from beneath his arm.

Alyssa recognized it, of course, as the one written by her father. "Papa's book on the subject of roses. I haven't seen a copy in years. Wherever did you find it?" she asked, wiping her hands on her skirt as she got to her feet. "I mustn't touch it," she lamented. "I'm covered with grass stains and dirt."

"I located this particular copy in the library, with the help of Sir Alfred," Miles told her. Then he added, "I first read your father's book when I was only fifteen years old."

"That was the summer you stayed with my parents here at the abbey?"

He nodded. "Something kept niggling at me the past day or two. I seemed to recall that your father had written in his book about a legendary white rose."

Alyssa went very still. "A legendary *white* rose? Most Old Roses were—are—pink."

"Precisely."

Her heart began to beat faster. "Surely you don't think—"

"It's possible," he said simply.

"But improbable."

"Perhaps."

"The dead vine," they said in unison.

"Have you seen the white rose yet?" he asked her.

Alyssa shook her head. She'd been waiting for him.

"I think it's time we took a look at this miraculous flower, don't you, my lady?" Miles offered her his arm, reassuring her that a little dirt wouldn't harm either him or his jacket.

They made their way along the flagstone path and through Milady's Bower toward the corner where the ancient vine rambled back and forth, seemingly at will, over the garden wall.

"There isn't one white rose," she exclaimed, the breath catching painfully in her lungs.

Miles finished the thought for her as they approached the stone wall. "My God, Alyssa, there are at least ten or twelve white roses."

Chapter Fifteen

"There is no mistake," Alyssa informed him, after speaking privately with her head gardener. "There *was* only one rose. Galsworthy swears it on his mother's grave, and he has three lads who will swear to it as well. Now look." She raised her arms chest high, extended her hands palms up, then dropped them to her sides.

"Yes. Now look," Miles echoed.

Alyssa counted them again. There were twelve large roses. "I don't understand."

"Neither do I."

They drew closer and inspected the blooms. Their color was pristine white, and in the center of each flower were several red petals in the shape of a teardrop.

"I've never seen a rose of this variety." Alyssa paused for a moment and reconsidered. "Except, I realize now, on my family crest. I wonder if it has a name."

"It does."

Her eyes flew to the man standing beside her. " 'O rose, who dares to name thee?' "

"Apparently someone dared a long time ago. I

found the name in your father's treatise on Old Roses." Miles opened the small book he'd taken from under his arm and began to read aloud to her: " 'Although I haven't been privileged to see it in my lifetime, nor does anyone in the region recall witnessing this particular variety in bloom, there is said to be a legendary white rose with blood-red petals at its heart. It grows in only one place, within the walled garden of Graystone Abbey, and the name of the rose is *Milady's Tears*.' "

"*Milady's Tears*," Alyssa repeated softly.

"You'll recognize some elements of the story your father relates, although it reads more like a fairy tale than actual history," Miles said, turning the page. " 'Once there was a beautiful and proud high-born lady who took refuge at the abbey when her beloved, a famed knight of the realm, rode off to the Holy Lands to fight at the side of his king, Richard the Lion-Hearted."

"*Coeur de Lion*," she murmured. "The knight must be Robert the Bold."

Miles looked up briefly. "He isn't mentioned by name, but I think we can assume that's who the earl meant." He continuing reading. " 'The lady was as devout as she was beautiful. She spent many hours praying in her chapel.' "

"The Lady Chapel," Alyssa said, clasping her dirt-streaked hands together.

" 'When she wasn't praying in her chapel, the lady tended her garden.' "

"Milady's Bower." The pieces of the puzzle were beginning to fit together.

" 'Before his departure, the knight had stones

placed around the well in the walled garden to form a shallow pool. That way the lady would always have fresh water for her flowers.' "

"The Knight's Well."

" 'The lady planted a rare white rose in honor of the absent knight. As she walked each day in her garden, she wept for her beloved, fearing for his safety in that faraway and foreign land.' "

"Her fears weren't groundless," Alyssa reminded him. "Thousands of knights died during the Crusades."

Miles nodded knowingly. "Even if a soldier was lucky enough to escape the slaughter on the battlefield, he often succumbed to disease before he could return home." He glanced down at the book in his hands. "Anyway, the story goes on to say that the lady's tears fell in such profusion that her garden never required watering."

"I'll wager that the red petals in the center of the rose are supposed to be her tears," Alyssa said, recalling all the times she had escaped to the garden to weep in private, especially after the deaths of her parents. She, too, had watered the flowers with her tears.

"You win your wager. That's precisely what your father writes in the next paragraph."

Her voice had an emotional edge to it when she said to Miles, "It was customary for the wife of an early Roman soldier riding off to war to collect her tears in a glass vial during his absence. There is such a vial in the abbey's Curiosities Room. It is small and made of blue glass, the top still plugged after eighteen hundred years, the woman's tears still inside." She took two deep, shuddering breaths. "Does my father tell what happened to the lady and the knight?"

He shook his head. "No."

"I wonder what her name was," Alyssa speculated.

"He doesn't say."

She shrugged tautly. "Perhaps he never knew."

Miles leaned toward the nearest rose and breathed in deeply. "*Milady's Tears* has a very fragrant scent." Inhaling again, he announced, "Unusual."

"Unusual?"

He frowned. "Yet familiar."

Alyssa bent over and took a whiff of the open flower directly in front of her. "Bittersweet." She straightened. "I've never smelled anything quite like it before."

"I have," he stated.

Frankly she didn't see how that could be. The story said *Milady's Tears* bloomed in only one place, and not in recent memory, certainly not in Miles St. Aldford's lifetime. "Perhaps the scent you remember was a similar one to this," she suggested.

Miles seemed disinclined to argue with her. "Perhaps."

She brightened. "It's fortunate we decided not to chop down the vine the day you arrived at the abbey."

"You mean the morning I made my dramatic entrance by bounding over the garden wall and promptly trampling your flowers?" he recounted with a self-deprecating smile.

"Under the circumstances, it couldn't be helped," Alyssa said. "You do have rather large feet, my lord."

They both stared down at Miles's oversized riding boots.

"I suppose I do," he muttered.

She hastened to reassure him, "Your feet aren't too large, of course. Indeed, they are entirely appropriate in size and proportion to the rest of you."

"In other words, I'm big all over," he said dryly.

Oh, dear, she was making a muddle of it. "Let's just say there are many things about you that could be described as larger than average," she elucidated.

An irreverent thought suddenly popped into Alyssa's head as she stood there beside the marquess. That moonlit night there in the rose garden, that night when he had first kissed her, that most masculine part of Miles St. Aldford's body had not only been large, it had been huge. Huge and hard.

She swallowed with some degree of difficulty. She supposed being huge and hard was preferable to being small and soft . . . if one were a man.

"You know what they say, my lady?"

Alyssa tried to avoid his eyes. "What do they say, my lord?"

There was something in his voice, something very much like laughter. "It's better to be too big than too small."

Heat flooded her cheeks. The man was a mind reader. It was as though he knew exactly what she'd been thinking. She was mortified.

Alyssa made a swipe across her overheated face with the back of her left wrist; it was the only part of her hands and forearms not streaked with dried mud.

Pish and piddle! There was nothing to be done about it now: She'd already opened her mouth and put her foot in it. And none too daintily, either.

"I've never thanked you for having the lamb's-ears and lady's mantle replaced," she said, abruptly changing the subject. "It was most kind of you."

"It was nothing." Miles stroked his jaw thoughtfully. "I must confess, however, I'm stumped by this recent development in your garden."

"As am I," she admitted.

"The vine appeared to be dead."

"It did."

"It was dead." A moment later the marquess contradicted himself. "Even if it is alive, why would it bloom now?"

"High Rose Tide," she pointed out.

He smiled ruefully. "And you did tell me that during the Middle Ages the water from the Knight's Well was reputed to be a cure for impotency. Maybe it works on flowers, too."

Alyssa didn't know what to say to that, so she merely bobbed her head several times. Truth to tell, she wasn't ordinarily a believer in the miraculous. Nevertheless, there were events in the course of human history that seemed to defy logic or rational explanation.

She leaned over and washed her hands in the cool water that sprang from the Knight's Well. She had no towel, but Miles politely offered the use of his handkerchief.

"Your father's book," he said, handing it over to her.

"It's been years since I've seen a copy." Her throat tightened. "I'd almost forgotten its existence."

"Doubtlessly you've had other things on your mind the past several years."

That was true.

Alyssa glanced down at the watch dangling from her waist. "Good heavens, look at the time. I'm going to be late."

He gave her a speculative look. "Late for what, if I may inquire?"

"A delivery. Then I'm off to meet with the land agent."

He reached out as if to touch her arm and then apparently thought better of it. "What delivery? What land agent?"

"The delivery is taking a used but serviceable suit of gentlemen's clothing to the hermit living in the Monk's Cave. Then I'm meeting with Mr. Worth, the land agent, because there are repairs that need be made to several of the cottages while the weather is still good," she explained. "After I meet with Mr. Worth, one of the lads is going to drive me into the village. The vicar and I intend to discuss a new roof for the church."

"What's wrong with the old roof?"

"It leaks like a sieve."

"I see." Miles nodded his head. He said nothing for a moment, then announced, "I'll accompany you on your rounds."

"I'm afraid it will be tedious for you, my lord," she said, very deliberately.

Miles squared his shoulders. "I'm no stranger to tedium." He added, "Besides, we're partners. You said so yourself."

She couldn't deny it. "So I did."

"Don't you agree that two pairs of eyes and ears, and two minds, are better than one?"

"Well . . . yes."

"You never know who or what we'll encounter that could be a clue in solving the mystery of your ghost."

"There is no ghost."

"I know that. You know that. Any halfway rational person knows that. Nevertheless, someone wants us to think there is."

"Ah, someone, no doubt, on your list of suspects."

"On *our* list of suspects."

"I must change," she said with a glance at her muddied gardening clothes.

"I'll have the carriage brought around," Miles volunteered as they headed for the house.

As she fairly flew across the Great Hall toward the bedroom wing of the abbey, Alyssa glanced back over her shoulder at him. "It will be rather nice to have you along for the ride, my lord."

Miles was as good as his word: For the next week, where Alyssa went, he went. If she decided to take a ride on Beauty, he accompanied her on Bulle Rock. If she worked in the garden, he was right there beside her, holding her basket, her garden sheers, her gloves. When she ventured into town, he drove the carriage.

They walked. They talked. They took breakfast,

lunch, and dinner together. They sipped coffee, tea, lemonade, even the occasional glass of champagne. They discussed art, travel, philosophy, gardening, and the ancient Greeks, as well as more mundane matters.

In the process, Miles made a few observations. Alyssa worked hard in her role as mistress of Graystone Abbey. She fed the hungry, tended to the sick, and cared for the poor. She was patient, kindhearted, and a sympathetic listener. People took to her: young and old, rich and poor alike.

There wasn't a deceitful bone in her lovely body. She possessed none of the artifice, the affectation, the studied coyness of so many young females in Society.

Miles had told her that night in Milady's Bower that she was different from the women he knew. He was only now beginning to understand how different she truly was.

It came to a head one afternoon. They were strolling in the abbey's formal statuary garden when Alyssa suddenly stopped on the gravel path. There was a life-size marble statue of the winged Pegasus on her right and Zeus himself looking down from Mount Olympus on her left. She gnawed on her bottom lip for a moment, lifted her chin a notch higher in the pleasant summer air, put her shoulders back—as if bracing herself for his reaction to whatever she was about to say—and looked at him from beneath a pale gray silk sunshade. "My lord, we must talk."

"My lady, we do little else," he countered.

"There seems to be a misunderstanding," she began.

Miles frowned. "A misunderstanding about what?"

"Our partnership."

"What is it you don't understand?"

"It is not I who do not understand, sir. It is you," she insisted.

Miles blinked. That didn't seem very likely to him. "What is it you think *I* don't understand?"

Alyssa seemed to be choosing her words with care. "When I suggested we become partners in this investigation, I didn't mean to imply we should be together continually."

His eyes narrowed. "What are you trying to say?"

"I need time alone."

"You are alone."

"When?" she challenged.

He thought. "When you're asleep."

"It scarcely counts as time alone if I'm not awake to appreciate the fact," she said with some emphasis.

Miles was practiced in the art of distraction. It was a necessary—and useful—tool of the Marlborough House Set. "Don't you enjoy my company?"

The lady's response was immediate and vehement. "Of course I enjoy your company. This has been the most wonderful week I've ever spent," she declared.

Miles started to smile and caught himself in the nick of time. It wouldn't do to let Alyssa know how much she'd given herself away. Still, he could hear the hesitation in her voice. "But?"

"I must be blunt."

"Blunt?"

"Candid, then."

He managed to keep the amusement out of his voice. "Naturally it is your privilege to say what is on your mind."

There was a short pause. "I need breathing room," she finally told him.

His mouth curved up at the corners. "Is there something wrong with your breathing?"

"I mean in a manner of speaking." Alyssa took in an exasperated breath and quickly released it. "Sir, you are sticking to me like glue," she complained.

"Madam, I know." It would be foolish to deny his actions. Alyssa was neither a foolish young woman, nor did she suffer fools gladly.

She seemed taken aback by his candor. "Then it was your intent all along?"

"It was."

Gray eyes regarded him with a speculative look. "Why?"

Why, indeed? The first rule in the successful spy's handbook was to tell the truth whenever possible. The second was to lie only when absolutely necessary. Since he had no intentions of telling Alyssa about his investigations or about the warning he had received from "a true friend," he would stick with *a* truth, if not *the* truth. Miles shrugged and said, "I enjoy your company."

"As I have already stated, I enjoy yours as well." Alyssa lowered the silk parasol until it rested lightly on her shoulder, then idly twirled the carved bamboo handle in her hands. "And?" she prompted.

"And what?"

"There must be more to it than that."

Miles had thought his answer would satisfy her. He should have known better. "There is no more." It sounded feeble even to him.

Alyssa gave him an insightful glance. "It's about the incident at the Grotto, isn't it?" She didn't give him an opportunity to respond. "You're trying to protect me."

She was quick. Too quick.

She straightened her already ramrod-straight shoulders. "I release you, my lord."

"Release me, my lady?"

"From your vow to protect me."

"Now, see here, Alyssa—"

"I do not need a keeper, sir."

"I am not keeping you, madam," he replied, his voice rising slightly in both tone and volume.

"Nor do I need a self-appointed guardian," she went on.

"That is a matter of opinion," he shot back.

Her chin came up. Her eyes widened slightly. Her lips firmed. "I'm not a child. I'm a full-grown woman. I have been in charge of this estate and my own life for nearly two years now. And somehow I have managed quite well without your help." She snapped her parasol shut and swept past him with a haughty "You will have to excuse me. I have a prior engagement."

Miles heard himself inquire, "What prior engagement?"

He noticed Alyssa didn't bother to look back at him. "A game of croquet."

"With whom are you playing croquet?" It better not be with that twit Sir Hugh Pureheart.

"It's none of your business," she flung over her shoulder. "But, if you must know, I'm playing with Miss Chubb."

"I'll join you."

Alyssa stopped on the gravel pathway and spun around on her heel. "You haven't been invited."

"Then invite me."

She shook her head. "No. I won't. We ladies make a pleasant pastime of the activity. We chat and laugh and remark upon the fine weather and compliment each other on our shots, whether good or bad. Gentlemen, on the other hand, take their game far more seriously. They insist upon keeping score, counting every wicket, and, in the end, declaring someone the winner and someone the loser."

"What's the sense in playing if one doesn't keep score?"

"There. That is it exactly. You may not play."

"I'll sit quietly on the sidelines and watch."

"You will make us feel self-conscious and uncomfortable. We won't be able to enjoy ourselves."

'Then I'll retire to my rooms and spend an interminably long, dull afternoon writing letters."

"An excellent idea. I bid you good day, my lord."

Miles did not retreat to the Knight's Chambers to answer his correspondence. He went only as far as the Celestial Room, where he stood staring out the floor-to-ceiling windows at the vast expanse of green lawn beyond.

It wasn't long before the two young ladies appeared. Charmel Chubb with her lustrous dark brown hair, refined mannerisms, fashionable emerald green gown with matching hat, gloves, slippers, and parasol—the latter with which to shield her milk-white complexion from the sun. And Alyssa with her pale hair, unaffected ways, unadorned gray dress, straw hat askew, shoes still dusty from their walk, gloves—no doubt at Emma Pibble's insistence—and her parasol, which was soon dispensed with altogether and left on a lawn chaise.

The pastoral scene brought a smile to Miles's face. The smile was immediately replaced by a frown. He should have handled this latest encounter with more tact. Alyssa wasn't like other young ladies. She took great pride in being self-sufficient and independent, in standing on her own two feet. He'd handled her all wrong. He could see that now.

"You're a bloody fool, Cork," he muttered under his breath.

"You mustn't be too hard on yourself, my lord," came a sophisticated female voice from behind him.

Miles turned. Caroline Chubb was approaching the row of windows. He could hear the swish of her gown as she glided across the marble floor, a vision in blue satin and cream-colored lace.

"Most men—and women—make fools of themselves at one time or another," she said, closing a matching satin and lace fan with a single expert motion of her wrist.

"Lady Chubb," he said in greeting.

"Lord Cork," she responded, circling around him until she stopped somewhere in the vicinity of his elbow. For a moment she posed, her picture-perfect profile to him, and gazed out at the afternoon's croquet match. "The two of them make an enchanting *tableau vivant,* don't they?"

"Enchanting," he agreed.

"Yet they are as different as night and day."

"They are, indeed."

"A study in contrasts."

He merely nodded this time.

"Of course, Miss Chubb is the younger of the two, being only eighteen on her last birthday. I believe Lady Alyssa is twenty-three"—the woman tapped an elegant fingernail against her chin as if to draw his attention to the fact that her flesh was still as young and supple as that of the girls they were observing—"possibly even twenty-four." Her voice was irreproachably pleasant. "Lady Alyssa will soon be an old maid, I fear."

"She is twenty-one, and I understand she has had numerous offers of marriage," he said in Alyssa's defense.

Caroline Chubb made a sympathetic sound. "Ah yes. I have heard she is intended for Sir Hugh."

Miles ground his teeth. "She is intended for no one. She is still in mourning."

A bejeweled hand was pressed dramatically to an ample breast. Miles wondered if Lady Chubb realized the outline of her nipples was clearly visible through the diaphanous bodice of her blue tea gown. Something told him that she was well aware of it. Just as she was well aware of her other "charms."

"Poor child. Losing both parents at once." After a moment she remarked, "Surely Lady Alyssa will put her bereavement aside now and accept Sir

Hugh. A gentleman doesn't like to be kept waiting too long."

Miles wondered how long *she* had kept Sir Alfred waiting.

Beguiling blue-violet eyes regarded him. "Perhaps you will soon take a bride yourself, Lord Cork."

"Perhaps."

"You are the fourth Marquess of Cork and your wife will be the fourth marchioness."

"So they tell me," he said in a dry voice.

"You are a respected peer of the Realm with an old and honored title. It is also said that you are among the wealthiest landowners in England. You are considered a handsome man, and one presumes you are in excellent health."

"One presumes."

"You are a member of the coveted Marlborough House Set, and a close friend and confidant to His Royal Highness, the Prince of Wales." Caroline Chubb pursed her lips with satisfaction. "What more could any young woman desire in a husband?"

"What more, indeed?"

"With all that to recommend you, Lord Cork, you will be free to choose from any female in the Empire. There will be a dozen, a hundred—" here she laughed, and the sound of her laughter was like the trill of a fancy-plumed, exotic bird," even a thousand eligible ladies vying for your attentions."

The prospect made Miles St. Aldford's blood run cold. "If that's the case, Lady Chubb, time is of the essence."

A furrow appeared on the beautiful creature's otherwise wrinkle-free brow. "It is?"

"I am thirty years old." And, as Blunt was fond of reminding him, he wasn't getting any younger.

She splayed her fan and began to waft it back and forth in front of her face. "Thirty is the perfect age for a gentleman to marry, my lord."

"So I have been informed." At least in this, Lady Chubb and his valet were in agreement.

She raised another issue. "There are certain requirements for the position of marchioness, naturally."

"Naturally." Not that Miles knew or particularly cared what they were.

"The lady must be young."

"But not too young, of course," he said, playing along with Caroline Chubb's game, all the while his eyes following the slender figure in dove gray as she frolicked across the green lawn, swinging here and there with her mallet, once missing altogether. When that happened, Alyssa put her head back and laughed good-naturedly at herself. Miles chuckled softly along with her.

"The lady must be in good health, herself, so that she may bear you healthy children: an heir and a spare, at the very least."

He merely grunted in response. Lady Chubb was right, but it sounded so disagreeable when she said it.

"The lady must be a great beauty."

" 'Beauty is in the eye of the beholder,' " he quoted.

"Come, come, Lord Cork. We both know that some people are more beautiful to behold than others," she said, lowering her voice to a whisper, as if they were somehow conspirators in a common cause. "It's a simple fact of life."

In his experience, beauty had never been simple. Perhaps because he had seen so much ugliness. Beauty could be for good or ill; rarely was it neutral.

Lady Chubb chattered on about the qualifications for his bride. "Any female who would attain to the position of marchioness of Cork should also be intelligent, possess impeccable manners, a lovely figure, execute the social graces to perfection, and, of course, she must be a complete innocent."

Miles exhaled on a long-suffering sigh. "Where does a man find such a paragon?"

"Charmel is a great beauty."

"Your daughter is beautiful."

"She will have her season in London next year."

"I predict that Miss Chubb will dazzle the gentlemen of Society," he said.

That seemed a foregone conclusion to Lady Chubb. "Charmel is too intelligent, too refined, perhaps too perfect for the average gentleman," boasted her mother.

The woman had more than her share of audacity. "Indeed—"

"Thankfully there are gentlemen who are not average, gentlemen who are themselves *above* average, who can appreciate the truly finer things in life, including an exquisite young girl. You are one of those gentlemen, are you not, my lord?"

He was tempted to answer Lady Chubb, but managed to restrain himself. There was more she had to say, and he wanted to hear it all before he replied.

"Understandably, someone with your breeding

and background requires the same breeding and background in his wife. I want you to know in a very short time it will be made clear that Charmel's blood is as blue, perhaps even bluer, than that of, say . . . Lady Alyssa herself."

God's mercy! What the devil was she talking about? Were the Chubbs somehow descended from ancient lords and ladies, the very nobility that had founded this great island nation? Was Miss Charmel Chubb the final expression, then, of all that was good and fine and true of the British aristocracy?

Another favored quote of of Blunt's popped unbidden into his head, this one from *Hamlet*.

" 'Something is rotten in the state of Denmark,' " Miles muttered to himself.

A flicker of annoyance crossed Caroline Chubb's face. "I beg your pardon, my lord."

"It is I who beg yours, Lady Chubb. I was reciting one of my lines for the play."

"The play?"

"Yes." He concocted the story as he went. "Blunt and I thought it might be amusing to put on a masque, and I was rehearsing my part just before you entered the Celestial Room."

There was a raised eyebrow from his female companion. "I've heard nothing about a play."

"I'm certain you will once we have the details worked out. Blunt is a thespian, you know."

"Blunt?"

"My companion."

"Do you mean your valet?"

"He serves that function as well. Anyway, Blunt is studying dramatics. His idol has been Sir Henry

Irving ever since he saw the actor play Hamlet several years ago with Ellen Terry as his leading lady."

Miles cleared his throat. "You certainly have the beauty and the demeanor to appear on the stage yourself."

Caroline Chubb was flattered, but she never lost sight of her original goal. "Charmel has the same beauty and demeanor, I must point out. And she is, of course, a complete innocent."

It suddenly dawned on Miles. Lady Chubb was offering her daughter as a bridal candidate. He'd been so engrossed in watching Alyssa and then in extracting himself from a potentially awkward situation that he'd only been listening with one ear.

Of course, it wasn't the first time he'd found himself cornered by a strong-willed *maman* with matrimony on her mind. But here in the country, he had to confess, he'd let his guard down.

"Charmel is an angelic creature," he was told.

Miles made no attempt at subtlety. "Speaking of angels, have you gazed upon the magnificent ceiling of the Celestial Room, Lady Chubb? It was painted nearly two hundred years ago by an Italian artist for the fourth Earl of Graystone." He put his head back and made a production of looking up at the murals.

"They are magnificent," she conceded. "Sensual. Voluptuous." She gave him a sidelong glance. "One might even say inspiring."

Miles nearly choked on his saliva. He knew full well that Caroline Chubb was referring to the trio of figures depicted directly over their heads. In the center of the grouping was a muscular *and* nude male. Rubenesque females hovered on either side of him, their bare breasts carefully drawn so as to be out of reach of his outstretched hands.

Without blinking an eyelash, the woman beside him stated: "You are a man of the world, my lord. I am a woman of the world. Therefore, I will speak plainly. If you were to marry Charmel, you would be getting much more than a beautiful, innocent young wife."

Hell-kite! What was she talking about?

Lady Chubb continued. "I understand that the married ladies of the Marlborough House Set enjoy certain freedoms and privileges."

"Some choose to."

"And that love affairs are a reward for, not a prelude to, getting married."

"Again, it is true for some."

"Then you wouldn't have far to look, my lord—say, no farther than your own *famille*—to find a mistress willing, even eager, to share your bed."

The night of the dinner party, when Sir Hugh had been singing the praises of Lady Chubb, Miles had remarked that the woman seemed too good to be true. He'd been right. For in the same breath, Caroline Chubb had just made him an incredible offer: her daughter as his wife, and herself as his mistress.

His mouth curved derisively. "You know what they say, madam."

"What do they say, sir?"

"Beauty's but skin deep."

She scowled. It was the first he had seen her look her age. "I'm afraid I don't understand."

"I know you don't." There was a distinct chill in

the air. "I must excuse myself. I have a great many letters awaiting my attention." With a curt nod, he turned and headed for the door.

"Lord Cork, we haven't finished our conversation."

"I believe we have, Lady Chubb," Miles said, never looking back. He kept right on walking. Indeed, he didn't stop until he'd reached the safety of the Knight's Chambers.

"Pack only my small valise, Blunt."

"How long will you be gone, my lord?"

"I'm not certain." Miles was sitting at the desk in the Knight's Chambers, fountain pen in hand, trying to find the words to write to Alyssa. So far they had eluded him. "One change of clothing should do, since I'm traveling straight to London on the train. Whatever else I require will be available at Cork House."

Blunt's ears perked up. "If you're on your way to London, my lord, I should be accompanying you."

Miles turned around halfway in his chair. "This time you'll be of far greater service to me here. I need someone I trust to keep an eye on Lady Alyssa and the Chubbs."

Blunt's expression darkened. "Then something *is* amiss."

Miles had never lied to his friend and companion; he never would. "Something is definitely amiss. That's why I'm going to London. I need some answers and I need them fast. There are those in the city who owe me a favor or two." Miles St. Aldford smiled, but there was no mirth in his smile. "You know what they say, Blunt."

"What do they say, my lord?"

" 'A cock has great influence on his own dung-hill.' " He crumpled up the piece of writing paper and dropped it into the waste receptacle beside the desk. "Tell Lady Alyssa that I have been called away for several days and that I will return as soon as possible."

"Wouldn't you rather tell her yourself?"

Miles shook his head. "The lady is feeling peevish toward me at the moment."

"Peevish, my lord?"

He took in a deep breath and slowly released it. "She seems to think I've become something of a nuisance. She even accused me of sticking to her like glue."

Blunt appeared to be biting his tongue. "I will relay your message, my lord."

Miles stood and slipped his arms into the suit coat his valet was holding for him. "By the way, we're doing a masque."

"We are?"

He nodded and made a sweeping gesture toward the bookcase filled with plays. "I thought you might get together with Miss Pibble and come up with something suitably Shakespearean."

"When are we performing this masque, my lord?"

Miles hadn't planned that far ahead. "At the end of next week, or possibly the week after."

"That is scarcely enough time to do Shakespeare justice," his valet felt compelled to point out.

"I'm not interested in doing Shakespeare justice.

I'm interested in using Shakespeare to see that justice is done," Miles informed his longtime companion.

Blunt took a stiff-bristled brush to the shoulders and back of the dark jacket. "Do we have a wolf by the ears, my lord?"

"If not a wolf," Miles said as he bade his friend farewell and strode out the door, "then most assuredly a sheep in wolf's clothing."

Chapter Sixteen

"Another sweet cake?" Alyssa inquired politely.

Hugh shook his head and patted his soft midriff. "I'd better not. I've already had three."

Actually, Sir Hugh had devoured at least four sweet cakes in the last half hour, but who was counting?

"More tea?"

"No, thank you." Setting his cup and saucer down on the table at his elbow, Hugh went to stand at the window. He looked out for a moment and then turned to her. "Alyssa—"

"We could use some fresh tea. I'll ring for the housemaid." She started to rise to her feet. "Better yet, I'll just run along to the kitchen and fetch it myself."

"Please sit down," the baronet insisted in his high-pitched tenor. "I have a matter of importance to us both I would like to discuss with you, my dear."

Oh, dear.

Alyssa knew what the matter of importance was. There was always a certain unyielding tone underlying Hugh's voice when he was about to bring up the subject of matrimony. She did not, however, wish to talk to him about anything even remotely connected to marriage.

Now now. Not ever.

She had already refused Hugh Babington Pureheart's offer several times in the past six months. When a straightforward yet polite no had failed to dissuade the gentleman, she had attempted to use logic, pointing out to him the many and varied reasons why they would never make an ideal couple.

"We aren't well suited to each other, Hugh," she had argued on one occasion. "You are a gentleman who prefers the city and I am a country lady born and bred."

"Then we will compromise and spend part of the year in London and part of the year here in Devon," he had countered.

On the surface it had appeared to be a workable solution, but Alyssa knew what it really meant: She would be utterly miserable half of the time and Hugh would be impossible the other half.

"I'm most content when left to my own devices: gardening or taking a quiet walk through Milady's Bower or curling up with a book," she had continued on that not-so-long-ago afternoon. "You prefer parties and fancy dress balls, games of chance and horse racing, sailing and Society, in general."

"There is no need for a husband and wife to have any interests in common," Hugh had declared while she'd stared at him in disbelief. "After all, a woman's domain is her household and her children; a man's is the world."

"I have always wanted to travel and see the world," she had piped up then.

"One encounters a great deal of bad food, bad accommodations, bad company, and bad manners when traveling outside England," he had informed her.

Alyssa had bitten her tongue and tried a different tack altogether. "What of love?"

"Love is nothing more than a lower class schoolgirl's fantasy," Hugh had scoffed. "A wife should respect her husband's wishes, follow his instructions to the letter, and satisfy his needs. In return, it is his duty to protect her."

"Protect her from what?"

Here, Hugh Pureheart had frowned in thought. "Harm."

"You mean act as her knight in shining armor?"

"That's a rather romantic way of viewing it. It is a husband's duty to weed out certain kinds of people and places, ideas and events that he deems unsuitable for his lady wife."

Alyssa had narrowed her eyes. "In other words, a woman shouldn't go or do or say—or, for that matter, even think—unless she had discussed the matter first with her husband."

"Exactly," Hugh had said, nodding his weak chin. Popinjay!

After that, Alyssa hadn't even tried to explain why the man she would marry—if she ever married, and that possibility seemed less likely with each passing year—must accept her as a true partner. At its very best, marriage was a meeting of minds. It was two people sharing their thoughts, their feelings, their ideas. It was a joining of two hearts, two souls, two bodies.

That was the kind of marriage her parents had. Alyssa would settle for nothing less for herself. If she were to marry someone like Hugh Pureheart, she feared something inside her would wither and die.

Sir Hugh moved away from the window and made an unspecific gesture with his hand. "Please, Alyssa, sit down."

Alyssa sat down.

She racked her brain. She needed a topic of conversation that would divert Hugh's attention. She finally found one. "Are you aware that the marquess has gone to London?"

A thoroughly smug and somewhat condescending masculine smile was bestowed upon her. "Everyone in the village, in the valley, possibly in the entire West Country, knows that the Marquess of Cork took the five o'clock train to London on Tuesday last. There has been talk of little else for the past three or four days."

The people of this valley did not have enough to keep them busy, Alyssa decided.

Hugh took a seat across from her. "Did the marquess say how long he'd be away?"

"No, he did not," she replied.

In fact, Miles had left without so much as a word or a note or a proper good-bye; just a cryptic message delivered through Blunt saying that he would be back as soon as possible.

Hugh picked up his teacup, took a sip, apparently discovered his drink had cooled while he had been wandering about the formal parlor, and put the china cup and saucer down with a most disagreeable expression on his handsome face. He leaned toward her and, lowering his voice, said, "There has been talk, Alyssa."

"Talk?"

"Gossip. Rumors."

"About what?" Not about her ghost, she hoped.

"Not about *what*," Hugh said. "*Who*."

"Who, then?"

"Miles St. Aldford, fourth Marquess of Cork, soldier, decorated war hero, supposed spy, confidant to the Prince of Wales, notorious womanizer, and libertine."

"Libertine?"

Hugh made a small production of plucking at an imaginary thread on his coat lapel. "So they say."

"Who is they?"

Hugh shrugged his well-padded shoulders. "People."

"I don't believe it."

Tilting his head to one side, he said, "There is speculation that the marquess has gone to London to visit a woman."

She hadn't heard that. Alyssa leaned toward him. "A woman? What woman?"

Hugh reached out and patted her hand. "It's not for the delicate ears of a lady."

Why did Hugh Pureheart insist upon treating her as if she were a child? It was most galling.

"You mean the marquess has gone to London to visit his mistress," she blurted out.

That earned Alyssa a censorious look and a scolding. "You shouldn't speak of such matters."

"Why not?" she retorted stubbornly.

The baronet sniffed his disapproval. "It isn't proper. You are a well-bred young lady and you are unmarried."

That again.

Hugh's soft jaw tightened. "Which brings me to the subject I wish to discuss with you."

Alyssa permitted herself a small sigh. It seemed she had only delayed the inevitable. "What subject?"

"Marriage."

She did not wish to discuss marriage, especially not with Sir Hugh Pureheart.

"I know you still mourn your beloved parents, but the time has come to put grief aside and embrace joy once again," sir Hugh said with all the solemnity he apparently felt the occasion called for. "Frankly, my dear, I have seen you wear nothing but shades of gray or black for nearly two years. Your attire has taken on the semblance of a uniform or a habit." He clearly didn't mean it as a compliment.

Alyssa sat up straight in her chair and folded her hands demurely on her lap. Bless him, Hugh had given her an idea. She wet her lips. "Perhaps this is the appropriate time to tell you."

"Tell me what?"

"I have reached a painful decision."

Hugh appeared slightly nonplussed. "Painful?"

"For both of us," she assured him. "But, in time, I believe you will find a suitable replacement."

"A suitable replacement for what?"

"Not for *what*. For *who*."

"Who, then?"

"Me." Alyssa took in a deep breath and released it. "I wasn't intended to be your wife, Sir Hugh. I have been called:"

"Called where?"

"To the quiet life, the contemplative life, the cloistered life," she explained.

Hugh frowned at her. "You mean like a convent?"

"Yes, like a convent." Heaven forgive her. "Only since I already live in an abbey, I won't actually have to go away. I will simply make Graystone Abbey into what it once was."

Pale eyebrows arched over soft masculine features. "A nunnery?"

"Something like that."

A muscle in Hugh Babington Pureheart's face began to twitch. "I don't believe you."

"Believe me," Alyssa said firmly.

Hugh regarded her coolly. "You'll change your mind."

"I won't."

He snorted. "You'll want to marry me within the month."

"I vow I will not."

"You don't know what you're saying, much less what you're doing," the gentleman sitting opposite her concluded, shaking his head from side to side.

Sir Hugh Pureheart was a selective listener. He only heard what he wanted to hear. He filtered out the rest. He conveniently and immediately forgot it.

He was also single-minded. He had made a decision some time ago to marry her. It would take a concerted effort to set him on a new and different course, but Alyssa knew she must try. She would begin by planting a tiny seed.

She cleared her throat. "I think you deserve a different kind of woman altogether, Sir Hugh. A beautiful young woman. One who is socially polished and thoroughly accomplished in all the wifely virtues. One who will bring to your marriage the respect and adulation you deserve. Someone like . . ." Alyssa paused and tapped a finger against her bottom lip in thought, "Miss Chubb."

There was a moment of silence.

Then Hugh Pureheart responded, "Miss Chubb is beautiful."

"She is."

"She is very polished."

"Very."

"Her family is rich."

"Excessively so."

"Her mother is certain to be the toast of Society."

"Certain to be."

"But she is untitled."

"You were untitled until your uncle died," Alyssa reminded him. Hugh had been Sir Hugh for a relatively short period of time.

Her rejected suitor rose to his feet and began to pace back and forth across the Aubusson carpet. Then he stopped and pointed a finger at her. "Sir Alfred was once in trade."

There was no denying the fact. "Apparently that doesn't bother the Duke of B—. Miss Chubb's brother is traveling on holiday in Italy with Lord Peter."

"Lord Peter is the duke's youngest son."

Alyssa nodded. "I understand, too, that Miss Chubb will be presented at court this year."

"So I've heard."

"With her beauty, her grace, her exquisite manners, Miss Charmel Chubb will, undoubtedly, be very popular with the ladies and gentlemen in town," Alyssa pointed out to him.

Hugh scowled. "Undoubtedly."

"A dozen young gallants will shadow her every step."

His scowl deepened. "Her every step."

"Of course, Miss Chubb is quite unattended this summer here in the country." Alyssa consulted the clock on the mantel. "Look at the time," she exclaimed. "I will soon be at my prayers."

Hugh gave her an appraising glance. "Don't let me keep you, my lady. I have important business to attend to, and I find I must beg your leave."

"Then I bid you a good afternoon, sir."

Hugh Pureheart paused in the doorway of the formal parlor and looked back at her. "In many ways, the abbey has been a nunnery since your parents died."

"In many ways," Alyssa agreed. "By the by, I believe I saw Miss Chubb strolling by the fountain."

The minute Sir Hugh was gone from her presence, Alyssa headed for the cemetery behind the Lady Chapel. Her family graveyard wasn't a morbid or depressing place, contrary to what some might think. At least it wasn't on a beautiful summer afternoon. Indeed, the view of the valley from this spot was magnificent. It was a view that had changed very little in the past century or the past millennium.

Alyssa put her head back, shaded her eyes from the bright sunlight with her hand, and gazed up at the Norman Tower. Constructed during the frenzy of building that had followed William the Conqueror's conquest of the West Country, it had walls of stone six feet thick in some places, twelve feet thick in others. There were windows at regular intervals, openings large enough for a man and his bow.

The only access to the Norman Tower was through the Lady Chapel. Beside the chapel's altar was a concealed door. Behind the door was a staircase that wended its way up and up, around and around, until it reached the lookout.

Alyssa knew this only from her family's stories. She had never actually been in the Norman Tower. The staircase was considered unsafe and no one had been allowed inside for as long as she could remember.

Alyssa walked toward the headstone of her parents' final resting place, bowed her head, and said a silent prayer for her mother and father. Then she looked up and gazed out over the valley.

"Mama. Papa. I've told a lie," she said aloud. "Well, I like to think of it as more of a fib, really. I'm not in love with Sir Hugh. I could never be in love with Sir Hugh. And I could certainly never marry him." She let out a long-suffering sigh. "But he refuses to listen when I tell him no. At least he did until today. At tea this afternoon I informed Sir Hugh that I was thinking of entering the contemplative life." Alyssa threw up her hands. "I know what our family motto states: *Vincit omnia veritas.* Truth conquers all. But Hugh Pureheart wouldn't listen to the truth. I know you would understand if you were here."

She bent over, placed a bouquet of fresh flowers on her parents' graves, and straightened again.

If she were going to marry—and she wasn't—she would rather marry Miles St. Aldford, and frankly even the marquess had become something of a nuisance before he'd left for London.

Still, Miles was broad-shouldered and handsome, and he did make her heart pound like a timpani when he kissed her, when he touched her, when he caressed her. . . .

She wasn't going to think about that now. That was all over and done with. The Marquess of Cork had behaved like a perfect gentleman since the incident in the Grotto.

Pity.

Alyssa sighed again and closed her eyes. She could smell the damp earth, the green grass, a hint of burning wood in the distance, the fragile scent of the flowers at her feet, the telltale odor of sheep grazing on the lawn and ducks nesting by the pond.

She opened her eyes. The sky was pure blue overhead. The trees were green. The woods were dark. There wasn't another human being in sight.

Then Alyssa happened to glance up again at the Norman Tower. There was a face in the window. A man's face. But of no man that she had ever seen before.

Chapter Seventeen

She was called Alyssa.

At least that's what the dark-haired man had called her, the dangerous one, the one who had stood guard at the entrance to the Monk's Cave while she had personally delivered the second basket. The basket had contained, among other things, a complete suit of men's clothing, a razor, and a bar of soap.

He'd wanted to shout for joy.

Then the lady had smiled at him and inquired, "What is your name, sir?"

"I'm called the Hermit, my lady."

"But surely that can't be your Christian name, can it," she had pointed out with all politeness and kindness."

The Hermit had shaken his shaggy mane and stuffed his clenched fists into the pockets of his threadbare jacket. He had been ashamed. He hadn't wanted her to see his hands and fingernails; they were still dirty despite his efforts to scrub them clean in the pond.

At last he had looked at her and confessed, "I don't remember my name."

She had appeared to be truly concerned for him. "Do you recall where your family lives? Where your home is?"

He'd shrugged his shoulders. Vague images had formed in his head, but he had no words to put with the pictures. Somehow it had seemed presumptuous to say that he thought his family and his home were here. If they were, surely someone would have recognized him by now.

He'd wanted to thank the young woman for her generosity, to tell her how much the razor and the soap meant to him, but he had become tongue-tied when she'd looked up at him.

It was her eyes.

Something about her eyes had held him mesmerized. The Hermit hadn't realized what it was until he had gone to the pond the next afternoon to bathe. For a moment, he had paused and gazed down into the crystal-clear water at his own reflection.

And then he had understood.

The mistress of Graystone Abbey had given him so much. Indeed, everything he had came from her: the clothes he wore, the food he ate, the blanket he slept on, the wood he burned for warmth on cool summer nights, even the cave he lived in. His only regret was that he had nothing of value to give to her in return.

The Hermit mulled it over.

He thought.

He listened.

He watched.

And he waited.

Then one day he knew what he could give to the lady with the voice of an angel: his protection. He would watch over her as a father watches over his child. He would make certain no harm came to her. He would safeguard her with his life, if need be.

After all, he'd been the one to set her free the day she had been trapped in the Grotto. He had made certain the gentleman—he now knew the gentleman to be the Marquess of Cork—was warned that it wasn't an accident, that a villain had intentionally locked her inside that cold, dark, dank place.

The marquess had taken the warning to heart. For an entire week, he had stuck to the lady like glue. Where she went, he went. No further harm came to her. Then, inexplicably, the gentleman had packed his bag and departed from Graystone Abbey, and Lady Alyssa had been left alone.

Alone and vulnerable.

That same day the Hermit had taken up his vigil. His eyes and ears had become her eyes and ears, although he made certain Lady Alyssa never saw him, never heard him, never knew of his presence.

It was the afternoon of the fourth day. The Hermit was crouched behind the honeysuckle when Lady Alyssa came strolling across the grassy mounds toward the cemetery. She stopped at the double headstone, then moved forward and traced, letter by letter, the names etched into the hard granite. As she stepped back, he could read: ANNEMARIE, BE-LOVED WIFE AND MOTHER. THOMAS, BELOVED HUSBAND AND FATHER.

A feeling of loss and sadness washed over the Hermit. Perhaps because he sensed that coming to the cemetery made the lady a little sad. He had seen her kneel and fold her hands in prayer. He had watched as she stood and bowed her head. He had witnessed the tears that sometimes streamed down her pale face.

Today Lady Alyssa spoke aloud, loud enough for him to hear. "Mama. Papa. I've told a lie," she confessed. Then she dropped her voice and he missed many of the words, grasping only," . . . not in love with Sir Hugh . . . never marry him . . . understand if you were here."

The Hermit did not care for Sir Hugh. Several times, while walking along the country roads, he had witnessed the gentleman astride his horse. Sir Hugh rode his mount too long and too hard, and it was his custom to use the whip far too often.

Lady Alyssa threw up her hands. "I know what our family motto states: *Vincit omnia veritas*."

"Truth conquers all things," the Hermit silently translated from the Latin. He hoped so. He prayed so.

The lady bent over, placed a bouquet of brightly colored summer flowers on her parents' graves, and straightened again. Then she looked up at the Norman Tower. There was a studied expression on her face; she appeared to be staring at something . . . or someone.

The Hermit saw nothing unusual or out of the ordinary. Therefore, he was more than faintly surprised when Lady Alyssa quickly gathered up her skirts and scurried into the chapel.

He had no choice but to follow her.

He moved without making a sound. It seemed to be a particular talent of his, or maybe it was a learned skill, a necessary skill if he wanted to survive.

The Hermit pushed aside niggling thoughts of his own past, and observed Lady Alyssa as she made directly for the wall behind the altar. She knew what she was about. She lightly ran her fingertips over the carved wooden panels—they were very old and very primitive, and depicted the Twelve Apostles at that last supper with their Lord—until she found what she was looking for.

"Aha," the lady cried out triumphantly.

She pressed the upper right corner firmly with her hand, the wooden panels moved as one, and a doorway was revealed.

The Hermit's mouth dropped open in astonishment. It was like something out of *The Thousand Nights and a Night*.

Lady Alyssa opened the door and peered inside the Norman Tower. From his hiding place behind a fifteenth-century Flemish tapestry, the Hermit could see thick stone walls—they were as thick as a man was tall—barred windows, and a flight of roughly quarried stone stairs. There seemed to be centuries of accumulated dust and cobwebs, fallen timbers and crumbling rock.

The young woman hesitated for no more than an instant, then she stepped across the threshold and entered the medieval tower. Behind her, the door was left ajar only an inch or two.

The Hermit was still debating the wisdom or folly

of following Lady Alyssa into the close confines of the tower when he heard footsteps in the hallway outside the chapel

Thump.

Thump. Thump.

Heavy boots. A man's boots. But who was their uninvited guest? Was he friend or foe?

The Hermit's heart began to beat in double time. He wanted to call out, to warn the young woman that somebody was approaching. But it was too late. The doors to the Lady Chapel were flung open and a gentleman entered.

The Hermit recognized him immediately. It was the man in the fancy coach, the one traveling with the fancy ladies, the one with the unpleasant, ruddy face and the muttonchop whiskers, the one who had sworn at him that day on the abbey road and told the driver to go on, leaving him covered from head to toe with mud sprayed from their carriage wheels. This was the man who had treated the Hermit as if he were the lowest of the low, a *Panchama*, an Untouchable.

Sinking into the wall at his back, the Hermit kept one eye on the door through which Lady Alyssa had passed and one eye on the newcomer. The gentleman took a linen handkerchief from his coat pocket and wiped his mouth and nostrils as he advanced toward the altar. He did not behave as though this were a holy place.

His presence in the chapel was no accident, however. It was clear the intruder had a purpose in mind. Stuffing the used handkerchief into his pocket, the man took out a scrap of writing paper, muttering all the while to himself, "According to my notes on the original drawings of the structure, it should be somewhere near the altar."

He advanced down the center aisle of the chapel, past the Saxon font that dated to the eleventh century, past St. Wilfrid's chair, once literally the seat of sanctuary in the valley, past the medieval carvings on the roodscreen, past the windows with their magnificent stained glass, to the front altar.

The gentleman circled the altar. He examined it from every angle. He stood back and scratched his head, then looked down at the paper in his hand.

"Blast and hellfire! This isn't going to be quite the one-man show that I'd hoped for," came the bitter complaint. "It's going to take a good-sized lever and several men to move the bloody thing." He took out his handkerchief and mopped his brow again. He was sweating like a hairless, pink swine.

The Hermit didn't dare even to breathe. He prayed that the lady remained where she was for another moment or two, and that the intruder stayed ignorant of her presence so close by.

"Just have to return another time," the man grumbled as he retreated toward the chapel doors. "Mustn't forget why you're here, Chubb. It'll be worth the effort." He seemed to console himself with a final thought. "After all, it's worth a king's ransom."

Chapter Eighteen

"Has the lady stayed out of trouble in my absence, Blunt?"

"She has, my lord."

"And the Chubbs?"

"Sir Alfred spends his days sequestered in the abbey's library, devoting himself to historical research, while his wife gads about the valley playing Lady Bountiful. She visits the shops in the village—where she manages to squander exorbitant sums of money—stops for tea and cakes with the local gentry, and, regardless of the weather, takes daily outings with Miss Chubb in their fancy liveried coach. The Chubbs spend their evenings gossiping with one another and playing endless hands of baccarat. Each night they retire to the Cloisters before ten o'clock," Miles's second-in-command reported.

Miles went to stand at the window of the Knight's Chambers. It was late afternoon. He was still dressed in the suit of clothes he had worn to travel down from London. Indeed, he had come directly from the train station at Exeter, not even taking time to stop for refreshments along the way. "Where is Lady Alyssa?"

"She is taking tea with Sir Hugh in the Blue Room, my lord."

Miles turned and bestowed a skeptical look upon his valet. "I passed Sir Hugh Pureheart leaving the abbey as I was coming in. Although the young baronet was in a decided hurry, he was more than willing to halt his horse and carriage in the middle of the road so he could tell me about the latest development."

Blunt regarded him with a puzzled expression on his face. "The latest development, my lord?"

"You haven't heard, then?"

"Heard what, my lord?"

Hortense Horatio Blunt was an accomplished actor, but Miles could see that his bewilderment was real.

He looked at his companion with steady eyes. "Sir Hugh informed me that he will *not* be marrying Lady Alyssa."

Blunt smiled thinly. "That is scarcely news, my lord. Lady Alyssa doesn't wish to marry Sir Hugh. She never has. Indeed, on at least three separate occasions in the past six months, she has rejected the gentleman's offer of marriage. I have it on the best authority."

"Miss Pibble?"

Blunt nodded adamantly. "Miss Pibble."

Miles was gratified. "I know that. You know that. Obviously Miss Pibble knows that. However, the reason Sir Hugh gave today for Lady Alyssa's refusal came as something of a surprise even to me."

Blunt blinked. "I would think the lady's reason is apparent enough: She can't abide the gentleman."

That was no reason. Half of the wives Miles was acquainted with in Society couldn't abide their husbands.

He went on with ill-concealed impatience. "Hugh Pureheart informed me that Lady Alyssa has said she will not—indeed, she cannot—marry him because she intends to turn Graystone Abbey into a nunnery."

"I thought it already was a nunnery, my lord, in a manner of speaking."

Miles waved away this consideration. "There is more to the story. The baronet claims that Lady Alyssa has been called."

"Called where, my lord?"

"Apparently to the quiet, contemplative, cloistered life." Miles ran a hand through his hair and muttered under his breath, "Which, according to my information, is the kind of life she has been living for the past twenty-one years. Anyway, before they parted company this afternoon, Lady Alyssa strongly suggested to Sir Hugh that he look elsewhere for a suitable bride."

"Miss Chubb."

"That's my guess."

"Perhaps this is simply part and parcel of the lady's scheme to rid herself of an unwelcome suitor," Blunt said after consideration.

"Perhaps." Scowling, Miles crossed his arms. "If so, there is just one hitch."

"What is it?"

Miles uncrossed his arms and dropped them to his sides. "Apparently Sir Hugh isn't entirely convinced that Lady Alyssa knows her own mind in this matter."

Blunt offered, "Sir Hugh doesn't know the lady very well, then, does he, my lord?"

Miles was in complete agreement. Hugh Pureheart was a man of limited imagination. He saw the world in literal terms and only on his own terms.

He told his valet, "Nonetheless, before he drove away, Sir Hugh confided to me, with an arrogant laugh"—in truth, Miles had found himself sorely tempted to drag the braying jackass down from his carriage and teach him a lesson in courtly manners—"that Lady Alyssa would be begging him to marry her within the month."

Blunt paused in his duties, the travel valise open and half unpacked. "If I were Sir Hugh, I wouldn't bet the castle on it." A flicker of a smile came and went. "Lady Alyssa, a nun."

Miles recovered his sense of humor. "You did say in the beginning, as I recall, that the lady was an angel, a saint, a paragon."

"I did, my lord. But, frankly, at the time, I was thinking she would make an excellent marchioness."

Miles coughed several times in quick succession and then made a small production of clearing his throat. "Where do you think Lady Alyssa would be now?"

"If tea has concluded, then she is undoubtedly at her prayers," came the answer.

"In the Lady Chapel?"

"She usually visits her parents' graves first, my lord."

Miles gave a decisive nod of his head. "I'm off to the graveyard, Blunt."

No trace of his parents had ever been found after the treacherous storm at sea which had swept them and most of the other passengers and crew overboard on that fateful night more than fifteen years ago, Miles reflected as he hiked up the hill toward the Gray family cemetery. Although his grandfather had insisted that the rituals be observed, including the erection of two elaborate headstones at Cork Castle, his family's ancestral country estate, no one was actually buried beneath the markers bearing the names of his mother and father.

Miles never visited the cemetery at Cork Castle.

In fact, he made a conscious effort to avoid cemeteries at every opportunity. But not this afternoon. This afternoon he was a man on a mission.

Miles reached the cemetery and stood for a moment before the double tombstone that read ANNE-MARIE, BELOVED WIFE AND MOTHER, and THOMAS, BELOVED HUSBAND AND FATHER. He bowed his head for a moment, out of respect for the gentleman and the lady who had been unfailingly kind to a lost boy after he'd lost both his mother and father.

It was years later—perhaps it had not been until quite recently—that Miles recognized the true value of the gift Annemarie and Thomas Gray had given him during that long-ago summer. They had welcomed him into their home. They had treated him like a son. They had allowed him to catch a glimpse of their personal lives, to see a married couple who were happily in love with each other.

Marriage could be so much more than most men and women, especially most men and women of the British aristocracy, made of it. That was the secret the earl and countess had shared with him.

It had created a gnawing hunger in Miles, a hunger that had yet to be assuaged. He dreamed of finding a very special woman who would love him for what he was, who would see the light and dark sides of his soul—what he had been, what he had done—and still accept him, nay, embrace him, because it was all part of the man he had become.

" 'If wishes were horses, beggars might ride,' " he murmured as he leaned over and touched the bouquet of brightly colored fresh flowers on the gravestone.

Alyssa had been here.

She wasn't here now.

Miles raised his head and gazed out over the verdant valley that seemed to stretch in all directions for as far as the eye could see. The Lady Chapel, the Norman Tower, and the surrounding landscape had changed very little in the past century, he surmised. Perhaps very little in the past millennium.

Then, just at the outer edge of his field of vision, he thought he saw something—or someone—move.

Miles quickly turned and looked up at the stone fortification built during the reign of the first King William. There, in the window at the top of the tower, he thought he saw a lady's face behind the grillwork of iron bars.

Could it be Alyssa?

No, it wasn't Alyssa. This young woman had dark—nearly black—hair, and, although he had caught only a glimpse of her, he was certain she was a stranger.

Miles circled the Norman Tower. He could find no way in from the outside; the entrance must be through the Lady Chapel.

Five minutes later he was inside. He stood, motionless, soundless, at the rear of the small medieval church and gave his eyes a chance to adjust to the dim light.

Someone had been here.

Someone was here now.

Miles could feel it.

The distinctive squeak of a door slowly opening registered on his brain. It was coming from the front of the chapel, somewhere behind the altar.

Silently, Miles glided from shadow to shadow, his back to the wall. He crouched as he approached the high altar, ready to spring into action if action was called for. He watched and he waited as a concealed door opened behind an elaborately carved panel.

He was poised to strike, his arm raised, as a head poked around the edge of the doorframe. The hair on that head was a familiar color: not yellow-gold, not white-gold, but something in between. It was hair the color of the finest champagne.

"Alyssa!" he said, making no attempt to hide the exasperation in his voice. "What the devil are you doing in there?"

Alyssa's hand flew to her breast. "My lord, you quite startled me!" That was putting it mildly. Miles St. Aldford had scared her witless. Her heart was racing. Her legs were quivering like jellied fish aspic. And she could scarcely find her breath.

"You quite startled me, my lady." His dark eyes narrowed. "What are you doing lurking about the Lady Chapel?"

"I am not lurking," she informed him with an indignant sniff. "I am investigating."

Frowning, Miles crossed his arms and looked down at her. "I thought we agreed you wouldn't on your own."

"I recall no such agreement."

His eyelids lowered. "We're partners, remember?"

Alyssa gave him a meaning-filled glance. "Ah, well, that no doubt explains why you took me into your confidence, my lord, before you up and vanished four days ago."

There was a short, brittle pause.

"That was different," he claimed.

She put her nose in the air. "That was precisely what I expected you to say."

Miles St. Aldford abruptly changed the subject. "Did you hear anything?"

She tilted her head to one side. "When?"

"Within the past five minutes," he said.

She nodded. "Footsteps."

"Where?"

Alyssa raised her hand—she noticed it had stopped shaking—and pointed behind him. "In the chapel."

His face was drawn in lines of deep concentration. "Could you tell if the footsteps were those of a man or a woman?"

"I could." She tried to swallow the lump suddenly lodged in her throat. "They were those of a man."

"Are you certain?"

"There can be no mistake about it," Alyssa told him. "In fact, I heard a man's voice."

Miles stared at her. "Who was he talking to?"

"From all accounts, he was talking to himself. I was intent upon keeping my presence behind the door a secret, so I dared not move any closer to hear what he was saying."

Another question was fired at her. "Did you see or hear anything else while you were inside the tower?"

Alyssa wet her lips with her tongue and drew in a deep breath. "No." Then she inquired warily, "Why?"

Miles massaged the back of his neck with one hand. "I was in the cemetery a few minutes ago. I happened to glance up at the window, the one at the top of the tower. I thought I saw something."

"Something?"

A tense frown bracketed his lips. He seemed to be questioning the wisdom of saying any more. "Someone."

Alyssa's heart began to pick up speed. "A man?"

He shook his head. "A woman."

"I thought I saw a man," she whispered.

She wasn't certain if Miles had heard her until he said, "I thought I saw a woman."

"He was a stranger."

"She was a stranger, too."

"I only caught a glimpse of him."

Miles nodded, but said nothing.

"Do you suspect somebody is playing a prank on

us?" Alyssa finally said. There didn't seem to be any other rational explanation for what had occurred.

"I don't know."

"I don't believe there is any malicious intent involved," she added as an afterthought. She couldn't explain why she believed that. It was just a feeling she had.

"I'm going to take a look," Miles announced, indicating the door behind her.

"That's what I was about to do when I heard the footsteps in the chapel. I decided it would be sensible to wait until he left before proceeding with my investigation."

Miles gave her a long measuring look. "It would be sensible for you to wait *here*"—he pointed to the spot where she was standing—"while I make sure the tower is safe."

She stood her ground, using his own words against him. "We're partners, remember?"

Alyssa could tell from his expression that Miles didn't like it. He didn't have to like it. After all, it was *her* chapel, *her* tower, and *her* mystery.

"All right, we'll go together," he finally agreed reluctantly. Then he snapped his orders as if she were a new recruit serving under him in Her Majesty's service. "Be careful where you step. Watch your skirts. Stay right behind me. Don't take any unnecessary chances. If I indicate you should stop, then you immediately stop." He held out his hand, expecting her to take it.

Alyssa did.

They proceeded hand in hand. Miles went ahead.

She was one step behind him. He tested each stone stair first with his weight. Then she followed.

"Seems safe enough," he said, as much to himself as to her.

They began to climb, up and up, around and around. Slowly in the beginning, then more quickly once they realized the basic structure of the stone stairs was solid. The climb still required great care on their part, for the same could not be said of the tower walls. They were crumbling in places and whole stones were occasionally missing, leaving gaping holes to the outside.

Despite the possible danger, Alyssa was enjoying herself. It was the first real physical contact she'd had with Miles since the day she had been trapped in the Grotto. Oh, there had been the polite steadying of her arm as they'd walked, or the unintentional brush of his hand against hers, but those had been fleeting moments and impersonal touches. She suddenly realized how much she had missed Miles.

She'd missed the sound of his voice, his laughter, his footfall on the garden path coming toward her. She had missed their walks, their rides on Beauty and Bulle Rock along the estate's wooded trails, their conversations about matters large and small, their companionable silences.

And she had missed so much more.

She'd missed the touch of his lips on hers. She'd missed the tastes and textures of his mouth, his teeth, his tongue; the erotic thrill of his kiss, the muscular strength of his arms and shoulders, the solid strength of his chest, the long line of his thighs pressed against her.

She'd missed the way Miles could make her feel: beautiful, desirable, exciting. There were things she had thought about this man that she had thought about no other. There were dreams she had dreamt. There were things she had done. There was even more she wanted to do. All with Miles.

Alyssa's reverie was interrupted when he paused and asked her, "Do you know where these stairs lead?"

"To a lookout of sorts, or so I've been told."

He frowned. "Haven't you been up here before?"

She shook her head. "The tower was considered too old and too unsafe."

"When was it built?"

"Original construction was begun around 1100, but extensive repairs were made more recently."

"How recent?" he asked.

She shrugged. "Two, maybe three hundred years ago."

"It doesn't look like anyone has been here since," Miles remarked in a dry tone. "The dust on these stairs is undisturbed." He observed, "I don't see any evidence of footprints."

"Neither do I."

Miles must have been thinking the same thing she was. If the staircase was the only way in or out of the Norman Tower, if there was no evidence that the stairs had been used, then how could a man— or a woman—have reached the tower window?

"I am not a fanciful female," Alyssa stated aloud. "I don't think I conjured up a man's face."

"I admit I've seen some strange things, some horrific things, even some inexplicable things in my soldiering days," Miles confessed, "but this one has me stumped."

"Then we'll simply have to see what we find once we reach the lookout," she said.

The lookout was nothing more than a small square room at the top of the Norman Tower. Lookouts, or windows originally tall enough for a man to crouch in with his bow and arrow or his spear were cut into the thick stone on each of the tower's four sides. Iron bars were embedded in each window. Miles went from one to the next and gazed out.

Alyssa moved around the room. "As a soldier—"

"Ex-soldier," Miles corrected her.

"As an ex-soldier, you must appreciate the strategic benefits of building a fortification on this site."

Miles gazed out over the valley. "The men who built the Norman Tower knew exactly what we know today. There's no way to sneak up on Graystone Abbey without being seen from here."

"How very interesting." Alyssa drew his attention to the window overlooking the cemetery. "The iron bars appear to have been forged into an elaborate design." She took a step back and studied the intricate grillwork. There was something naggingly familiar about the pattern. "What does this look like to you?"

Miles came up beside her. "It looks like the Crusader's cross on your family crest."

Alyssa's hand flew to her mouth. "Of course! That's it!"

"Now, *this* is interesting," her partner said with a strange air of speaking at random.

Naturally, he had her undivided attention. "What is?" she inquired eagerly.

Miles stood directly behind her. Alyssa could feel his warm breath wafting the tiny hairs back and forth on her nape. She was suddenly, inexplicably, covered with gooseflesh.

"If you squint while you're looking out through the design in the window, you can trace part of the Crusader's cross on those grassy mounds just beyond the cemetery. It appears as though the pattern was once repeated below in the landscape. This may have been the medieval turf maze you and Miss Pibble found reference to in your research," he suggested.

Alyssa was excited. "It may well be. Emma and I have long suspected that the turf maze was on this side of the abbey because it's the oldest part of the grounds."

"I've seen the pavement maze in Chartres Cathedral, of course. It's a traditional medieval Christian design, circular, with a symbolic cross in the center," Miles related to her. "And I recall a childhood outing when my mother took me to see the hedge maze at Hampton Court."

"How old would you have been?"

He shrugged. "Six or seven. I got lost, of course. I was frightened. Yet I remember being fascinated and intrigued by the winding passageways, all the same."

"The Lappa Maze in Cornwall forms the shape of a steam locomotive," Alyssa told him. "And there is an unusual hedge maze set on the hillside at Glendurgan. It's cut from waist-high laurel." Her voice took on a wistful quality. "But what truly fascinates me are the lost turf mazes, the ones with names like Robin Hood's Race and Walls of Troy." She gazed out the window at what may have been the site of Graystone Abbey's turf maze. "Deep in the Middle Ages, unknown men with unknown motives carved mazes in the green turf of villages and churchyards, and left them to mystify future generations." Then she became animated again. "Did you know that historians recently discovered a piece of ancient mosaic tile they think was part of a Roman labyrinth? They could still read the inscription scratched on the back."

"What did the inscription say?"

" *'Labyrinthus hic habit Minotaurus.'* "

"The Minotaur in his labyrinth."

"The Minoan legend was very popular with the ancient Romans," she confirmed. "Of course, their mazes were often purely contemplative or decorative. Not like the early turf mazes that were designed to be walked or run along."

"Supposedly monks and nuns did penance by traversing the paths on their knees," Miles said, rubbing his leg as if the thought alone had somehow caused him pain.

An inspired thought suddenly occurred to Alyssa. She approached the window overlooking her family cemetery and felt along the ledge with her fingertips. She found it on her second attempt. Bending down, skirts billowing around her in a cloud of gray silk, she carefully brushed at the inscription etched in the cornerstone.

Miles crouched beside her. "What have you found?"

"Writing."

"An inscription?"

She nodded. "In Latin."

"Can you make it out?"

"I think so." She peered at the words and translated aloud: " 'Man wanders in a dark labyrinth.' "

Miles grimaced. "A typically depressing adage passed down from the medieval church, no doubt. Is that it?"

Alyssa shook her head. "There's more." This time she read the Latin phrase out loud. " '*Amor vincit omnia.*' "

" 'Love conquers all things.' " Miles turned and stared long into her eyes. "Not your family motto: *Vincit omnia veritas*, truth conquers all things?"

"It says love." Her voice broke on the last word. She cleared her throat and tried to sound philosophical. "But aren't love and truth simply different sides of the same coin?"

"Do you believe that?"

"Yes." Alyssa quickly dropped her eyes before Miles St. Aldford saw something in them she wasn't ready to admit even to herself, and certainly not to him. Perhaps never to him. "There is one more phrase etched in the stone."

"What is it?"

"Just two words," she said meaningfully.

This time Miles studied the centuries-old plaque and finally translated in a husky voice: " 'Ariadne's Thread.' "

"Ariadne's Thread," she echoed.

He sighed, stood, and held out his hand to her. "Now we know."

Alyssa placed her hand in his and rose to her feet. "Now we know what Ariadne's Thread is." Somehow the knowing was bittersweet. "What it was."

"A medieval turf maze."

"All but gone, all but forgotten," she said a little sadly.

One question had been answered today. More questions had been raised. Questions to which they might never know the answers.

Had someone been at the tower window?

Who was he?

Who was she?

How had the man and woman found their way in and out of the Norman Tower without being seen, without leaving a trace of their presence?

Miles looked around the small tower room. "There's nothing more to be discovered here, Alyssa. I think it might be safer if we went back down now," he coaxed.

"All right."

Then he paused and sniffed the air. "Did you smell that?"

Alyssa took a whiff. "Fresh air. A hint of wood smoke." She put her nose up and inhaled deeply. "Dust." She could see by the expression on his face that it was none of these things. "What did you think you smelled?"

Miles shook his head. "For a moment I thought I could detect the scent of roses."

Alyssa shivered despite the warmth of the afternoon sun pouring in the lookout. "Yes, I think I'd like to go now."

Miles led the way. They were soon at the bottom of the stairs, the door to the tower closed behind them, the wooden panels securely in place, the entrance once more concealed.

"Have you had your tea?" Alyssa inquired as they left the Lady Chapel and strolled along the deserted corridors toward the main living section of the sprawling country house.

"No, I have not," he replied. "I came looking for you the minute I returned to the abbey."

"Why, pray tell?"

Miles stopped and gazed down into her face. He was standing entirely too close to her for comfort. "I ran into Sir Hugh as he was leaving."

Alyssa resisted the temptation to lick her lips or drop her gaze or make a mad dash for cover. There was something in the marquess's eyes, something that looked suspiciously like amusement.

"We had tea together," she said with simplicity.

"So I gather." Broad, black shoulders were lifted and dropped again. "Sir Hugh had some interesting tidbits."

"Interesting tidbits?"

He raised an eyebrow. "The baronet informed me that you are not going to marry him."

She gave a single laugh. "That is scarcely news. I told you that myself weeks ago."

"So you did."

Alyssa fingered the watch dangling from her waist; it had belonged to her mother. "Did Sir Hugh mention anything else?"

"Not much. Simply that you've been called to the cloistered life and that you're going to turn the abbey into some sort of nunnery," he spelled out.

"Oh, dear."

"Yes—oh, dear." Miles chuckled and wagged his finger at her. "You'll be doing penance, my lady."

"It wasn't exactly a lie." Her face became suffused with warmth. "It was more of a harmless fabrication."

"Harmless?"

She sighed. "I had hoped Hugh wouldn't tell anyone."

Miles put his head back and laughed heartily. "Sir Hugh Pureheart, for your information, is the biggest gossip in the West Country."

Alyssa groaned. "It will be all over the valley by morning."

"At the latest."

"I wasn't certain I'd convinced him," she admitted.

"I'm not certain you did. He seems to have the impression you'll still come around to his way of thinking."

She could feel the heat of embarrassment flood her cheeks. "he didn't tell you everything, did he?"

"He did."

"The unmitigated gall . . ." she sputtered. "The absolute nerve . . ."

"If it makes you feel any better, I, for one, don't believe for a minute that you'll ever beg Sir Hugh to marry you."

"Oh, Lord!"

"On the other hand, I don't believe you would make a good nun, either, Alyssa."

She looked up at him. "What makes you say that?"

"This."

Without further ado, Miles St. Aldford swooped down and covered her mouth with his. It was like a dash of cold water on the face upon first awakening and leaving a warm bed. It caught her off guard and it left her gasping. She blinked several times in rapid succession. A shiver ran down the length of her, from the hair on her head to the toes curling up in her shoes.

He took her breath away and gave her his in exchange. It was an intimate gesture, one she had never engaged in with any man but Miles. One moment he was kissing her as if to prove a point; the next she was kissing him back and proving him correct.

Something niggled at Alyssa even as she realized Miles was slipping his arms around her waist. Something Sir Hugh had said at tea this very afternoon. Something to do with Miles's visit to London.

"There has been talk, Alyssa. Gossip. Rumors," Hugh had taken delight in telling her.

"About who?" she had inquired.

"Miles St. Aldford, fourth Marquess of Cork, soldier, decorated war hero, supposed spy, confidant to the Prince of Wales, notorious womanizer, and libertine." Then Hugh had added, *"There is speculation that the marquess has gone to London to visit a woman."*

Alyssa went cold in Miles's arms.

Miles lifted his head and gazed down at her. "What is it?"

She would not be made a fool of—not by this man, not by any man. "You may unhand me now, my lord."

"Alyssa?"

She couldn't keep the sarcasm from her voice. "Did you have a successful trip to London, sir?"

He frowned. "Yes, madam, I did."

She wiggled free of him. "And how did you find your mistress, my lord? Well, I presume."

Chapter Nineteen

"Mistress?" For a moment Miles's mind went blank. He didn't have a mistress. He hadn't had a mistress in nearly a year. And God knows, he hadn't sought the services of a professional courtesan since he was a very young and inexperienced man.

"Mistress," she repeated. "Paramour. Concubine. Kept woman. *Fille de joie.*"

Miles momentarily lost his composure. Where would Alyssa get a tomfool, addlebrained idea like that? "Where did you get a tom—" He caught himself in the nick of time and began again. "Where did you get an idea like that?"

One delicately drawn eyebrow arched in an inverted V. "Common knowledge."

"Common it may be. Knowledge it is not. Who in the world would make up such a story?" Miles knew the answer the instant the words were out of his mouth. "Lady Chubb."

"Lady Chubb?" Alyssa's surprise was not feigned; he was certain it was genuine.

"Then you must have heard it from that horse's . . . mouth: Sir Hugh," he said through gritted teeth.

"As a matter of fact, I did," she replied tartly.

Miles was speaking as much to himself as to her when he muttered, "Who better to tell, if you want a rumor spread, than the biggest gossip in the West Country?"

"Why," Alyssa inquired, with more than a suspicion of curiosity in her voice, "would Lady Chubb want to have a falsehood spread about you?"

Miles's mind was brimming with possibilities. If the information he had garnered about the Chubbs while he was in London was even partially accurate, then Sir Alfred had always been something of a clod—outside of building a vast empire upon the demand for men's pink silk stockinette drawers, that is—and Lady Chubb was the true brains. She was the dangerous one of the pair: Caroline Chubb was ambitious and she had no conscience.

"Never trust a man who doesn't pay his gambling debts," Miles advised.

"What do gambling debts have to do with it?" Alyssa inquired.

"Sir Alfred owes me nearly twenty pounds," he told her.

Her pale brows congealed into a scowl. "You think Lady Chubb is having lies spread about you throughout the Devon countryside because Sir Alfred doesn't wish to pay the twenty pounds he has lost to you playing baccarat?"

Miles shook his head. "Of course not. It isn't the money; it's the principle of the thing." He realized he wasn't making himself understood. "An enemy can smell weakness. He won't stop looking until he's found out what it is."

"The principle of *what* thing? *What* enemy? *What*

weakness?" Alyssa stomped her foot on the mosaic floor. "What are you talking about, my lord?"

Miles had no intentions of explaining to her any more than was absolutely necessary. "Let's just say, my dear Alyssa, that Lady Chubb and I don't see eye to eye on certain subjects."

"What subjects?"

"Marriage, for one."

That stopped her cold. Alyssa blinked several times in rapid succession and mouthed, "Marriage?"

"Miss Charmel Chubb, for another."

Finally, it seemed to dawn on her what he was talking about. "You don't mean to tell me that Lady Chubb has been trying to snare you as her son-in-law?"

"That is exactly what I'm telling you."

The truth slowly sank in. He could see it on Alyssa's lovely face. Then she took a deep breath and said with genuine admiration, "Miss Chubb *is* beautiful."

"Miss Chubb's beauty is but skin deep," Miles said. He added for good measure, "Frankly, the young lady bores me to tears."

" 'Tears, such as angels weep'?" Alyssa quoted. A hint of a smile tugged at the corners of her mouth.

He raised his eyebrows fractionally. "Shakespeare?"

"Milton."

The immediate crisis having passed, Miles looked around. They were standing in a long, secluded corridor. At one time, perhaps four or five hundred years in the past, it must have been part of a cloister: walled on one side, open to the elements on the other.

The walls of the corridor were painted mortar. The floor was covered with medieval heraldic tiles honoring the aristocratic families of the region. The graceful arches between the traditional Roman colonnades had been transformed into large, paned windows, one of which looked out on a private courtyard. There was a window seat filled with embroidered pillows, a stack of books, a small knitted ball, such as a cat would play with, and a lady's hanky.

Miles indicated the feminine hideaway. "Yours?"

"Mine," said Alyssa with simplicity.

"Shall we sit for a few minutes?"

Her head came up. "Don't you want your tea?"

He did.

Eventually.

"There are more important matters that need to be resolved first," he told her.

They sat down side by side. Miles picked up one of the leatherbound volumes from the pile and read the title aloud: "*Le Chanson de Roland*. In French, I see." Somehow he wasn't surprised to find Alyssa reading the epic poem about the Emperor Charlemagne, the medieval knight Roland, and their exploits.

"Do you read French?" she inquired.

Miles nodded but admitted, "I haven't in some time." He replaced the book on top of the stack. "Did you know that the only manuscript of *The Song of Roland* is at Oxford?"

"No." His companion permitted herself a small

sigh and said wistfully, "I would like to have studied at a university."

"You have a wonderful library here."

A shadow flitted across her face. "But it's not the same, is it?"

"It's not the same," he agreed.

Alyssa picked up her copy of the epic poem. "Tell me more about the manuscript at Oxford."

"It's written in Anglo-Norman."

"The French spoken by the early Normans in England," she clarified.

He nodded. "The historians think it dates to 1170, although there were probably oral versions fifty years before the written one." He racked his brain for anything else he could recall. "The name of the scribe given at the end is Turoldus."

Alyssa seemed satisfied. "Can you imagine writing down over four thousand lines of poetry?"

"No, I can't." Miles knew he had put off the inevitable long enough. He reached for Alyssa's hand, the one not holding *La Chanson de Roland*, and gazed intently into her eyes. "I did not go to London to see my mistress."

His confession apparently made her uncomfortable; she began to fidget. "You don't have to explain yourself to me."

"I know, but I want to." It was going to take a concerted effort, Miles realized, to undo the mischief done by Lady Chubb and Sir Hugh Pureheart. One day they would both be made to answer for their actions. "The reason is simple, Alyssa. I don't have a mistress." He went a step further in his explanation. "In fact, I haven't had a mistress for a very long time."

She looked at him with huge gray eyes. "Why not?"

Miles wasn't certain he could explain it to her—she was such an innocent when it came to men and women—but he had to try.

He cleared his throat and commenced. "In his youth, a man may find that his needs, his desires, his appetites can be satisfied by almost any willing female."

Alyssa appeared to be all ears. "Rather like a starving person put before a banquet table filled with food."

"Something like that, I suppose." Miles lost his train of thought. "Maybe this isn't the time or the place."

"Of course it is. Please go on," she urged.

Miles searched for the right words. "A young male may prove himself indiscriminate."

Alyssa offered her own translation. "He may gorge himself on whatever food and drink he can get his hands on."

Miles felt as though he were standing on quicksand, but he plowed ahead all the same. "On the other hand, a mature male—one with intelligence, taste, and breeding, may discover, at some point in his life, that he desires to do more than simply eat his fill. He finds himself interested in quality rather than quantity."

"He becomes a kind of gourmet," she suggested.

Miles brightened. "Yes, he becomes a gourmet."

"All this talk of food is making me hungry," Alyssa

confessed as she placed the *chanson de geste* with the other books.

Miles frowned. "I thought you had your tea with Sir Hugh."

"I had a cup of tea. I did not eat anything." Then she admitted to him, "I still don't understand why you haven't had a mistress in a very long time."

He might as well be honest with her. "I haven't met a woman who intrigues me." Alyssa intrigued him, but she was hardly a candidate for his mistress.

What was she a candidate for?

To his surprise, Miles had missed her while he was away. She'd been on his mind during the train trip to London. At night, he had returned to Cork House from his club, or a dinner party with friends, or an outing to the theater, and lain awake thinking about her.

Each morning he had awakened fully aroused, her scent in his nostrils, her taste on his lips, and he had known he'd spent the night dreaming about her.

In fact, he had concluded his business, made his excuses, and hurried straight back to her.

Alyssa regarded him with uncertainty. "Why are you looking at me like that?"

He shouldn't ask, but he couldn't seem to help himself. "Did you miss me while I was gone?"

The slightest tinge of color appeared on her cheeks. "I kept very busy while you were in London."

"You didn't answer my question," he pointed out.

"Then, no, I didn't miss you," she declared. But her lower lip was trembling slightly, so that she had to steady it with her small, straight white teeth.

The lady was lying.

She was irresistible. She lied so prettily and so badly. Miles raised his hand and tipped her chin toward him. "Alyssa, you aren't telling me the truth."

"No, I'm not," she admitted in a whisper. She raised her eyes. "I did miss you."

Miles's heart began to thud in his chest. The large muscles in his arms contracted. The legs of his trousers were suddenly uncomfortably snug. His body began to stir in ways he had hoped to avoid, under the circumstances. Any gentleman knew this wasn't the time or the place.

"I missed you," he said.

Then he bent his head with the intention of brushing his lips across the lady's forehead, changed his mind at the last moment and chose her mouth, changed his mind yet again and took her mouth with his in a long, drugging kiss.

That was Miles's first mistake.

His second mistake was gathering Alyssa in his arms and drawing her slender body against his. She was delicious to taste, soft and inviting to touch. She smelled faintly of something sweet, something slightly musky, something indescribable.

He'd lied.

He'd told himself that he was interested in something more than the mere physical aspect of a man and woman's relationship. Yet, at the moment, all he could think about was kissing this woman and peeling away the layers of her clothing until she fell into his eager and awaiting hands. He itched to touch her. His mouth was hungry for the taste of her nipples, her breasts, the delicate skin around her navel, and lower to that virgin female fruit, ripe for the picking.

As a man and as a soldier, Miles St. Aldford had always prided himself on being in control of his mind, of his body, of his emotions. It was a matter of conditioning and self-discipline.

He kissed Alyssa and his self-discipline vanished. Suddenly he had to kiss her. He had to taste her lips, nibble with his teeth, plumb the honeyed depths of her mouth with his tongue.

He had to touch her; the shell of her ear, the curve of her chin, the long, slender length of her neck. His hand was at her nape, her shoulder, her back, her waist.

It wasn't enough.

He had to caress her. He found the small indentation near the bottom of her spine, the sensitive nerve on the underside of her wrist, the rhythmic pulse beating in the tiny hollow at the base of her throat, the soft breast beneath the layers of clothing.

It still wasn't enough.

Miles wasn't certain later how he managed it. Perhaps a country lady wore fewer or simpler undergarments than the fashionable females of Society. To his relief, the buttons down the front of Alyssa's bodice effortlessly surrendered. The satin ribbons of her chemise came undone. Fine lawn gave way; lacings parted, and she was his to kiss, his to caress, his to fondle.

His hand covered her breast, and she gasped. His fingers gently trailed across her nipples, and she groaned. He tore himself away from her mouth, settled on her hungrily with his lips and teeth and tongue, suckling her, and she cried out his name.

"Miles!"

Christ, she was sweet. Instinctively, she arched her back as she grasped at his shoulders, pawing at his coat, his shirt, his chest. She inadvertently drove her breast deeper and deeper into his mouth until he thought—had there ever been a sweeter morsel?—that he would surely swallow whole that lush kernel of female flesh.

Then he uncovered her other breast, and dragged the arrowed tip of his tongue back and forth from one sensitive nub to the other. He felt her shatter in his arms. She fell back among the pillows on the window seat and he followed her down.

There were questions in her eyes; some of which he could not answer. "Miles—?"

"You are irresistible."

"I want . . . I need . . . I desire . . ."

"I know," he muttered as he buried his face in the side of her neck and inhaled the scent of her.

"I've never felt like this before," Alyssa confessed when they both came up for air the next time.

Neither had he.

She was rambling, only occasionally making sense to him, stopping to catch her breath in irregular places. "I never . . . knew. I . . . never imagined. I never dreamt."

He hoped not.

She must have found her arms growing heavy. She dropped them to his waist. In her ignorance, and in her innocence, she allowed her hand to brush against him. His turgid flesh leaped for joy.

It would never be enough.

It was then Miles nearly begged Alyssa to touch him, to put him out of this heavenly misery. Beads of sweat broke out in a fine line on his brow. He was shaking. She was trembling.

He moved his hand lower, pushing her skirt and petticoats aside, and then slowly—it was pure agony and pure ecstasy—drew his hand up her silk-stockinged leg.

When Miles finally settled his palm on the soft mound at the apex of her thighs, only a thin layer of damp cotton separated him from his ultimate goal.

It was enough.

Alyssa began to move against his hand, seeking something for which she had no name and of which she had no knowledge. Surrounded by a fine white linen fabric, now wet through and nearly transparent, Miles eased one finger inside her. She drenched his hand, her body clenched around his cloth-shrouded finger, and she let out a small shout of surprise, of exaltation, of release.

It was more than enough.

The sound of her soft cries, the realization that this was the first time for her, sent Miles catapulting over the edge and past the point of no return. He exploded in his trousers.

Miles borrowed *La Chanson de Roland* to see him back to the Knight's Chambers. A copy of the medieval epic poem had never been put to better employment, in his opinion.

As Alyssa left him, intent upon retreating to the privacy of her own rooms, her hair in a tangle of soft gold and silver, her skirts rumpled, her cheeks aflame, each with a big round dot of color in the center, a general air of distraction about her—nay, not distraction but panic—Miles spoke up. "Alyssa, we must talk."

She refused to look at him. "Please, Miles, not now," she implored, clutching at her bodice. The lady's garment seemed to be missing several buttons.

In truth, he had not meant now. He was standing in a hallway, where half a dozen servants might pass by at any given moment of the day, a book clutched to the front of his clothing, the remnants of his climax drying on his leg. "Soon."

Her eyes were frantic. Her answer was meant only to placate him. "Yes."

"Very soon."

"All right."

Miles snapped to attention. "Madam, this is a formal request to speak to you."

Alyssa seemed to gather some semblance of her wits about her. "Then we will meet tomorrow morning, sir, at ten o'clock in the formal sitting room."

What had she done?

What could she have been thinking of?

"You weren't thinking. That was the problem," Alyssa muttered under her breath as she closed the door of her suite, sank back against the solid wood panels for a moment, then quickly reached behind her and turned the lock to make certain she would be undisturbed.

With legs still trembling and hands as cold as

ice, she walked across the sitting room and into her bedroom. She came up to the mirror standing in the corner and regarded her reflection.

She wasn't altogether certain she understood what had just transpired between herself and Miles St. Aldford, but it had been frightening, glorious, thrilling beyond her wildest imaginings.

Was she still a virgin?

No matter, she was no longer an innocent. Not that she had any regrets. She had none.

She would, however, send her regrets to her houseguests for dinner tonight. She had no wish to share this moment, this occasion, this feeling with the likes of Lady Chubb or Sir Alfred.

She wasn't a coward, Alyssa told herself.

"Yes, you are," she declared to the doe-eyed creature in the looking glass. "But tomorrow will be soon enough, I think, to face yourself and the Marquess of Cork."

Chapter Twenty

The formal drawing room was flooded with morning light. The windows faced due east and avoided the setting sun during the evening hours, when it was most often in use. Or it would be in a house like Graystone Abbey if one were attending the weekend house parties and soirees of former years.

Alyssa sat clutching an ivory linen handkerchief—trimmed in black lace to mark it for mourning—in her right hand. She smoothed the skirt of her gray silk dress with her left. Her hair was meticulously piled on top of her head in a rather severe hairdo. She had especially asked Emma for help with her coiffeur, rather than allow her usual girl to stick a hairpin in here and there.

Most mornings, of course, there was little reason to have her hair done. She was usually in the garden at this hour, weeding her flower beds or deadheading the roses or digging in the dirt for the sheer joy of feeling the cool earth in her hands, some sort of covering plunked down on her head to keep the sun from burning her skin.

Alyssa did not wear makeup. No woman of her class or breeding did. Or at least no woman of her class and breeding would admit to it. Nevertheless, this morning she'd had to resort to a touch of rouge on her lips and cheeks. She had appeared so pale in the mirror.

Yesterday her cheeks had been bright red and she'd had to press a cool cloth to them in the privacy of her bath to reduce their heat and color.

Yesterday had never happened.

That was the tack Alyssa had decided to take. It was the only way to handle an otherwise embarrassing situation.

"I understand from Miss Pibble that we are going to do a masque, my lord," Alyssa remarked to Miles St. Aldford, her back stiff against the stiff back of the formal Queen Anne chair.

The marquess was seated opposite her in an identical Queen Anne piece. However, since he was so tall and his legs were so long, he did not quite fit the furniture.

He did not quite fit the room, either.

It was all pinks and lavenders and plums—the seventh Countess of Graystone had had a penchant for the rose tones—and Miles St. Aldford was dressed this morning in severe black with a gray vest.

Not that Alyssa was anything but a peahen in her gray moire silk. She had, however, picked the loveliest and the most expensive of her mourning dresses for the occasion.

There was no occasion, she admonished herself. It would be foolish—it would be utter folly—to think otherwise.

Miles failed to respond to her first attempt at conversation. She wasn't certain he had heard her comment; he seemed to be studying the design in the carpeting. So Alyssa tried again.

"Is the masque the subject you wished to discuss with me this morning, my lord?"

"It is not, my lady."

Alyssa suddenly realized that the Marquess of Cork might be nervous. It was an intriguing notion.

Miles cleared his throat, rested one hand on his knee, looked out the window at the formal gardens—rather longingly, she thought—and began. "Madam, you may well have asked yourself why I have not married."

She hadn't. "No, actually, I haven't, sir."

He frowned. "That wasn't a question. That was my opening statement."

"My apologies, sir."

He picked up his train of thought. "There are many reasons why I have chosen not to marry since coming of age some nine years ago. I was committed to serving my Queen and country as a soldier. This commitment frequently required that I leave England and venture to foreign countries, often with danger and Blunt as my only companions."

Momentarily, Alyssa forgot where they were and what they were about. She clapped her hands together. "Oh, do tell me more about your adventures, Miles."

"Another time, Alyssa."

She immediately settled down again.

"As I was saying, it has only been the past two or three years since leaving Her Majesty's service and returning full-time to my country that I have given any serious consideration to the prospect of marriage and children."

Children.

The word sent the oddest thrill through Alyssa. She had thought very little about having children. Perhaps because she could never imagine who her children's father would be. . . .

"As the fourth Marquess of Cork," Miles continued, "I have always been aware, naturally, of my duty to one day marry and produce the fifth Marquess of Cork. I am a man who has always stood by his duties."

"I have no doubt of that."

"But I would not choose to marry out of duty," he told her. "That is why I have waited until the age of thirty. It has become increasingly clear to me—indeed, I saw it in your own parents, dear lady, as well as my close friends Lawrence and Juliet, Jonathan and Elizabeth, that 'whoso findeth a good wife findeth a good thing.' "

"Proverbs?"

Miles nodded. "You have stated your own requirements in this matter."

Alyssa frowned. "What matter?"

"The matter of marriage."

"I don't wish to marry. I don't intend to marry. I have stated that my choice is the contemplative life."

Miles waved this aside. "It's perfectly clear to everyone it was merely a ruse to rid yourself of that twit Sir Hugh Pureheart. I can't say I blame you, madam, having met the gentleman on several occasions myself." He took a deep breath and went on.

"I once asked what you wanted in a gentleman and you answered me."

"I did?"

"The night of the welcoming dinner party for the Chubbs."

"I did."

Miles apparently had her answers committed to memory. "You require a gentleman who respects your mind."

"I remember now," she acknowledged.

"I do, madam."

"You do *what*, sir?"

"I respect your mind. I respect your intelligence. In fact, I find you mentally superior to most of your sex."

Alyssa returned the compliment. "And I find you a notch above the average gentleman."

"You also mentioned that you would like a gentleman who finds joy in music, literature, nature—"

"And gardening," she said, smiling.

Miles nodded. "And gardening. I do enjoy music, reading, and the outdoors, madam. I am convinced that I could come to appreciate the finer points of gardening, as well."

"Especially roses."

"Especially roses." He heaved a sigh. "You have also indicated a desire for travel. I have seen the world, and I possess both the resources and the interest in showing it to you."

"Miles—"

"Please let me finish, Alyssa."

She nodded.

"I can offer you more than you realize," he said

in a perfectly serious tone. "There are always the obvious advantages: the title of marchioness, the ancestral homes, Cork House and Cork Castle, the respect—and, I think, the affection—of friends and acquaintances from the lowest to the highest, even as high as the Queen herself. All of this will be yours, madam."

"Miles, I—"

"I am still not finished, madam."

"Please go on, sir."

"I am willing to offer you a marriage in which you would be an equal partner."

Alyssa knew her face lit up. "You mean, like the partnership we have for investigating?"

He nodded. "I believe I can offer you compatibility that few husbands and wives find in the marriage bed."

Heat rushed to her cheeks. "We seem to get on rather well together in that area."

For the first time Miles seemed to relax. He laughed and said, "Yes, we seem to." He grew serious again. "And I can offer you one very important thing."

"What is that?"

"Freedom."

Freedom. Freedom to go. Freedom to do. Freedom to be exactly what she was. It was a heady thought. And an attractive one to her, as Miles must have known it would be.

"I want freedom above all else," she told him.

"I know," he said. "Now we must discuss something of great importance to us both, madam."

"What is that, sir?"

"The question of honor."

"Yours or mine?"

"Yours *and* mine." Miles ran his hand through his hair. "I very nearly seduced you yesterday in a window seat of this very house."

Very nearly. She was under the impression that he had. Alyssa could think of nothing to say. She sat there and fingered the handkerchief in her palm.

"I am not to be trusted."

Alyssa's head flew up. "Of course you are. I trust you above all men."

"I'm not to be trusted when it comes to you, Alyssa." His eyes darkened. "I'll be frank. I can't keep my bloody hands off you."

"Oh—"

"This presents me with something of a dilemma."

"What kind of dilemma?"

"If I stay at Graystone Abbey, I can guarantee that we will consummate our relationship with or without the sanctity of marriage."

She sat there, stunned, silent, knowing it was true.

"If we do so outside the bonds of matrimony, it will dishonor both of us," Miles pointed out needlessly. "We have two choices: I stay, and we marry by special license as soon as possible. Or I leave, and we promise not to see each other again."

Promise never to see each other?

He went on. "Neither of us has families to consider. Neither of us has other attachments of the heart. If you agree to marry me, madam, I would like to do so within the week."

"Within the week?"

"I don't know a better way of handling the whole affair. I laid awake all night going over and over the courses of action open to us. It always came down to the same thing in the end: We must either marry quickly . . . or we must part."

Alyssa, too, had lain awake most of the night, facing the truth of her feelings. She could think of a dozen good reasons why she shouldn't marry him. She could think of one good reason why she should marry him: She was in love with Miles St. Aldford.

"My dear lady, what are you doing?" he inquired some minutes later. He had rarely talked so much or so long in his entire life, Miles realized. He had tried to present his points logically and convincingly. Now he had reached the end of his proposal and was waiting for Alyssa to say something.

"My lord, I'm thinking." she tugged on a wisp of her hair. "Well, actually I'm making a list."

"A list?"

"I would write it all down if I had pen and paper handy, but since I don't, I must make do with what I have."

"Which is?"

"I am committing it to memory."

"What are you memorizing a list of, madam?"

"Questions, for one thing."

"And for another?"

"Conditions, I believe you might call them."

"Conditions for what?"

"Marrying you."

Egods, the woman had her nerve. Miles felt a rush of heat speed to his face. Despite his best intentions, he gave himself away. "Conditions?" he repeated.

Alyssa nodded her head. "I'll begin with a few simple requests, sir."

"Do, madam."

"I would like your permission to create a rose garden at Cork Castle, if there is not one there already."

"Done."

"I would like to bring my cat, Tom, to live with us."

"Done." This was much easier and much simpler than he had anticipated.

"I have some personal belongings—a number of books, a few special pieces of furniture and bric-a-brac, and, of course, Beauty—that I would not like to have to leave behind."

"It isn't necessary for you to ask permission concerning these things, Alyssa. You may bring with you whatever and whomever you wish."

"Which brings me to the subject of Miss Pibble, my lord."

Miles unbuttoned his coat and crossed one leg over the other. This was going to take longer than he had expected and this infernal chair was bloody uncomfortable. "Miss Pibble?"

"Emma has been my teacher, my friend, my bosom companion for most of my life. I couldn't possibly leave her behind."

"Then Miss Pibble may come to live with us." He reconsidered. "She may have her own suite of rooms in another part of the house. Near the schoolrooms.

She may wish to oversee the education of the next Marquess of Cork."

"Thank you. I would also like permission to return to Graystone Abbey whenever I need or desire to. You must understand, my lord, that I have lived here all my life and my parents are buried here."

"Done. As long as you bring me with you, or you don't stay away too long."

"I promise."

"Is there anything else?"

"One other matter."

"Yes, well, what is it?" he prodded when she didn't speak.

Alyssa dropped her eyes and concentrated on her hands for a moment. "You spoke of freedom, my lord."

"Yes."

"Does that mean freedom for both of us?"

He hesitated. She was getting at something and he didn't know what it was. "Yes."

"I see."

"I am speaking of freedom of spirit, of thought, of intellectual pursuit, freedom to express oneself," he clarified. "I don't mean to imply that either of us is free to dishonor or hurt the other one, or to come and go without consulting our partner first."

She was still mulling something over, Miles could tell.

"And what of freedom to take lovers?" Alyssa blurted out.

Miles saw red. No other man would ever touch his Alyssa. He was going to be her first and last lover.

She went on. "I understand that kind of thing is done all the time in the Marlborough House Set."

"It is not done by everyone, madam. It will not be done by the Marchioness of Cork."

Her voice grew soft. "And what of the Marquess of Cork?"

"What are you saying, Alyssa?"

"What's sauce for the goose is sauce for the gander, Miles."

"Are we back to a discussion of food, my dear?"

"You may make a jest, sir. But I am serious. If the marchioness is be loyal, then so is the marquess. We're partners, remember?"

"I remember. Done."

"Than you may ask me, sir."

"Ask you what, madam?"

"You may ask me to marry you."

Miles asked.

Alyssa accepted.

They agreed to be married quickly and discreetly—indeed, the word they agreed on was *secretly*—and as soon as possible by special license. They would exchange their vows in the Lady Chapel, late at night, after the household was abed.

Miles would make the necessary arrangements and then send word to Alyssa when all was in readiness.

The summons came six nights later.

Chapter Twenty-one

Lawrence Grenfell Wicke, the eighth Duke of Deakin, looked around the small, candlelit chapel as it filled with guests. He gave an amused grunt, leaned toward his best friend and fellow former soldier, and, lowering his voice to a whisper, inquired: "Who are all these people, Cork? I thought this was supposed to be a secret wedding."

Miles St. Aldford, Marquess of Cork, turned to his best man and, with no small amount of chagrin, admitted: "It was. But you know better than I what happens when a man gets involved with a beautiful, intelligent, *and* headstrong woman."

"I do, indeed," Lawrence heartily agreed.

"I refused to have the odious Lady Caroline Chubb or any of her family or friends at our wedding. Since the Chubbs are in residence here at the abbey, the only way to handle the affair, as I explained to the young lady, was to keep it a secret. I knew you and Juliet would stand up for us. But Alyssa insisted that she could not leave out those near and dear to her. So we compromised."

"Compromised, huh?"

Miles nodded. "Lady Chubb et al., were *not* invited. Practically everyone else was."

"Interesting compromise."

Miles sighed and shook his head. "Interesting young woman."

Lawrence grinned and patted him affectionately on the shoulder. "She's going to lead you on a merry chase, Cork."

Miles grinned right back. "I seem to recall that Juliet led you on a merry chase not so long ago, Deakin."

He was referring to their visit last winter to New York City and Knickerbocker society. It was there that the Duke had met his match in Miss Juliet Jones, America's wealthiest heiress. Several months after dancing together at Mrs. Astor's famous annual ball, Lawrence had made Juliet his duchess.

Miles turned to check the chapel door for the tenth time in as many minutes. "What can be keeping her?"

Lawrence made a valiant attempt to sooth his friend's nerves. "Your bride will be along directly. Perhaps the dress required a nip or a tuck here and there. And Juliet will insist on observing the custom of 'something old, something new, something borrowed, something blue.' You didn't give us much notice, old chap. From the moment Blunt appeared at the door of Grantley Manor with your letter, we had but three days to put the whole business altogether. I saw to commandeering the bishop and obtaining the special license. Juliet dealt with the wedding dress and other bridal accoutrements."

Miles was grateful. He had expressed his gratitude to Lawrence several times already since entering the Lady Chapel. "I won't forget this, Deakin."

"You would have done the same for me. As a matter of fact, you did." The duke regarded the latest wedding guests. "Who are the two gentlemen sitting down now?"

Miles peered toward the back pews. The hour was nearing midnight, and the votive candles lent more glow than light to the rear of the small chapel. "One is the vicar, Mr. Blackmore. The other is the village doctor, Aristotle Symthe. I take it both were lifelong friends of the late earl and his countess."

"And the uncomfortable-appearing fellow with the woolen cap clasped in his hand?"

"Galsworthy. Head gardener. Been here since the time of the eleventh Earl of Graystone. Works wonders with roses." He might as well explain the rest of the gathering while they were waiting for Juliet and Alyssa. "The two middle-aged women are the housekeeper and the cook. By the way, the cook rivals your own for the preparation and serving of hot dishes. I have seriously been thinking of stealing her from the abbey."

"How will you manage that? Double her wages?"

Miles shook his head. "Alyssa will be the carrot I dangle in front of Cook's nose. She first came to this house as a scullery maid the week the lady was born."

"Clever devil," muttered Deakin. "Ah, I see Blunt has joined the wedding guests."

"That is Miss Emma Pibble with him. She was Alyssa's governess at one time, but over the years they have become confidantes and the very dearest of friends. They are inseparable now, I understand. Miss Pibble will be moving to Cork Castle with the bride."

"Your lady appears to be well loved."

"She is, indeed. And there is someone else who will eventually be making the move to Cork Castle with us."

"Someone?"

"Perhaps I should have said some*thing*. The creature's name is Tom, but don't be misled by the simple, friendly nature of the appellation. Tom is a force to be reckoned with in this household."

"That is the largest domestic cat I have ever seen," declared Lawrence.

"That is exactly what I said the first time I saw Tom," Miles concurred, thinking back to that night in Milady's Bower. In many ways, he realized, that was when it all began.

Lawrence gave him a discreet nudge. "Now, there's an odd chap if I ever saw one."

At first Miles didn't recognize the latest arrival to the chapel. Then he muttered under his breath, "My God, it's the Hermit."

"The Hermit?"

"He lives in the Monk's Cave."

Lawrence Grenfell Wicke—wisely, perhaps—did not ask any more questions.

Miles stood there, staring at the man he had—like everyone else—been calling the Hermit for the past month. Gone was the scraggly beard and the shoulder-length hair. He had obviously bathed. Several layers of dirt and grime were missing as well.

The man was dressed in the suit of gentleman's

clothes Alyssa had given to him several weeks earlier. It was the first time since his sudden appearance at the abbey that the stranger looked human.

Miles was genuinely shocked to find that the gentleman was only a handful of years older than he
was. He had thought of the Hermit as old. And
although the man was still very thin, his face and
his physique showed signs of filling out. No doubt
thanks to the baskets of food Alyssa had delivered
to him on a regular basis.

For some inexplicable reason, a line of poetry—
Miles couldn't remember where he had read the
poem or even who had written it—flitted through
his mind: " 'And all my nightly dreams are where
thy gray eye glances.' "

"You must be nervous," said Lawrence. "Quoting
pretty words at a time like this." The duke reconsidered. "Or does your lovely bride have gray eyes and
occupy your nightly dreams?"

Miles found himself distracted by the questions.
"As it happens, the answer to both is yes."

"Here comes the bishop," his best man pointed
out unnecessarily. "Are you certain this is what you
want to do, Cork? It's still not too late to call it off."

"I'm certain, Deakin," Miles said unwaveringly.

"I want only the best for you," his friend stated,
suddenly quite serious.

"I know. You'll see," Miles reassured him. "The
lady is an angel."

"A pair of angels have just entered the chapel,"
Lawrence Grenfell Wicke informed him.

There was no wedding march, no organ music, no
clarion calls, only the sound of the summer breeze

swaying the treetops, the soft murmur of a prayer from somewhere in the small church, the *swish, swish* of Juliet and Alyssa's gowns as they floated into the Lady Chapel.

The duchess was a vision in soft blue silk that matched the blue of her eyes. Her dress was simply but beautifully cut. As usual, Juliet wore no jewelry other than a pair of discreet earrings.

Then Alyssa came into view, and all eyes were on her.

Miles couldn't take his eyes off her. Lord, she was lovely. As lovely as he'd ever seen her. He watched as she came down the church aisle toward him. Tall and slender, head held high, chin up, hair like silvery gold in the candlelight, skin a creamy perfection beneath her veil, dressed in purest white with a bouquet of pure white roses in her arms, roses that cascaded over her sleeve and became silk roses down the length of her bridal dress.

Miles was dumbstruck.

He realized that he had never seen Alyssa in anything but gray or black for mourning. Gray and black were *not* her colors. The lady was beautiful in white.

The lady was magnificent.

For the first time in a very long time, Miles St. Aldford felt the sting of tears in his eyes. His mother and father would have found joy in this moment.

Alyssa came to him and they knelt together before the bishop.

Something old: Alyssa was wearing her mother's, her grandmother's, her great-grandmother's wedding veil, lovingly passed down from woman to woman, from one generation to the next.

Something new: she was gowned in white silk and satin, the most beautiful wedding dress she had ever seen, miraculously produced from a trunk just a half hour ago by Juliet, Duchess of Deakin.

Something borrowed: her earrings. Perfect white pearls. Precious pearls from the Orient. They had been given to Emma Pibble upon the occasion of her eighteenth birthday by her father, a ship's captain, a gentleman who had sailed the seven seas.

Something blue: At Juliet's insistence, she had quickly tied a small blue satin ribbon to her bodice. It was the only thing she was wearing that wasn't white.

Everyone that she cared about was in the chapel with her tonight. Everyone that she cared about heard the bishop's prayer, his sermon on the sanctity of marriage, the exchange of vows between Miles Mountbank St. Aldford and Alyssa Constance Gray.

"I, Miles Mountbank, take thee, Alyssa Constance, to be my wedded wife. And I do promise and covenant before God and these witnesses to be thy loving and faithful husband, in plenty and in want, in joy and in sorrow, in sickness and in health, as long as we both shall live."

Then it was her turn to speak. Alyssa heard her voice ring out soft and clear, gaining strength and conviction as she went. "I, Alyssa Constance, take thee, Miles Mountbank, to be my wedding husband. And I do promise and covenant before God and these witnesses to be thy loving and faithful wife, in plenty and in want, in joy and in sorrow, in sickness and in health, as long as we both shall live."

Miles placed a ring on her finger. The bishop gave them his blessing and declared they were man and wife. Alyssa's veil was lifted and she was kissed for the first time by her husband.

It was the way she had always dreamed of being married—when she allowed herself to dream about it at all. The chapel at her home filled with candles and familiar faces, loving faces.

All but two, of course. But she liked to believe that her mother and father were with her in spirit.

Then, one by one, each guest in the chapel came up to them and said a word of congratulations or best wishes. More than a few tears were hastily brushed aside.

Mrs. Fetchett pressed a quick kiss to her cheek in a rare show of emotion.

Cook said nothing, just patted her hand and dabbed at her own weepy eyes.

Galsworthy shuffled his feet, of course, and clasped his cap in his hand. Then he reached into his coat pocket and removed a perfect new rose, a *Milady's Joy*, he said he called it, since *Milady's Tears* wouldn't be right somehow for a wedding celebration.

Dr. Symthe beamed with pride and remarked how he remembered the night he had been called to the abbey because there was a baby about to be born to the Countess of Graystone. That baby was, of course, Alyssa.

The vicar gave his own sweet and unaffected

blessing, and Alyssa went up on her tiptoes and pressed a kiss to his blushing cheek.

Blunt vigorously shook Miles's hand and gallantly bowed to her, even as Tom tried to wrap himself around her skirts.

Emma came to her at last. "I have never seen a more beautiful, a more radiant bride," she pressed to Alyssa's ear.

"Thank you, my dear Emma."

"You have been the daughter I was never to have," she whispered. "I'm so proud of you and so filled with happiness for you. May God go with you always."

They were both blinking back tears when they drew apart.

The chapel emptied, each person quietly slipping away as they had arrived. The bishop disappeared to his carriage, a generous token of appreciation in his pocket from both the duke and the marquess. He would receive another expression of appreciation several weeks later from Her Majesty, Queen Victoria.

It was just the four of them, then: Lawrence and Juliet, Miles and Alyssa. Or so they thought until Alyssa glanced up and spied the Hermit standing in the shadows.

For the first time he smiled at her. His smile seemed so familiar. She couldn't quite imagine why. Then the gentleman bowed to the group and took his leave.

"We are going to be great friends," Juliet, Duchess of Deakin, promised Alyssa as she and the duke prepared to return to their private railroad car.

"I hope so," Alyssa told her. She'd never had a friend her own age. "Your generosity tonight has left me feeling overwhelmed."

"It was little enough to do for you and for the man who made my own wedding possible," Juliet declared.

Alyssa looked to where Miles was standing some short distance away talking to Lawrence. "Was Miles truly instrumental in bringing you and the duke together?"

"I think we can say he was *indispensable*." Then the duchess put her head back and laughed softly. "If I hadn't overheard the two of them talking on my wedding night and bragging about how clever they were and how wonderful it was to have snared Lawrence an heiress—not just any heiress, mind you, but the wealthiest spinster in all of New York, perhaps in all of the Americas—then I would never have gotten mad as a hornet and realized that I loved my husband."

Alyssa's eyes were huge by now.

"More important, perhaps he would not have realized how much he loved me," Juliet declared.

The Duchess of Deakin was different. Perhaps it was because she was an American. Alyssa had never met an American before. She was certain now she would like to meet more.

Juliet dropped an affectionate kiss on each of Alyssa's cheeks in turn. "But that is a story for another time and another place, my dear Alyssa. I will tell the whole thing to you one day." She lowered her beautiful contralto voice. "And you must tell me how Miles St. Aldford came to Graystone Abbey to find a ghost and ended up finding himself a bride."

"I will," she whispered back.

"It's time to go, Juliet," came the loving reminder from her husband as he came up and slipped an arm around her waist.

Miles and Alyssa stood in the back of the Lady Chapel for a moment after everyone else had departed. There was no sound. There was no movement. And yet they both felt it: They had been blessed.

Miles gazed down intently into her face and offered her his arm. "Come, lady wife. The hour grows late and our bed awaits us."

Chapter Twenty-two

Men *were* a different species altogether, Alyssa concluded as her husband escorted her through the dark house. There was not another soul about at this hour, just the two of them, and the only light to see by was that of the full moon streaming in the windows.

"It must be late," Alyssa whispered; she was surprised to hear her own voice come out sounding so husky.

"It's nearly two o'clock," Miles informed her.

"I'm not the least bit sleepy," she added.

He seemed to find that amusing. She could hear a low male chuckle, followed by: "That's good."

She racked her brain for something, anything, to say. "It was a lovely ceremony."

"Yes, it was," Miles agreed.

Alyssa paused and picked up her trailing skirts, draping them over her left arm. Her veil was a cloud of intricate antique lace around her head and shoulders. "I like your friends Lawrence and Juliet very much."

"They like you very much."

"Do you think so?"

"I know so," he stated. "Everyone likes you. In fact, everyone loves you."

Alyssa grew genuinely curious in spite of herself. "How do you know?" she asked.

Miles gave a private laugh. "Common knowledge."

"Pish!" She felt herself flush a dull red and pointed out—modesty insisted that she do so: "Besides, it isn't true. Lady Chubb doesn't love me. Sometimes I have the feeling she doesn't even like me."

"That can only be a compliment to you," Miles said in a hard, dry tone.

Alyssa wished she hadn't mentioned Lady Chubb. After all, it was their wedding night and she would have no unpleasantness associated with it. To that end, she put the woman from her mind and changed the subject. "Juliet is very beautiful."

Miles came to a halt in front of a moon-washed window, turned to her, cupped her chin in his palm, and vowed in a voice that sent shivers of pleasure racing down her spine, "You are beautiful, lady wife."

There was a meaningful pause.

"On their wedding day, a bridegroom is required to tell his bride that she's beautiful."

"How do you know?"

"Common knowledge," Alyssa answered, teasing him just a little.

"It may be common knowledge," Miles said, his eyes never leaving hers, "but you are uncommonly lovely."

Alyssa wasn't used to compliments. At least not a gentleman's compliments, and certainly not a husband's compliments. She dropped her gaze. "I've never had such a beautiful dress."

"From this day forward, Lady Cork, I order you to never wear gray or black again," he said.

"*Order*, Lord Cork?"

Miles St. Aldford took a moment to reconsider his hasty choice of words. "Request?"

"I will honor your request. For, if the truth be told, I am heartily sick of wearing nothing but gray or black." Alyssa's features settled into an expression of puzzlement. "What will I do with all my clothes?"

"Give them away."

"What will I wear?"

Her husband arched one rakish eyebrow in her direction and suggested, "A smile?"

She failed to comprehend his meaning. If she wore only a smile, then she would be as bare as a newborn babe. "I will have nothing to wear at all, sir."

"Do not despair, madam. If necessary, the best dressmakers in London—indeed, in all of Europe—will be brought here to the abbey posthaste. They will design, concoct, construct, and sew a wardrobe fit for a queen. You will have day dresses and evening dresses, morning dresses and tea dresses, informal dresses and formal dresses, and whatever else you require in every color of the rainbow." Miles paused for a breath. "What is your favorite color?"

Alyssa's head was swimming. "Pink, I think."

"Then you shall have a dozen pink dresses."

She tapped a finger against her chin and rethought her choice. "No. I believe it is blue."

"Then you will have a dozen blue gowns as well."

She'd never been particularly interested *in* or concerned *with* what she wore. But Alyssa realized that she wouldn't mind being pretty for her husband. After all, Miles knew—Miles had known—so many pretty women in his time.

She gave him a sideways glance. "What if I changed my mind again and told you that my favorite color is yellow?"

Miles seemed to find that vastly amusing. He put his head back and laughed. Indeed, for a moment his quiet laughter was the only sound in the moonlit hall. She loved the sound of her husband's laugh, Alyssa realized with a heartfelt pang.

"I'll buy you a hundred dresses, lady wife, a thousand dresses, if that is what you desire."

Alyssa gave a most unladylike snort. "I wouldn't know what to do with a hundred dresses, my lord, let alone a thousand. There is scarcely room for a dozen in my dressing room."

"Perhaps you need a different dressing room, then," Miles suggested. "There are unused chambers at both Cork House and Cork Castle that dwarf this hall."

It boggled the mind.

At least, it boggled her mind.

It suddenly occurred to Alyssa that she might be regarded as something of a country bumpkin in her husband's exalted social circles. She wondered if it mattered to him. Just in case, she'd better watch her manners. After all, she was the Marchioness of Cork and chatelaine of several grand houses now.

Without further ado, Miles reached for her hand and urged her up the great staircase toward their wing of the house. They came to the door of her suite first.

"I will leave you now, my lady."

Alyssa's spirits plummeted. Her heart sank all the way down to her white satin wedding slippers. Miles was leaving her. She was being returned to her own rooms as if nothing had happened, as if nothing had changed, as if she were still Lady Alyssa Gray, spinster, instead of Lady Cork.

She felt like she had a mouthful of ashes. "Good night, then, my lord."

Miles frowned slightly and responded, "Not good night. Simply *a bientôt.*"

Alyssa opened the familiar door and swept into the sitting room of her suite. Her disappointment was beyond belief. Then she looked up and immediately realized why Miles had not seemed particularly concerned. Everything had been changed. Everything had been put into readiness while they were gone. No doubt at the marquess's request, Emma Pibble and Mr. Blunt had seen to the details themselves.

A transformation had taken place. The long-locked double doors connecting her sitting room and the sitting room of the Knight's Chambers—she had quite forgotten the doors' existence since on her side they were concealed behind a large antique screen—had been unlocked and opened wide.

The screen, an exotic scene of spiraling pagodas and delicate cherry trees in blossom, carved from dark wood inlaid with precious jade—the colors of the precious jade ranging from alabaster to Ming green, from pale pink to black—had been acquired by the fifth Earl of Graystone and presented to his bride as a wedding gift. The screen now stood in a far corner of the room.

Alyssa could see straight through into the Knight's Chambers. There was a beautifully laid supper table, complete with candlelight, gleaming silver, sparkling crystal champagne flutes, a bowl of pure white roses—their fragrance detectable from where she stood—and a bottle of fine champagne chilling in a silver bucket beside the table set for two.

It was the most romantic setting she had ever beheld.

Alyssa turned and went back through the sitting room to her bedroom. She carefully removed the heirloom lace wedding veil and placed it on the milliner's form for safekeeping until it could be packed away for the day when her daughter would wear it to be married in. It was then she noticed the nightdress and wrapper laid out on her bed.

The material of the nightgown was finest lawn, with intricate flowers embroidered at the neck, at the wrists, and encircling the row of tiny pearl buttons down the front. The wrapper was of the same fine lawn, also embroidered with flowers and accented at the neck, the waist, and the hem with satin ribbons of palest pink, palest yellow, and palest blue.

"Now I have something else to thank you for, Juliet," Alyssa said aloud, knowing full well that the lovely things were a gift from the Duchess of Deakin.

Alyssa paused in front of the mirror and studied

her reflection with surprising detachment. She looked the same; she did not feel the same. Except for a slightly pink cast to her cheeks—and the magnificent wedding gown, of course—her appearance was as it had always been. It was on the inside where she was different. She was all expectation and brimming curiosity, trepidation and nervous excitement. After all, this was her wedding night.

She knew nothing about wedding nights.

There was so much that she still didn't know about men and women. So many questions that were still unanswered. Where could she find the answers now? Who could she turn to at this late hour?

There was a soft knock from the other room and then she heard her name being called out in a familiar baritone.

"Alyssa?"

She took in a deep breath and slowly released it, patted her hair once or twice, licked her lips, put her shoulders back, and went to greet her husband.

Miles was leaning against the open double doors. He had dispensed with his dress coat, his collar, his necktie. Several buttons had been undone down the front of his white evening shirt. He appeared comfortable and at ease. He was rakishly handsome, cutting a fine figure of a man—in truth, the finest Alyssa had ever seen—with his broad shoulders, his muscular arms, his slim waist, and his long legs.

He took her breath away.

"Madam, would you care to join me for a glass of champagne and perhaps a little late supper?"

Alyssa was quite certain she would be sick if she

tried to eat, but a glass of champagne might well settle the odd flutterings in her stomach. "I accept your gracious offer, sir," she replied, walking across the sitting room toward him, praying all the while that her legs wouldn't give way beneath her.

Miles was excruciatingly polite as he seated her on one side of the intimate table and then sat down opposite her.

"Everything is so beautiful," she exclaimed, her tongue thick in her mouth.

Miles contemplated her and the supper table without any change in his expression. "It was the joint effort of Blunt, Miss Pibble, Mrs. Fetchett, and Cook, I believe."

"I must be sure to thank them all in the morning."

"We'll both thank them."

"Of course, that's what I meant to say," Alyssa stammered. "We'll both thank them." She regarded the numerous silver platters and covered dishes. "I suppose their feelings will be hurt if we don't eat and drink something."

"I suppose they will." Miles poured two glasses of vintage champagne and handed one to her before he announced, "I would like to propose a toast."

Alyssa waited with the crystal flute in her hand.

Miles raised his glass and looked intently into her eyes. "To Alyssa, my lady, my wife, 'who walks in beauty like the night.' "

"Lord Byron?"

"Lord Byron."

Then they sipped their champagne.

Alyssa found that it warmed her insides and

helped her to relax. In fact, she soon spoke up. "I would like to propose a toast this time."

Miles regarded her, his eyebrows raised in surprise. "Very well. Allow me to refill our glasses."

Once her glass was replenished, she held it up to the candlelight and studied the rise of lovely bubbles for a minute. Then she gazed across the table at him. "To Miles, my husband, my lord, my knight in shining armor."

There was an eloquent silence.

"May I serve you supper?" he inquired after some time.

Alyssa fixed a pleasant smile on her face. "Yes, thank you."

Miles heaped two plates with sumptuous treats: thin slices of beef fillet and succulent lobster salad, buttered sole and baked quail and savory breasts of partridge, imported ortolan, caviar from the Russias, fresh fruits of all types and description.

He placed one gold-rimmed plate in front of her, and the second in front of himself. They sat for several minutes without speaking *and* without eating.

Miles finally broke the silence. "Alyssa, I think we need to talk."

He had once said that was all they did.

He went on. "We spoke of freedom as being an important part of our marriage."

"We did."

"Freedom may take many forms. For example, the freedom to say 'I wish to wait,' or even the freedom to say no. Do you understand what I'm trying to tell you?"

"No."

Miles ran his hand through his hair. "Perhaps we should start at the beginning. If there was one thing you could say to me right now, what would it be?"

Alyssa hesitated.

He reminded her. "You are free to say whatever is on your mind."

She swallowed hard. "I am quite nervous, my lord."

"So am I, my lady."

Encouraged by his candor, she continued. "I know nothing about being a wife."

"I know nothing about being a husband."

"That isn't true. That can't be true," she pointed out. "You know a great deal about the relationship between men and women, between a man and a woman."

"But I am just as ignorant of the relationship between us as you are," he said. "We're going to have to learn together."

"She's beautiful and therefore to be wooed. She is woman, therefore to be won."

Shakespeare may have been right, but Alyssa was also as nervous as a kitten, Miles realized. He was going to have to take it slow and easy, for both their sakes.

He tried to imagine the whole affair from Alyssa's point of view. Even if a woman was in love with a man—and the subject of love had certainly never been spoken of between the lady and himself—it must be frightening to enter marriage ignorant of its physical aspects.

He watched as Alyssa raised the crystal champagne flute to her lips and took several more sips. She was, no doubt, attempting to 'screw her courage to the sticking-place' with the aid of the fine French vintage.

"This freedom you speak of," she said, concentrating on her hands, "does it extend to asking questions?"

They were husband and wife now. Miles knew he must do his best to satisfy his wife's curiosity without utterly destroying her innocence. Alyssa was such a curious creature. He took a swallow from his own glass of champagne. "Naturally."

"Then I would like to know exactly what happens between a husband and a wife in the marriage bed."

Miles thought for moment. "They kiss."

"I surmised as much."

"They caress each other."

"I am familiar with that aspect as well."

"They explore the basic physical differences between the male and female human form."

She frowned. "Why can't you just tell me in plain, simple anatomical terms, sir?"

"It is not done, madam."

"Why not?" Alyssa asked, catching the tip of her tongue between her teeth.

Her tongue was pink and pointed. Her teeth were small and white, and they could, they would, drive a man to distraction if she were to suddenly nibble on the lobe of his ear or his sensitive lower lip, or take a taste of a male nipple or move even lower. . . .

Miles gave himself a shake. "Why not *what*?"

"Why isn't it done?" she asked begrudgingly.

"It would be considered highly irregular and most inappropriate," he said, wishing he had never started this damnable business.

He should have taken Alyssa straight to bed and demonstrated what it was about. Actions frequently spoke louder than words. As a former military man, he should have remembered that. Hell and blast, he had made a grave strategical error.

She wouldn't leave it alone. "Because I'm unmarried? Or because I'm a female?"

"You are married," he reminded her.

"Then we're back to gender?"

Miles cautioned himself to patience. "So it would seem."

She put her glass down and stared at a single drop poised on the rim. "I must confess that I didn't expect to remain ignorant after marriage, sir."

"You won't remain ignorant, madam," he guaranteed her. "Experience will teach you everything you wish to know." Miles fell silent, musing. Then he decided to try a different approach with the lady. "Think of the possibilities between a man and a woman as a sensual feast."

Alyssa raised her head and there was more than a hint of interest in her eyes as they stared into his. "Are you using food again, my lord, as a metaphor?"

"I am." Miles reached across the table and, with a small flourish, uncovered again a number of the silver serving dishes. "I promise you that we will discover a smorgasbord of tastes and textures. Some, we may find, are not to our liking. Some may be too tart or too sweet to suit our tastes. Some we may decide to indulge ourselves in only occasionally."

Alyssa seemed intrigued. "Tell me more."

"We may wish to eat a quick, simple supper. Or there may be times when we are starved and we will linger at the dinner table all night long," he told her.

Her gray eyes grew huge. "All night long?"

"All night long."

Alyssa was obviously still mulling over the idea as Miles examined a platter of fruit. He selected a large, lush, red strawberry. He leaned toward the lady and offered her the choice morsel. "Grasp the strawberry with your front teeth. Close your lips around it. Appreciate its slightly prickly texture. Run your tongue over the tiny seeds on its surface. Now bite into the fruit and savor its sweet flavor."

Alyssa did as he instructed. Then she swallowed the strawberry, licked the juice from her lips, and declared, "That was delicious."

Miles took a second strawberry and ate it in the same manner himself. Then he looked into his wife's innocent eyes and said, "That isn't nearly as sweet, as delicious, as delectable as the fruit which your breasts offer me, madam."

Alyssa appeared to be momentarily speechless. But she recovered rather nicely, he had to concede. "Are there other foods on the table that have a similar metaphorical value?"

"There are."

She looked over the possibilities and selected a small brown hazelnut. "Explain this one, if you will."

Miles went warm inside. "A man has breasts, although they are not identical in size, shape, or function to a woman's, of course."

"Does a man have nipples as well?"

He nodded. "They are not unlike this small brown nut."

Alyssa popped the hazelnut into her mouth and began to chew. "Do you taste like a nut?"

"I don't know."

"Then I'll have to find out for myself, won't I?" she murmured in an unintentionally seductive manner.

"Yes, you will," Miles answered huskily.

Next Alyssa selected a plump ripe plum. She held it in her palm for a moment and turned it over with her fingertips. "I have never seen an unclothed flesh-and-blood gentleman before. Do you have plums, sir?"

Miles reminded himself to breathe. "I do, madam."

"Am I to nibble on them?"

Miles went hot. "Only if it appeals to you."

"I'm sure it will." Then Alyssa sank her teeth into the ripe flesh and took a bite.

Miles groaned aloud.

Her head came up. "What is it, sir?"

He waved her question aside with his hand.

She blithely went on. "I understand from my reading that the banana is a popular fruit grown in tropical regions of the world. Although we have none of the tapered, elongated variety on our table tonight, will it be included in our sensual repast?"

Miles nodded.

"Do I eat it?"

Miles choked.

"Are you quite all right, my lord?"

The linen napkin covering his lap proved to be

his salvation. "I hadn't realized just how arousing a plate of fruit could be, my lady."

"Arousing?"

"Stimulating."

"Are you stimulated?"

"Yes." He'd had quite his fill of discussing food as a metaphor for sex. He was as hard as a bloody rock. "Madam, the hour grows ever later. It's time we prepared for bed."

Alyssa rose from her chair, her skirts cutting a wide satin swath as she moved between the supper table and the sitting room door. At least she was too preoccupied with her own maneuverings to notice that he kept his dinner napkin dangling from his belt all the while, Miles thought sardonically.

He escorted the lady to her suite and then returned directly to his own. He went through to his dressing room and disrobed. Standing in front of the full-length mirror, Miles studied his reflection dispassionately.

How would a fully aroused male appear to a young woman who had never seen a nude man before? Other than the statues in the abbey's formal gardens, of course.

She might be frightened.

She might find herself repulsed.

She might think him something horrific out of the Brothers Grimm.

She might even laugh.

"Not quite the same thing as the well-endowed Apollo, hey, Cork?" he said with a self-deprecating smile.

Miles pulled on a dressing gown and firmly tied

the belt around his waist. He had bathed, shaved, scrubbed his teeth, and in general made himself presentable to the lady before he had dressed for the wedding ceremony. There was little left for him to do now but hope.

He covered the food, picked up their champagne glasses and the bottle of sparkling wine, and presented himself at the entrance to Alyssa's sitting room just as the lady emerged from her bedroom.

Alyssa was still dressed in her wedding gown and finery. In fact, she seemed to be in exactly the same state as when she'd left his suite some fifteen or twenty minutes ago.

Well, she wasn't exactly in the same state. Her hair was coming undone and tumbling around her shoulders in a mass of golden silk, and her cheeks were red with exasperation.

He stopped in his tracks. "What is it?"

Alyssa let out a frustrated sigh. "I have never understood haute couture, husband."

Was this the time to be discussing it? "Why haven't you changed out of your wedding gown?"

"I can't."

"You can't?" Miles repeated, surprised.

"I'm stuck."

"Stuck?"

"Must you repeat everything I say, sir? I tell you I am stuck. The maids have all long gone to their beds. I wouldn't think of disturbing Emma in the middle of the night, and I can't get out of this infernal contraption by myself."

"I see."

Miles suddenly realized his bride was on the verge

of tears. He had never seen Alyssa in such a state. Of course, it was her wedding night, she'd gulped down two glasses of champagne—and no supper to speak of—and she had been under considerable emotional strain of late.

She wasn't finished, either. "What drivel. What foolishness. What insanity, Miles!"

"What is, my dear?"

The first tears appeared like tiny dewdrops on the tips of her pale eyelashes. "That a full-grown woman should not be able to undress herself. It's a disgrace."

"I quite agree," Miles said, commiserating with her. "Mr. Charles Worth has much to answer for. But since he is in Paris and I am here, may I offer my assistance?"

She appeared somewhat mollified. "If you don't assist me, I will be forced to sleep in my wedding gown."

"We wouldn't want that, now, would we?" He certainly didn't. "Don't fret, Alyssa. I know exactly what to do." Miles set the glasses and champagne down on the table, took her by the elbow, and urged her in the direction of her bedroom.

It was the first time he'd seen the inner sanctum, of course. It was comfortable, feminine without being frilly, filled with interesting oddities: seashells, childhood memorabilia, family photographs, books and more books, a collection of china cats, pretty little bits of this and that.

"First, we get rid of this voluminous skirt," he proposed. "I'll undo the hooks down the back, and you step out of it."

"You will see me in my petticoats," she observed.

"Madam, before this night is over I will see you in far less than that," he pointed out.

The satin bodice was next.

"Hold up your hair, so I can get to the button at your nape," he ordered.

Alyssa silently obeyed and held up her hair.

Her nape was irresistible.

"Don't fidget, wife," he admonished her. "It will take me forever to undo the remainder of these ridiculously tiny buttons." Mr. Charles Worth had much to answer for, indeed.

"Now, lift your feet one at a time," Miles instructed, and swooped up the yards and yards of beautiful satin material.

He made a production of hanging the wedding gown over a chair and smoothing the skirt and train. He deliberately kept his back to her, knowing it would give Alyssa a needed minute or two to deal with her petticoats and chemise. Only one task remained. Unlacing the back of her corset.

"You may turn around now," she told him.

Alyssa stood in the middle of her bedroom, wrapped in a white cotton sheet, her back to him. She looked like a Greek goddess.

Her back was extraordinary: long and supple. Her skin appeared to be as soft and smooth as silk. It was ivory in color and perfect.

Miles began the task of undoing his wife's tight lacings. When he had finished, there was a whispered "Thank you, sir," and nothing more.

"It was my pleasure to be of assistance, madam." He gave a slight bow of his head, which she would only catch a glimpse of in her mirror, and returned to his rooms.

Miles St. Aldford stood at the window, looking out over the rose garden below, the moon illuminating that bower of scents and delights and he murmured to himself: " 'Go, lovely rose . . . tell her . . . when I resemble her to thee, how sweet and fair she seems to be.' "

She did not know the protocol in such matters, Alyssa realized as she slipped into her nightdress and wrapper, gave her hair a perfunctory brushing, and turned down the lamp in her bedroom. The problem was solved for her in an unexpected way.

"Alyssa, there is someone here to see you," Miles called out from his sitting room.

"Who?"

"An old friend," came the answer.

"Where?"

"In there," Miles answered, indicating behind him.

Alyssa walked into the bedroom of the Knight's Chambers. There, curled up in the middle of the bedcovers, legs tucked beneath him, eyes slitted, watching every move they were making, was Tom.

"Where have you been?" she said, sitting down on the edge of the mattress to pet her cat. "I haven't seen you since the chapel. Have you been out chasing mice in the garden?"

Miles watched from the doorway. "Is Tom a first-rate mouser?"

"Naturally. The real trick, however, has been teaching him to leave his catch outside. He keeps

bringing half-dead mice into the kitchen and dropping them at Cook's feet." She glanced up at her
husband. "Tom likes you."

"How can you tell?"

"He's in your room."

"He's in my room because you're in my room,"
Miles pointed out.

"Perhaps."

There was a minute or two of silence.

Alyssa realized her husband was watching her intently as she scratched Tom behind his ears and ran
her hand down the purring cat's body from head to
haunches. "What is it?"

"You look like an angel."

"But I'm not an angel. I'm a woman."

"And my wife."

"And your wife."

Miles came across the room to her, reached
down, and lightly combed his fingers through her
hair. "Silver. Gold."

"Which?"

"Both."

The hour was late. The setting was intimate. She
was garbed in her nightgown and wrapper, and
Miles was wearing only a dressing gown.

Alyssa reached up and touched the head of dark
hair. "Yours is like a thick pelt of sable."

His hand caressed her cheek. "Your skin is like
silk."

Alyssa brushed her fingertips along his chin.
"Your jaw is firm, but not entirely unyielding. You
have a fine brow and intelligent eyes. Your ears are
small and tucked close to your head. Your nose is

definitely patrician." She smiled with pleasure. "You're a handsome man, husband. I do believe I find greater pleasure in looking at you than I do any of the statues in the garden."

"Even the well-endowed Apollo?"

"Well, I shall have to see about that, won't I?"

"We'll take this one step at a time," Miles promised her. "If there is anything that frightens you, we'll stop."

Everything frightened her, but Alyssa had no intentions of stopping now. That first night in Milady's Bower she had known this was the man with the answers, if she only knew the questions to ask. She had been waiting for tonight. This was her chance to learn the answers and the questions.

"I'll take your wrapper," Miles politely offered as he slipped the garment down her arms and dropped it over the back of a chair.

"What of your dressing gown?"

"I don't have anything under my dressing gown."

"You don't?" A secret smile touched her lips. "It certainly appears as though you do."

"I mean, I have no other clothing under my dressing gown. I am nothing but skin and bone and muscle and—"

"Quite." Alyssa leaned back and ran her hand through Tom's fur. "I see, my lord, that a man may also be likened to a tree."

Miles scowled. "I don't comprehend your meaning, my lady."

"A tree has many branches or limbs: Some are large, some are small, some are merely twigs."

The expression on her husband's handsome face

was priceless. "Are you inferring that certain parts of my anatomy made be compared to a twig?"

"No, indeed. In fact, I was going to compare you to a mighty oak tree."

Miles began to laugh; it started as a low rumble in his chest and finally burst out into the room as a full-blown guffaw. "You, madam, are proving to be a delight."

"I simply believe in calling a fig a fig, sir."

"Don't tell me we're back to fruit," he teased.

"We aren't back to anything of the sort. But see what you've done: Your loud laughter has driven my cat away."

"It was time for Tom to find another napping spot, anyway," Miles said as he stretched out alongside her on the bed and gazed down into her eyes. The humor had faded from his. "I'm going to kiss you, Alyssa. I'm going to caress you. I'm going to make you my wife in every sense of the word. Come with me, and we'll discover a whole new wondrous world together."

Alyssa put herself in his hands and they did.

Miles kissed her. He tasted of champagne and sweet strawberries, something indefinable, something a little wild and wonderful, but mostly his taste was something all his own.

She loved the taste of him.

He smelled faintly of the summer night and the lingering scent of roses from their supper table, the masculine soap he must bathe with, but he also smelled like a man; he smelled like Miles.

She loved the way he smelled.

His body was firm and strong and muscular. His

skin was smooth where it should be, rough where it had to be, smattered with hair where it must be.

She loved his body.

Miles kissed her, urging her lips apart, teasing her with his tongue, then cajoling, then deadly serious as he delved into her mouth as if he could never get enough of her, never go far enough, never quite reach what he was seeking: to meld their lips and teeth and tongues into one.

She loved his kiss.

She loved his touch, his caress as he used his agile hands and fingers to take the clothes from her body, the breath from her lungs, the strength from her bones and muscles. She could deny him nothing, for she would only be denying herself as well.

She had once told him about the things she wanted from a man: one who would respect her mind, one who finds pleasure in books, music, and gardening. But she had never said that she wanted a man who would love her, adore her, make her blood sing in her veins with a wild hot song. She had not known about passion as a fever in the mind, or that a man could make a woman forget everything but the way he made her feel. If she had known, her list would have been much longer.

Then Miles's face was before her and his shoulders blocked out everything but him. He slipped between her legs. She could feel that part of him pressing against her. She reached down between their bodies and touched him for the first time. "Your skin is so soft!" she exclaimed as her eyes flew to his. "Yet you are so hard."

"It's a paradox," he agreed with a crooked smile.

Alyssa looked down at their naked bodies pressed together. She should have felt self-conscious, but she didn't. This was right. This was the right time, the right place, the right man.

"We're so different," she murmured, studying the male physique and the female counterpart. "We're like night and day."

"Where you are soft and inviting, I'm hard and ready," Miles said.

She touched her own breast for a moment and then his bare chest. She went up on one elbow and stuck out her tongue and ran it across his brown male nipple. She licked it several times, then took it into her mouth as he had done with hers and suckled. She heard a gasp from the man hovering over her. "You do taste a bit like a nut," she murmured in a husky voice.

Then Miles pushed her back onto the bedcovers, came down and took her nipple between his lips, and drew her deeper and deeper into his mouth. It was some time before he raised his head. She was moaning and moving beneath him. His eyes were glazed with passion as he declared, "You do taste as sweet as the sweetest strawberries."

"I want . . . I need . . . I desire . . ."

"What?" came the husky question.

Alyssa opened her eyes and gazed into his. "You, Miles."

"And I want you, Alyssa."

"Make me your wife," she pleaded.

"I will."

"Now, please."

"Now." He slipped his hand between her legs and

parted the soft flesh at the apex of her thighs. He eased a finger inside of her and it came away warm and wet with her fragrance. "I'll try not to hurt you, my lady wife, but—"

"I know. I know," she said soothingly. She wasn't totally ignorant. She knew there would be some pain, some discomfort. She had overheard housemaids gossiping once in the kitchens when she was a little girl and no one thought she was listening.

Then Miles was there with his mouth on hers, kissing her, drawing her into that spiral of excitement. Miles was there with his manhood between her thighs, pushing and prodding. Miles was there, his teeth nipping her breasts, her nipples, the tender flesh of her body.

When she was singing with need, when passion ran hot and heavy through her veins and she would have done anything for him, Miles spread her legs farther apart, raised her hips off the bed, positioned himself above her, and gazed down into her eyes with a burning intensity. Then, with her name on his lips, he plunged himself into her.

"Sweet Blessed Virgin!" she cried out.

"Not any more," he panted.

He filled her. She was no longer herself. She was Miles and she was Alyssa. She would never be just Alyssa again.

Miles made love to her with every part of his body, and when he thrust into her at the end and shouted her name over and over again, seeking his own release, spurting his seed into her womb, she knew a thrill and a sense of belonging that she had never known before.

Miles had made her his wife.

And she had made him her husband.

The world would never look quite the same to him after this moment, Miles realized as he lay atop his wife, waiting for his breathing to return to normal, waiting for his heart to stop pounding in his chest, waiting for his manhood to soften so he could slip from her lovely tight body without causing her any further discomfort.

He felt like he had never made love to a woman before. It was the damnedest thing. He had seen everything anew through Alyssa's eyes. It was a wondrous vision.

He had once complained—what a fool, what a boy he had been—that he had never married because he had never found a woman who was different, a woman who wasn't predictable, a woman who was fascinating and who would never bore him.

He had just gotten lucky. Very lucky.

Alyssa wiggled under him. His weight was too much to leave on her. Miles rolled carefully to one side and lay there, unconcerned for his nudity, feeling as relaxed as he had ever felt in his entire life, as fulfilled, as satisfied, as happy, as content.

He tried to move back onto his side so he could gaze at his wife beside him in the bed, but a cramp caught him in the leg. He groaned aloud.

Alyssa was immediately there, hovering over him, her bare breasts brushing against his chest, her hand on his arm, concern written on her lovely face. "What is it?"

"Pain," he gritted through his teeth. He knew it

would pass; it would simply take a few minutes. The knife wound in Zanzibar had done something to one of the thigh muscles. It rarely bothered him. But then he rarely used his legs in quite the way he had tonight.

"Where?"

"Leg."

"Which leg?"

"Left." The one next to her, as a matter of fact.

"Miles, the scar. How did it happen?"

"Knife."

"When?"

"Five years ago."

"Where?"

"Zanzibar."

She frowned. "For Queen and country?"

"Something like that."

"You could have been killed."

"Or worse," he said with sardonic humor.

She wasn't laughing. "What should I do?"

He reached up and pointed to his mouth. "Kiss me."

"At a time like this?"

He nodded his head and smiled at her. "It will take my mind off the pain until it passes."

"In other words, it will create a distraction."

"Yes."

"Then I have a better idea," Alyssa murmured as she swept her hair back over her shoulder, leaned down, and kissed his scar very tenderly, very carefully.

Miles moaned as her kisses continued along his thigh. "Now I know you're an angel, wife, and I have died and gone to heaven."

Chapter Twenty-three

"I will *not* say these lines," Lady Chubb stated dramatically. "What does 'Out, vile jelly!' mean, anyway? Who would write such a disgusting thing and call it prose?"

"William Shakespeare, my lady," Blunt informed her.

"And this one," she went on in a petulant tone, raising another objection. " 'Wisdom and goodness to the vile seem vile; Filths savor but themselves.' Where does that come from, I ask you?"

"*King Lear,* act four, scene two," Emma Pibble interjected, as she looked up from the script and peered over her spectacles. "We are doing scenes from the Bard, after all, Lady Chubb."

" 'O Romeo, Romeo! wherefore art thou Romeo?' " posed Miss Charmel Chubb from the alcove where she was rehearsing her lines with Hugh Pureheart.

" 'It is the east, and Juliet is the sun!' " declared Sir Hugh in a perfect monotone.

"Why can't I play the role of Juliet?" Lady Chubb proposed with a coquettish giggle.

"Juliet is a young, innocent girl of no more than

thirteen or fourteen," Emma Pibble pointed out with her usual no-nonsense manner. "You are a woman of mature years, madam."

"In other words, you're getting a bit long in the tooth, old thing," Sir Alfred mumbled in an aside to his wife. Then he spoke up and informed the entire assembled cast, "I can't be sitting here. It's a waste of my valuable time. I have important business to attend to." He pulled nervously on his muttonchop whiskers and mumbled under his breath again, "Don't see what the purpose of all this silly playacting is about."

"Where is Lady Alyssa?" Lady Chubb demanded to know, as if it were her right both to demand and to know. "She should be here to oversee this kind of thing. It was her idea."

"Actually, the masque was originally the marquess's idea, but my lady will be joining us shortly," Blunt assured the woman coolly.

"Why did she miss yesterday's rehearsal? We were all supposed to be here at three o'clock sharp and not a minute later. Has the lady of the manor taken to her bed with a headache again, or is she merely longer at her prayers?"

Miles would *not* appreciate being called a "headache" by Lady Chubb, Alyssa thought with some small amount of amusement. She had heard and seen quite enough through the crack in the ballroom door. She inhaled a fortifying breath, put her shoulders back and her chin up, opened the door wide, and prepared to enter the fray.

"Ah! There she is now. Didn't I tell you she would be arriving at any moment to clear up this business?" claimed Lady Chubb as she pranced toward Alyssa, resplendent in an afternoon tea gown of moss-green faille with lavender piping at the neck and sleeves.

"Good afternoon, Lady Chubb. Good afternoon, everyone. My apologies for being late." She would not explain the reason she was late. Any more than she would explain why she'd missed yesterday's rehearsal. The truth was, she had just gotten dressed for the first time in nearly two days. She had spent the past thirty-odd wonderful, scandalous hours without a stitch of clothing on. Her husband had found he liked her best in "flesh tones."

She'd had a dickens of a time this morning, sorting through her wardrobe from several seasons past, trying to find an acceptable gown to put on. The final selection was a simple pink muslin, markedly out of fashion even by West Country standards, but it was one of the few things she had unearthed that wasn't black or gray.

She had a few tender bruises, and there were certain parts of her body that were stiff and sore, as if she had gone horseback riding for hours and hours and it was her first time in the saddle.

Indeed, it had been.

Alyssa was delighted to discover, however, that she was an excellent horsewoman whether riding man *or* beast.

Caroline Chubb splayed a matching moss-green fan trimmed in lavender and began to flutter it back and forth in front of her ample bosom. "I don't wish to play a hag."

Alyssa looked at her and said in all innocence, "But you're perfect for the part."

The other woman looked briefly disconcerted. "I am better suited to the role of Juliet."

Alyssa looked from her guest to Blunt to Emma and back again. "I'm certain that Miss Pibble or Mr. Blunt has explained that the role of Juliet must be played by a young innocent girl like Miss Chubb."

Caroline made a condescending remark. "I don't see how your servants know so much about Shakespeare."

Alyssa felt hot anger rise inside her. It made its presence known by the bright color suddenly dotting her cheeks, the trembling in her voice and the shaking of her hands. "I am afraid, Lady Chubb, that you have been misinformed in this, as in so many other things," Alyssa stated in her best lady-of-the-manor tone.

"Misinformed?" came the haughty challenge.

"Mr. Blunt and Miss Pibble are not my servants, and you owe them an apology. Mr. Blunt has been many things in his long and illustrious career, and he is currently regarded as one of the finest amateur Thespians in all of England. Miss Emma Pibble is a scholar and historian of the first rank. Why, only recently a prestigious literary society published her essay discussing the irony in Shakespeare's light and dark comedies."

The resulting apology was perfunctory at best, but it would have to do, she supposed.

Lady Chubb was one of those women who always had to have the last word. "I understand you're playing a nun in our little theatrical production, Lady

Alyssa. The role is perfectly suited for you. You won't even have to pretend for the part." She added in a deliberately pointed tone, "The rest of us, of course, rehearsed for hours yesterday while you were malingering in bed."

She hadn't exactly been malingering, Alyssa reflected, amused.

"Is that a smile?" Lady Chubb demanded to know.

"Yes. It is."

"What kind of smile are you smiling, my lady?"

"It's just a smile," Alyssa said offhandedly.

Eventually the moment would present itself and she would have to tell Sir Hugh Pureheart and the Chubbs about her marriage to Miles. But this wasn't the time or the place, and Caroline Chubb was already in fine form this afternoon.

Suddenly a true-life drama was being playing out in the alcove.

Miss Charmel Chubb sprang to her feet, threw down her script, and declared, "I can't go on with this charade, Hugh."

Whereupon she burst into tears, covered her face, and ran for the balcony, where in seasons long past young ladies—fans and hearts aflutter—and their gentlemen retreated for a breath of fresh air and a moment of privacy.

Hugh Pureheart simply sat there, looking nonplussed, waiting for someone to explain to him what the devil was going on. He obviously didn't have a clue.

Blunt, ever the diplomat, drew the cast's attention away from the unhappy young woman. "Lady Chubb, perhaps you would consider reciting a few of Desdemona's wonderful lines from *Othello*. If you open your script to page thirty-four and read the first two speeches in scene two, I believe you will see what I mean."

Alyssa went to Charmel Chubb on the balcony. She sat down in a chair beside the beautiful young woman, who was even more beautiful with tears streaming down her face.

"Mother says I am to marry the marquess," the girl finally managed to get out, her mouth atremble.

"Which marquess?"

Charmel Chubb twisted the delicate handkerchief in her hand until it ripped down the center. "The Marquess of Cork, of course. She tells me I have no choice."

Alyssa was gentle. "Your mother cannot insist that you marry the marquess."

Charmel looked up. "Yes, she can. You don't know my mother. She can make people do whatever she wants them to. She is a very determined woman."

Alyssa regarded the girl with what she hoped was a calm demeanor. "Let me put it this way, Miss Chubb. You cannot marry the Marquess of Cork because he is already married."

Charmel's mouth dropped open. "The gentleman is married?"

"Yes."

The next words out of her young mouth were: "The cad! To present himself all this time as an eligible bachelor!"

"He isn't a cad. He has only very recently married." Alyssa patted her hand. "So you see, you are free to follow the dictates of your heart and wed Sir Hugh if that is what you wish."

"But it is not what *I* wish," came a haughty voice from behind them. "And I will beg you to keep your nose out of what is none of your business, Lady Alyssa."

"Mother, I don't—I can't—marry the marquess because he is already married," Charmel announced, trying to dry her tears and realizing only then that she had torn her hanky asunder.

She wasn't a bad sort, Alyssa thought. Not like the mother.

Lady Chubb appeared thunderstruck. Indeed, she appeared to be furious. Her violet eyes narrowed to two thin, almost colorless slits. "Who told you such nonsense?"

Alyssa stood and prepared for battle. "I told Miss Chubb. And it isn't nonsense."

"You told my daughter that Miles St. Aldford is married?"

Alyssa squared her shoulders. "I did."

Lady Chubb took a menacing step forward. "Why?"

Alyssa stood her ground. "It happens to be true."

An ugly sneer spread across the beautiful woman's features. "Where would you hear something like that? Don't tell me you're now privy to the marquess's private life."

Alyssa braced herself. "As a matter of fact, I am."

Lady Chubb's expression froze. "You are the marquess's hostess. Nothing more."

"That may have been true in the beginning. . . ."

The woman's mind was obviously working furiously. "Are you implying that *you* married the marquess?"

Alyssa took a slow, deep breath. "I'm implying nothing. I did marry the marquess."

"But you are to be a nun."

"I've changed my mind. Or I should say that Miles helped me change my mind."

Lady Chubb spoke loud enough to wake the dead. "You are the new Marchioness of Cork?"

This brought the entire assemblage to attention inside the ballroom. Hugh's mouth dropped open. Sir Alfred stood and blinked several times, not certain what was going on. Blunt and Miss Pibble turned and smiled at each other.

"I am the new Marchioness of Cork."

"It must be some kind of jest, some kind of practical joke."

"I assure you, it isn't. I don't play practical jokes on people. I don't like practical jokes." But Alyssa suddenly realized that Caroline Chubb was perfectly capable of doing so . . . and who knew how much more?

Lady Chubb wasn't finished with her interrogation. "Why would the marquess marry you?"

"Our reasons for marrying are no one's business but our own," she said.

The lady snapped her fan shut and made a most unpleasant sound. "He undoubtedly felt sorry for you."

"That was not one of the reasons."

There was a sly, superior air about Caroline Chubb when she next claimed, "There are things you know nothing about, Lady Alyssa."

"Lady Cork to you, Lady Chubb."

"Ask your husband why he went to London."

"It wasn't to see his mistress," Alyssa stated.

Lady Chubb shrugged. "Perhaps not. I wonder why he went, then. I wonder what he discovered while he was poking his bloody nose into other people's business. You, dear lady, may be more than a little surprised by the answer."

Sir Alfred came alive. "Caroline, don't! Not yet. It's too soon."

Lady Chubb snapped at her husband, "Shut up, Alfred." She seemed to turn her own bitterness into hateful accusations. "Miles St. Aldford married you because he knows you'll soon have no place to live."

Alyssa went still.

"The rightful owners will soon be coming to claim this magnificent old abbey that you have called home for your entire life." Lady Chubb laughed. "Your husband made you his wife because he felt sorry for a homeless young woman. Run along and find him. Ask him if it isn't true."

Alyssa's heart was pounding in her ears. She couldn't seem to breathe. She couldn't seem to think. Lady Chubb's attack had been so vicious and unexpected. It couldn't be true. Not about the abbey. Not about Miles and herself.

Alyssa regained momentary control of herself. "You'll have to excuse me, but I won't stay here and listen to this woman's lies." Then she put her head up and her shoulders back and exited the ballroom like a queen.

She bumped into Miles at the door. She could tell from the thunderous expression on her husband's face that he had heard every word exchanged between Lady Chubb and herself.

"Miles?"

"Not now, Alyssa." He was a stranger to her. "There is something I have to see to first."

Miles St. Aldford hadn't denied a thing. Every word was true. Alyssa picked up her skirts and ran.

Miles stormed into the ballroom, came to a halt, dropped his fists to his sides, and took it all in in a single glance.

"I'm so sorry, my lord," Blunt stepped forward first. "None of us saw it coming."

"I understand congratulations are in order, Lord Cork," Lady Chubb said sweetly—too sweetly. "I believe I saw your little bride run in that direction."

"You don't have time to worry about my wife, Lady Chubb. You are going to be busy."

"Busy, my lord?"

"Packing."

"Packing what, my lord?"

"Your belongings," Miles spit out. "You have made a grave error in judgment, madam." he said in a voice so frightening that it left the others trembling in their shoes. "I want you, your husband, your daughter, and your entire entourage gone from this house by morning."

"We don't always get what we *want*, my lord."

The woman's nerve was unbelievable. However, his military training was invaluable. Miles lowered his voice to nearly a whisper. "You will leave the abbey, the valley, the West Country. If you do not go willingly, I will personally assist the authorities in throwing you out."

Charmel Chubb burst into tears.

Sir Alfred's face was chalky white.

Caroline Chubb's voice dripped venom. "You will rue this day, my lord."

"I doubt it, my lady," Miles shot back with a cold sneer.

"Charmel. Alfred. Francesca. Come." Lady Chubb rallied her troops. When she reached the door of the ballroom, she paused and glanced back over her shoulder at him. "It isn't over yet, Lord Cork."

Chapter Twenty-four

The door to her bedroom was locked.

Miles knew because he had tried to turn the door handle and it wouldn't open.

Next, he knocked and softly called out her name. "Alyssa."

There was no answer, but he knew his lady wife was in there. Every now and then he could detect the sound of her footsteps pacing back and forth, and then occasionally what he sensed was a muffled sob.

Miles rammed his fingers through his hair in a frustrated gesture. Christ, she was crying.

He knocked again and spoke louder. "Alyssa. It's Miles."

"Go away," he heard in a voice that he scarcely recognized as being his wife's.

He sighed heavily and pressed his forehead to the door. "We need to talk, my lady."

"All we do is talk, my lord. You said so yourself." After a moment, she added, "Why didn't you tell me?"

Miles knew this was coming. He still didn't have a good answer—or what Alyssa would consider a good answer, anyway. He shrugged his shoulders. "I should have."

"But you didn't," came the irrefutable fact.

He soundlessly beat his fist against the wall on one side of the bedroom door. "I was trying to protect you, Alyssa."

"Oh, you mean 'ignorance is bliss.'"

"Sometimes it is. I didn't have enough information to proceed on. All my sources—"

"You mean spies, don't you?"

"All my sources could find out was that someone had been looking into the background of the Earls of Graystone and the legal writs for Graystone Abbey. That isn't considered a crime in this country," he reminded her. "It's usually just some harmless old historian doing his research."

"You suspected it was the Chubbs and you didn't even tell me. You didn't warn me."

"I was here to protect you."

"My knight in shining ar—mor."

Her voice broke on the last word, and Miles hated himself, hated Lady Chubb, hated all the rotten Chubbs for breaking the most uncorrupted heart he had ever known.

"Alyssa, please unlock the door and let me come in."

"No."

"I'm your husband."

There was a short, brittle pause. "Why did you marry me, Lord Cork?"

He'd known that one was coming, too. "I'll only be too happy to tell you, Lady Cork, if you will let me in."

There was silence. Then: "We were supposed to be partners. We were supposed to be equals."

"I know." He knew.

"You didn't mean any of it," came the damning accusation. "You lied to me."

"Alyssa?"

"Go away, my lord. I don't want to talk anymore."

"Alyssa, please!"

Silence greeted him.

Hell and damnation, if it were anyone but his wife inside that room, behind that door, he would kick the frigging thing in. But that wouldn't solve the problem. He had to see Alyssa face-to-face, not talk to her through a wooden door.

The lady was right. They talked too much. Sometimes it was better to let nature take its course. If only he could see her, kiss her, hold her. He could make everything all right again.

Miles St. Aldford looked around the feminine sitting room, spotted a chintz sofa that was about half his length, stretched out on it, and tried to make himself comfortable.

His lady wife had to come out of her bedroom eventually, and when she did, he would be waiting for her.

She must have fallen asleep. When Alyssa raised her head from the pillow and looked around, the room was dark. She sat up and peered at the carriage clock on the table beside her bed. It looked like twelve o'clock.

That meant it was twelve o'clock midnight.

She had slept for hours.

Well, first she'd lain awake for several hours, thinking. That was after her husband had ceased pounding on her bedroom door and had quit trying to "reason" with her.

Trust was a fragile thing between friends, between partners, between a husband and a wife. Once that trust had been broken, it wasn't easy to restore.

Miles should have told her everything. She told him everything.

Well, almost everything.

She had to confess that she'd never mentioned seeing the knight with the Crusader's cross on his tunic in the mist. It happened the day she'd found herself locked in the Grotto. One moment there he was across the lake, and the next he was gone.

Maybe she hadn't told Miles because she was afraid he wouldn't believe her. Or maybe she hadn't wanted him to worry about her. Whatever the reason, she'd tried to protect him by keeping him ignorant of the facts.

Just as he had tried to protect her.

But the same argument didn't hold true for their marriage. She had told the truth and he had lied.

That wasn't quite right, either.

She hadn't actually lied; she had simply omitted to tell him everything. He apparently had done the same. The difference was she had omitted to tell him that she loved him, that she adored him, that he was everything she had ever dreamed of in a husband.

Miles's sin was far graver. If what Lady Chubb said was true, Miles had married her to give her a home.

It wasn't the worst reason she had heard of for getting married.

Actually, it was rather sweet.

Tomorrow morning, at a reasonable hour, after they'd had their coffee and a light breakfast, she and the marquess would sit down and straighten a few things out between them. No more secrets. No more sins of omission. No more ignorance is protection.

In the meanwhile, Alyssa realized, the sound she heard was a growling coming from her own stomach. She was famished. Her appetite for food had been nonexistent the past few days. She blushed to think of the reason.

Cook would have something delectable in the pantry. Cook always did. Maybe a cherry tart, or a bit of pudding, or a loaf of fresh baked bread and homemade currant jam.

Alyssa's stomach growled louder.

She slipped off the bed and tiptoed across the room to the door. Years of experience in sneaking out to the rose garden had taught her where every telltale groan in the floorboards were, where every piece of furniture stuck out, and which doors squeaked. She always kept her doors well oiled.

In a matter of minutes, she was across the sitting room and out into the hallway. From there, it was a straight shot down the back stairs and into the kitchen.

The pantry was a veritable treasure trove: There were cherry and peach tarts, two kinds of pudding, leftover lamb, fresh bread and shortbread, fruit of every variety—she decided to pass on the fruit—

thick wedges of cheese under white cloth—she sliced off just a sliver of the Stilton—and a pitcher of buttermilk.

She had just poured herself a glass of buttermilk, with which to wash down her midnight repast, when she thought she heard something out in the hall. She held the milk in her mouth, not daring to even swallow, and waited.

There it was again.

Alyssa set the glass down, slipped across the kitchen, silently pushed the door open until it was ajar several inches, and peered around the corner.

Someone was there. Someone was tiptoeing through the house. From the size of the body, she guessed it was a man, and he was carrying something over one shoulder. She couldn't see what it was.

The figure stopped in front of a moonlit window and turned around. Alyssa quickly pulled back in the shadows and watched. She could see a face.

It was Sir Alfred Chubb, and he was up to no good.

Chapter Twenty-five

Alfred Chubb knew he was being followed.

At first he'd thought it was the lady's tomcat. She gave the monster free run of the abbey and the gardens at night. Then he realized it was the lady herself. She was as curious as a cat, that one.

Curiosity killed the cat; satisfaction brought it back. The childhood ditty ran through his head.

He could do without women or cats. They were both too bleeding independent, had minds of their own, went their own way and didn't come around unless they felt like it, and they were sneaky.

A friend once told him over a pint of ale at the Pea & Cock that there were two days when a woman was a pleasure: the day a man married her and the day he buried her.

That was the way Alfred felt right now.

Charmel hadn't stopped crying since the ugly scene in the ballroom this afternoon. He couldn't say he blamed Sir Hugh for turning tail and running at the first opportunity. Frankly, the baronet was smarter than Alfred had given him credit for.

Caroline and Francesca were packing. He didn't understand much *Français*—only a few basic words like *merci* and *bonsoir* and how much will you pay for a pair of chubbs; he used to know how to say that in six languages—but his wife's French maid was jabbering away to her and he didn't think any God-fearing church man would want to know what the two of them were saying to each other.

Miles St. Aldford was another piece of business, altogether. The marquess wasn't one of those namby-pamby aristocrats who refused to get his hands dirty. From what he'd heard, the man was trouble. Real trouble. Deadly trouble. Alfred couldn't imagine what Caroline had been thinking of, going after first Lady Alyssa and then Lord Cork like that. Sometimes he didn't understand the woman.

Sometimes he didn't understand women.

What was he going to do about the young woman following him?

This was his last chance to get down into Ariadne's Thread and take a good look around, thanks to Caroline. If only his wife had kept her mouth shut this afternoon—but she hadn't. She'd insulted their hostess, royally duked off the marquess, managed to get them kicked off the premises, and nearly gave the whole show away.

It didn't make his job any easier.

People didn't think he was clever. Not his wife. Not his daughter. Not his former business associates, most of whom he'd owned lock, stock and barrel before it was all over. It didn't bother him. Being underestimated gave a man an advantage, a slight edge, and sometimes that was the only difference between winning and losing. He'd come too long and too far and he'd worked too hard to lose now.

What was he going to do about the young woman following him?

He would lure the lady into Ariadne's Thread. People were always wandering into mazes, getting lost and never being heard from again. Or so he'd heard.

He knew just the spot for Lady Alyssa. Or should he say Lady Cork? It must have been used by a hermit or a religious recluse at one time, maybe as self-punishment or penance, certainly some kind of solitary confinement. Once his "shadow" was shut in, he could go about his work undisturbed. He'd let her out again, of course, before he closed the trapdoor.

Or, at least, he thought he would. . . .

Miles shot straight up in his bed and gave a shout.

Only he wasn't in his bed. As a matter of fact, he wasn't in a bed at all. He wasn't even on the chintz sofa in Alyssa's sitting room where he remembered lying down a few hours ago. In fact, he seemed to be stretched out on the floor of the sitting room: At least it was long enough for his legs.

What time was it?

What had awakened him?

Why couldn't he move?

He knew the answer to the last question. There was a weight on his chest. It moved. And it made a sound.

"Tom?" Miles reached up with one hand and encountered soft, thick fur. "Tom."

The rest of his questions weren't answered in order. Somewhere nearby a chiming clock sounded the hour.

One.

Jesus, Mary, and Joseph! He'd been asleep for hours. The last he recalled knowing the time, it had been ten o'clock in the evening. Three hours ago.

Miles suddenly knew what had awakened him, too. He'd had the dream. The one in which he was being chased by someone—or some*thing*—through the labyrinth. Ariadne's Thread. He wondered if by some awful chance Alyssa had had the same nightmare again as well.

"Sorry, Tom, I've got to move," he apologized, urging the cat off his chest and rolling onto his side in preparation for standing up. That's when Miles turned his head and saw the door to Alyssa's bedroom standing wide open.

He was on his feet in an instant.

In the next instant, he was at the door of his wife's bedroom and searching for the lamp, a candle, a match, anything. He settled for the moonlight. The bed was empty. The room was empty. Alyssa was gone. Apparently, while he'd slept, she had blithely walked right past him and out into the hallway.

Why?

Where would she go in the middle of the night?

Milady's Bower.

Miles raced to the window. There was no sign of her, or of anyone, in the moonlit garden below. That was no guarantee she wasn't there, of course . . . except for Tom's presence in the house. If she'd gone for a midnight walk in the rose garden, her guardian angel would have accompanied her.

"Where is she, Tom?" he asked the huge ginger-colored cat as it wrapped itself around his legs. "Do you know?"

Miles was getting that feeling again. The one he didn't like, the one that always meant trouble was close at hand, the one, however, that had saved his life—and Blunt's—on several past occasions.

The same two questions niggled at him. Why would Alyssa get up in the middle of the night? Where would she go?

She was too thoughtful of others to disturb Emma Pibble at this late hour. She had too much common sense to leave the abbey to go riding or visit the family cemetery.

The list was short. She was wide awake and had gone to the study to read. She was hungry and had gone to the kitchen to eat. She was troubled and had gone to the chapel to pray. Miles would not allow himself to consider any other possibilities. Not yet.

"We'll start with the study and work our way through the list," Miles heard himself say to his companion.

He caught a glimpse of himself in Alyssa's mirror. He looked like hell. He hadn't washed or shaved or brushed his hair. He *had* slept in his clothes.

A quick visit to the Knight's Chambers resulted in a favorite knife going into his boot and his revolver down the back of his belt. He didn't want to unnecessarily frighten anyone, so he kept his jacket on and brushed his fingers through his hair.

He was not an alarmist by nature, Miles reflected as he opened the door of the Knight's Chambers and noiselessly moved out into the hallway and through the sleeping abbey toward the study, but there were untrustworthy people and unexplained events in this house.

It wasn't until he'd slipped into the book-lined study, flattened himself against the wall, and looked around that Miles realized his wife's oversized tomcat was right beside him.

Alyssa wasn't in the study. It didn't appear as if she or anyone else had been here recently. The fire was laid for morning but remained unlit. The lamp was cold. There were no used candles. The papers were neatly stacked on the desk.

Keeping to the shadows and avoiding the revealing moonlight as much as possible, Miles headed in the direction of the kitchen. Here, it was another story altogether. The pantry door was ajar. A glass of buttermilk had been left on the table. Fresh crumbs—shortbread, from the looks of them—were scattered underfoot.

Miles went down on his haunches, reached out, and retrieved a single important clue from among the crumbs: It was a long, silky strand of blond hair.

Alyssa had been here, and not so long ago.

She wasn't here now.

His brow wrinkled in speculation. What had made the lady leave her midnight repast in such a hurry? There weren't any signs of a struggle, so he assumed she'd left voluntarily. Had she heard something? Had she seen something? If so, had she decided to investigate on her own rather than include her partner?

Miles knew Alyssa was sorely disappointed in him. He had vowed they would be partners and equals, and then he hadn't kept his vow. He hadn't told her the truth about his trip to London. He hadn't shared his suspicions concerning the Chubbs. He had never mentioned the incident in the library when he'd caught Sir Alfred poking his nose into her family history.

Of far greater importance, Miles knew, was his failure to tell Alyssa how much he loved the look of her, the feel of her, how he loved her eyes, her laugh, her kiss, her caress.

He had not told his lady wife that he loved her, that he couldn't imagine his life without her now, that he wouldn't have any life without her. He hadn't mentioned that she brought joy to his every moment, that she gladdened his heart, that she cast a brilliant light on the dark side of his soul.

He wouldn't make the same mistake twice. Miles only hoped and prayed it wasn't too late. The sin of omission could exact a high price: his wife's trust and affections, his marriage, her safety. If someone had harmed even one hair on Alyssa's precious head, he would make them pay a price they would never forget.

He made for the Lady Chapel. Two nights before, he had also come to the small medieval church at midnight—for his wedding. It had been a time of white roses and candlelight, holy solemnity and vows exchanged, gathered friends and the blessing of loved ones.

Now the chapel was dark and deserted.

Miles stepped inside and waited. From long years of training and habit, he stood without moving, without making a sound, almost without breathing.

He became part of the chapel: a block of the stone wall, a section of a wooden pew, a piece of an ancient statue.

He was right.

Alyssa wasn't here, either.

He was wrong.

The chapel wasn't deserted.

There was a faint light at the front of the church near the altar: the glow of a lantern, perhaps. Then the sound of metal scraping against metal could be heard. It sent chills down Miles's spine. But it was the oddest thing. The sound seemed to be coming *not* from behind the altar, but from *beneath* it.

It was time he took a closer look.

"For the love of God!" Miles exclaimed softly as he reached the front of the chapel and found the altar pushed to one side.

There was a gaping hole in the floor of the church and a flight of stone stairs leading to a subterranean vault. He could see down fifteen, maybe twenty feet to the bottom of the steps, where a second lantern illuminated a series of passageways.

He should have known.

He should have guessed.

It wasn't an uncommon practice five hundred, a thousand years ago. For beneath the Lady Chapel, perhaps lost to time and memory, were the crypts of the dead.

Catacombs.

Chapter Twenty-six

She should have known better.

It had been an obvious trap from the outset. Alyssa wasn't so much afraid as she was angry and displeased with herself. Not that she was particularly pleased with Sir Alfred Chubb. Emma Pibble had been right all along: He was *not* a gentleman.

She had followed him into the chapel and watched with fascination as he'd pushed the altar to one side and then employed a special steel crowbar to pry something open in the floor. To her amazement, several moments later, Sir Alfred seemed to simply disappear. Naturally, she had moved closer, discovered the entrance to the catacombs, and carefully made her way down the ancient stone steps.

She had taken the bait beautifully.

She had been peering curiously into the tiny cell at the bottom of the steps—it was no more than a niche carved out of the wall of the subterranean chamber—when a strong hand had caught her between the shoulder blades and propelled her forward. The door of the cell had been slammed shut behind her and the key turned in the lock.

She was a prisoner.

Then she had heard Sir Alfred mumbling under his breath as he shuffled off along the passageway of the underground mausoleum: "That should keep the young lady out of my hair. Now, where did I put my map of Ariadne's Thread?"

Ariadne's Thread?

An idea began to form in Alyssa's head. Actually, several were. The first one pertained to getting out of this ridiculously tiny room. She had no intentions of sitting here on a hard, cold stone bench and waiting docilely for a knight in shining armor to rescue her. This time she was going to rescue herself.

Alyssa stuck her fingers into the disheveled hair piled atop her head—most of her hair was tumbling down about her shoulders, anyway—and rummaged around for a hairpin. The first one was too small. But she found what she was looking for on her second attempt: a large, strong specimen with a pointed tip on one end.

She stuck the hairpin into the ancient lock and began to gingerly move it around. If thieves and pickpockets and all kinds of unsavory types could break into locked rooms, then, Alyssa reasoned, surely an intelligent and nimble-fingered woman could break out of one.

She was making some small amount of progress, she thought optimistically, when she suddenly heard a man's voice outside the recluse's cell.

"Alyssa, are you in there?" came the whispered query.

"Miles?"

"Yes."

"Yes, I am," she whispered back, her spirits soaring.

"What the devil are you doing?" She could hear the exasperation in her husband's voice and something else ... something that sounded to her like fear.

"I'm trying to pick the lock with my hairpin," she told him.

"Bloody hell, madam," Miles swore feelingly, forgetting to lower his voice.

"Keep your voice down, sir," she admonished from inside her small prison.

"Afraid I'll wake the dead?" came the sardonic whisper.

"No. But you could bring Sir Alfred rushing back from wherever he has gone."

"Stand back, wife," her husband instructed. "I'll attempt to open the door from this side."

Stand back? There was scarcely room in the tiny cell to *sit* back, Alyssa observed dryly.

A moment later, there was a solitary snap, and then the door swung open. What remained of the lock was dangling from the ancient doorframe; the rest was smashed into myriad pieces and scattered in the dust at their feet.

Miles leaned over and retrieved an object from the debris. "Your hairpin, madam."

"Thank you," she said politely, sticking it back at random in the mess on top of her head. "I must look a fright."

Miles shook his head and reached for her. "You gave me a hell of a fright."

Then Alyssa was being crushed to her husband's chest.

Dear Lord, it felt good to touch him, to cling to him, to feel his warmth, to hear the strong, steady rhythm of his heart beating beneath her ear. Alyssa realized she would like nothing better than to stand there forever with her arms wrapped around Miles's waist.

She finally put her head back and gazed up into his eyes. "How did you do that?"

"Do what?"

"Break the lock on the cell door."

He freed one arm, dove behind his back, and brought out his revolver. "I used the butt like a hammer. One good whack—"

"I thought you were going to pick the lock."

"That was my second choice."

"Do you know how to pick a lock?"

"Of course." Miles returned the revolver to his belt. "Picking locks was part of the standard training."

Alyssa arched her eyebrows. "For a spy?"

"For a spy."

"Were you any good at it?"

"I was the best," Miles informed her with an arrogant smile.

"Really?"

He held up his right hand and wiggled his fingers. "They used to say I had the magic touch."

Her husband certainly had the magic touch when it came to her, Alyssa thought to herself with a blush. "Thank you, sir, for setting me free."

"My pleasure, madam." He grasped her by the elbow. "Now, let's get out of here."

She dug in her heels. "We can't leave."

Miles frowned. "We can't? Why not?"

"I know what Ariadne's Thread is," she announced in an excited whisper.

Miles kept his voice low but audible. "So do I. It was a turf maze. We both saw what remained of it through the window of the Norman Tower. Now let's go."

Alyssa shook her head. "Sir Alfred was muttering to himself before he disappeared into the catacombs. I distinctly heard him say: 'Where did I put my map of Ariadne's Thread?'"

Her husband's eyes narrowed in speculation. He looked around at the warren of passageways, the small chamber they were standing in, the tiny recluse's cell. *"This?"*

"Yes, *this*," Alyssa confirmed. "The entire catacombs is a maze. Heaven knows how many chambers and recesses and passageways are down here. And I think it's the identical pattern repeated over and over and over again."

Miles obviously grasped the full implication of what she was telling him. "Your family crest. The medieval turf garden. The window of the Norman Tower. The layout of the catacombs." He slapped his thigh. "Of course."

"Of course," she repeated, delighted to find that they were in total agreement.

He shot her a frown. "That only leaves two questions."

"Two?"

"What is Sir Alfred doing down here?"

"I have no idea."

"Neither do I." Miles paused for effect. "And what is at the center of the labyrinth?"

Alyssa dug her teeth into her bottom lip. "I think I know. I have to find out for sure."

Miles exhaled. "I had a feeling you were going to say that."

She looked at him. "*Vincit omnia veritas.* Truth conquers all things. I believe the truth may also set us free."

"Us, madam?"

"All of us, sir."

"All right, but we'll have to stay alert and watch our step. Alfred Chubb is still down here wandering around looking for something," Miles cautioned, handing her a lantern.

"I wonder what he's looking for."

Miles shrugged. "The Minotaur?" He took a second lantern down from the wall and made sure both were working properly before they started into the labyrinth.

Alyssa whispered at his back. "With any luck, perhaps the Minotaur will find Sir Alfred."

"How well armed is Chubb?"

"I only saw a large steel crowbar."

"It's the weapons you didn't see that worry me." Miles slipped his hand under his jacket in the back. She knew he was double-checking the position of his revolver. "We will give this one chance, madam. Even if we don't find what you're looking for, we turn around and march out of here. Do you understand?"

Alyssa realized he was deadly serious. "I understand."

"Frankly, I don't mind telling you, it makes me nervous to be heading into a strategic situation where I know there's only one way out."

"I don't believe Sir Alfred is dangerous."

"Any man can be dangerous if he finds himself unexpectedly cornered," Miles informed her with a grim expression.

Alyssa sensed a familiar presence and glanced down to find Tom rubbing his face against her skirts. "You didn't tell me you'd brought help," she remarked to Miles.

"Help?"

Reaching down, she scratched behind the tomcat's ear. "Tom has a wonderful sense of direction. He's going to help us find our way to the center of the maze."

Lanterns in hand, they set off through Ariadne's Thread—Miles in the lead, Alyssa one step behind him. Tom wound back and forth between them, occasionally scouting ahead, only to return and seemingly wait for the humans to catch up with him.

Fifteen minutes later, they came to a crossroads. It was a high-ceilinged chamber with narrow passageways spreading out in four different directions.

"They all look the same," Miles said unnecessarily.

"They look the same, but they aren't the same," Alyssa told him, knowing she had no choice now but to trust her instincts. She closed her eyes and stood there.

"Madam," her husband inquired after three or four minutes of dead silence, "what are you doing?"

"I'm thinking," she mouthed.

"Do you think this is the time or place?"

Alyssa nodded her head and kept her eyes shut. "I'm trying to picture Ariadne's Thread."

"A damned fine sense of direction and a compass would hold you in better stead."

She disagreed. "You once confided to me that it was your instinct for trouble that had saved your life several times. My instincts tell me now that if we want to find the heart of the maze, we have to go on faith, intuition, trust, whatever name you wish to put to it." Alyssa opened her eyes. "It's this way."

"We're approaching something," Miles warned her. "Let's be very quiet until we see what it is."

Alyssa knew that he was concerned it might include the missing Sir Alfred.

They came to an arched doorway that opened up into a larger chamber. Even with only their lanterns to shed light on the room, Alyssa could still see it was a small church. There were carved figures along the walls and an elaborate chandelier overhead. An altar stood at the front with a magnificent stone cross in the center.

"What is this place?" Miles asked in a hushed voice. "It looks like a church."

"It is a church," she whispered back.

"There," he said, raising his arm to point. "There's something in the center."

Lanterns held high, they approached the very heart of the maze together.

Alyssa could see two huge blocks of granite. Then

a distinct and unmistakable outline. "Dear God, Miles"—she grabbed his arm with her free hand—"it's a body."

"Not a body," Miles corrected her as they advanced toward the tombs, "but an effigy. Actually, two effigies. I want you to stay put, Alyssa. I'm going to see if the torches along the walls of the crypt still have anything left in them that will burn."

They did.

The torches appeared to be made of some kind of oil-soaked material. Miles soon had three or four lit. They didn't burn brightly, but it was enough to see by.

He returned to his wife's side. She was like a statue. She didn't move. She didn't speak. She simply stood and stared at the two burial vaults and the two marble effigies carved into their tops.

The first figure was that of a handsome knight. His features were strong, intelligent, surprisingly youthful. He was portrayed wearing a Crusader's tunic with the familiar cross on the front. His carved hands were placed one over the other, and he was grasping a great stone sword.

Miles studied the effigy of the man in front of him, then glanced over at the second figure. It was a woman and there was something vaguely familiar about her. He circled around the knight's tomb, held his lantern up, and stared in amazement.

The lady was beautiful. Her face was young, serene, intelligent. She was dressed in a long, flowing gown. Her hands were posed in front of her, clasping a bouquet of stone roses.

"It's the face in the ~~window~~," he said.

"It's *his* face," Alyssa said in a hoarse whisper as she stood and stared at the knight.

"It's *her* face," Miles said, not understanding. "I only caught a glimpse of it that afternoon, but it's her face all the same."

"The lady and her knight."

Miles moved to the corner of the granite tombs. "There are Latin inscriptions on the end of each coffin."

Together, they translated the words etched into the stone centuries before.

"*Hic jacet*—here lies," Alyssa read aloud, "Robert the Bold, loyal knight and king's Crusader, dedicated servant to his God, devoted father and loving husband." Her voice broke on the last two words. "Born 1166. Died 1209."

Miles read aloud the inscription on the lady's tomb. "Her lies Ariadne, brave heart and queen's lady, dedicated servant to her God, devoted mother and loving wife. Born 1169. Died 1209."

"She was only twenty, a year younger than I am now, when Robert left her to accompany King Richard to Jerusalem," Alyssa murmured.

Miles checked the dates on Robert's sarcophagus. "He was only twenty-three."

"They were so young."

"Younger than we are now." He was already thirty.

Alyssa slipped her hand into his and said, "Robert did come back to her."

Miles looked down into his wife's rapt face. "Yes, he did come back to her."

He understood now why the love of the right woman could, would keep a man alive through the horrors of war, the awful stench of death on the battlefield, raging fire, famine, pestilence. None of it mattered if a man had something, some*one*, to return to. He would walk through hell itself to get back to Alyssa.

His lady wife finished the story of the lady and the knight for him. "They were married. They had children. They lived happily, and when the time came, they were buried here together in this sacred place so they could be together throughout all eternity."

"Throughout all eternity," Miles repeated as if it were a scared vow. He turned to Alyssa. "I understand how Robert the Bold felt. I want to spend eternity with you, my love."

Alyssa smiled at him through her tears. "And I want to spend eternity with you—"

There was a harsh laugh from the door of the crypt. "Odd as that may seem, it can be arranged."

They both jumped to their feet and turned.

"Damn you, Chubb!" Miles swore.

"Sir Alfred!" came a feminine gasp from beside him.

The man sneered unpleasantly. "At your service, Lady Alyssa. Or should I say Lady Cork?"

Chapter Twenty-seven

When he'd needed it most, his instinct for trouble had failed him, Miles St. Aldford reflected harshly as he stood and watched Alfred Chubb point a revolver at Alyssa.

He fought to compose himself. "This is a mistake, Chubb," Miles said in a deadly soft voice that more than one enemy would have recognized and trembled at the sound of.

"It certainly is. First, the mistake was your lady's. She should never have followed me tonight. Then the mistake was yours coming to look for her. If the two of you had stayed put in your rooms, none of this would have happened."

"Sir Alfred, what are you doing down here in the catacombs?" Alyssa asked.

The man's attention turned away from Miles and centered on Alyssa. "You are the curious one, aren't you?" Alfred Chubb laughed, but it wasn't a very pleasant sound. "That is precisely what I was thinking to myself when I realized it was you, my lady, following me and not that bloody awful cat of yours. I said to myself, 'She's as curious as a cat, that one.'

Then I remembered a childhood ditty that used to go through my head: *Curiosity killed the cat . . .*"

"Satisfaction brought it back," Alyssa finished for him.

"Well, now, I don't know if I can promise you satisfaction, Lady Cork. It is Lady Cork, isn't it? You went through a legal wedding ceremony, I presume?"

Alyssa put her nose a notch higher in the stagnant air of the catacombs and stated, "As a matter of fact, Sir Alfred, the marquess and I were married by special license upstairs in the Lady Chapel just two nights ago."

Time, Miles thought to himself. He needed time. Time to think. Time to plan. Time to come up with a strategy that would get them out of this unholy mess without anyone ending up hurt . . . or dead. He hoped his bride could manage to keep the man talking. Alfred Chubb wasn't likely to use his weapon if he was busy chatting.

"I know you're a respected amateur historian, Sir Alfred," Alyssa remarked as if she were sitting in her formal parlor and entertaining the gentleman for tea. "These catacombs must be a virtual treasure trove for you. Why, you'll be famous for having discovered them. I would think that historical societies all over the British Isles, perhaps even on the Continent, would be clamoring to hear your story and learn your research techniques. You, Sir Alfred, have written your own place in history tonight," she declared with a definite flair for the melodramatic.

"I'm not interested in the history of the crypts," the red-faced gentleman confessed; apparently the exertion of hunting through the catacombs had been more than he was used to. "But I am interested in finding the treasure you mentioned."

Alyssa's face went blank. "Treasure?"

Alfred Chubb waved his revolver in a threatening manner. "The treasure trove."

"But, sir, I was speaking in metaphorical terms."

"I don't care what terms you were speaking in, my lady. I want to know where the treasure is hidden."

"What treasure?"

His face screwed up into a furious scowl. "The treasure that Robert the Bold brought back with him from the Crusades."

She blinked several times in rapid succession. "Did he?"

"He did."

Alyssa shrugged her shoulders. "I've been hearing that fairy tale since I was a little girl, of course. I assumed it was nothing more than the usual family legend," she confessed. "I wouldn't put much stock in it if I were you, Sir Alfred."

"The usual family legend?" he repeated, incredulous.

"Everyone I know has a family legend or two; usually it involves treasure. Sometimes it's a family ghost." She bestowed a brilliant smile on her surely unwanted and certainly now undesirable houseguest. "We at Graystone Abbey are most fortunate. We have both."

Miles noticed that Sir Alfred was beginning to sweat profusely despite the cool temperature in the underground chamber. With any luck, the man's hands would perspire as well. Chubb's grasp on his revolver might well start to slip.

"You don't have a ghost at the abbey," Alfred Chubb contradicted her with a snicker, as if he were in on some private joke.

"We don't?"

He shook his head and laughed out loud this time. "I only found out tonight myself. It's some third-rate actor Caroline hired to play the part. Every now and then he dresses up in his Crusader's costume, prances around on his horse, and waves his sword in the air. She said it was meant to be a diversion, that it was intended to keep the marquess here busy chasing after shadows."

"That was not very kind of you, Sir Alfred."

"I'm not a very kind man, Lady Cork. And, in case you failed to notice, my wife is not a kind woman."

Miles could see Alyssa's cheeks were quite pink. She would not enjoy being made a fool of. "I assume it was supposed to divert our attention from the fact that you were intending to steal my ancestral home from me."

Sir Alfred smiled. "Oh, I still intend to take Graystone Abbey from you," he announced. "But I won't have to steal it. It will all be above board and legal."

Alyssa swayed. Miles wanted to reach out and steady her, but any movement on his part would draw Alfred's eye, and that was the last thing he wanted. He would make his move soon. For Chubb would eventually run out of patience with Alyssa and that was when *he* intended to strike.

Alyssa pulled herself up to her full height. "Would you care to explain your last statement, sir?"

"I have the proof I need."

Gray eyes narrowed. "The proof you need for what?"

The man's expression was pure wickedness. "To show that I'm the next in line for the title of Earl of Graystone."

His wife didn't even flinch. Miles was proud of her. He slowly moved to his left. He was going to get himself in position now.

"How can you be in line for anything, let alone for the ancestral title belonging to my family?" Alyssa demanded to know.

"We're related."

"We, sir, most certainly are not," she shot back.

Alfred Chubb dug in his pocket for a handkerchief and mopped his brow with it. If he put it back, the split second of distraction would be enough. Miles was going to dive for his ankles. Unfortunately, the man didn't.

"Whether you like it or not, Lady Cork, we are sixteenth cousins on your father's side."

"Everyone in England is undoubtedly my sixteenth cousin on my father's side," Alyssa said, trying to make light of his claim. "I will see to it, Sir Alfred, that you never inherit the title, this house, or anything that belongs to the rightful Earl of Graystone."

"And who do you think is the rightful Earl of Graystone?" he asked, his mouth twisting into an ugly line.

"My uncle, James Gray."

"Your uncle is long dead, if not buried," claimed her opponent.

"He is alive and well."

"How do you know?" came the demand.

"Because I would know it here"—Alyssa pointed to the spot above her heart—"if he were dead."

"Cock and bull!" swore Alfred Chubb.

"You will never be the Earl of Graystone," she stated determinedly.

Miles didn't like the tone of their conversation. Alyssa was pushing the man too hard. He was about to crack. Surely she saw that.

"I had intended to take you two out of here with me," Chubb said. "Now I'm reconsidering. It might make my plans go more smoothly if the current resident of the abbey was, sadly, to disappear."

Miles had to say something. "If your claim to the title is half as solid as it sounds, you don't have to do anything drastic, Chubb."

"Almost forgot you were here, Cork. You haven't had much to say for yourself."

It was time, Miles told himself.

Then it seemed to happen all at once. He spotted Tom as the cat came sashaying into the chamber, casting a huge shadow against the wall of the crypt.

"My God, Chubb!" he said, pointing.

Alfred Chubb must have caught a glimpse of something just out of range. He took his eyes off Alyssa. That was all the time Miles needed. He dove for the man's ankles and Sir Alfred tumbled to the ground like a dead weight, his revolver flying out of his hand.

"No!" he shrieked. "You'll ruin everything."

362

"You would never have been the Earl of Graystone," came another voice from the door of the chamber.

"It's the Hermit," Alyssa said.

"I don't think so," Miles told her as he got to his feet, dragging Sir Alfred with him.

"Who are you?" demanded the defeated man.

"I'm James Gray, Earl of Graystone."

Chapter Twenty-eight

"It was my eyes that told you?" James Gray repeated to Miles St. Aldford with bemusement as he sat in the study of Graystone Abbey sipping a glass of very good Napoleon brandy. The hour was late, but none of the three were interested in parting company. The events of the long night had left them wide awake.

"It was a line of poetry that kept running through my head: 'And all my nightly dreams are where thy gray eye glances.'" Miles took a sip of his brandy and turned to her. "I thought it was your gray eyes, my dear. Now I realize you and your uncle have the same gray eyes."

"I should have known you," Alyssa lamented to the man who seemed so familiar and yet was a stranger to her.

"There was no reason you should recognize me," James consoled her. "I left for India when I was a young man of nineteen. You would have been only five years old at the time."

"That was the summer before I came to stay at the abbey with your brother and his wife," Miles said. "Otherwise, we might have met as young men."

James Gray grew pensive. "I'm sorry I won't be seeing Thomas and Annemarie again."

"Father and Mother often spoke of you," Alyssa reassured him. "They would take turns reading your letters out loud during the evenings. So, you see, Uncle, I feel as though I do know you."

Miles reached for her hand on the sofa between them. "I think, in your heart, you recognized James from the first."

"Perhaps that's why you allowed me to stay in the Monk's Cave and brought me provisions," the new Earl of Graystone suggested. "All I know is it was the first decent food I'd had in . . ." a pained expression crossed his gaunt but handsome features, "I can't remember how long."

"What is the last thing you remember before you arrived here in the valley?" Alyssa inquired kindly, knowing that her uncle's memory was sporadic at best.

James Gray set his brandy glass down on the Queen Anne table at his elbow and raised his hand to his head. He massaged a spot behind his ear. "I remember the letter arriving telling me about Thomas and Annemarie. I immediately began to make arrangements to return to England, but it took several months to put my business in order. We set sail. I think there must have been a storm at sea." He rubbed his head again. "I don't recall much after that until I found my way here."

"You didn't know who you were, or even your own name?" she said softly.

"Not until yesterday," her uncle confirmed. "Somehow—only God knows how—I found my way to Graystone Abbey. I seemed to belong here. At times there would be small flashes of memory. I was swimming in the pond one evening and suddenly I knew I'd been there before, doing exactly the same thing. I stood up in the water, saw the Grotto across the pond, and I knew."

Something occurred to Alyssa. "You were the one who let me out of the Grotto that day."

James Gray nodded his head.

She stared at him in amazement. "Have you been watching over me?"

"Yes," said the earl with simplicity.

"Then you must also be 'a true friend,' " Miles interjected.

Alyssa wrinkled up her brow. "A true friend?"

Her husband turned and told her. "After the incident in the Grotto, I received a message telling me that it had been no accident and that I should protect you. It was signed 'a true friend.' "

James Gray's face took on hard lines. "I didn't suspect the Chubbs at that point, but I didn't trust them, either. Not from that first meeting on the road."

Alyssa concentrated on her small glass of brandy. It was painful to think of her uncle, Papa's younger brother, the rightful heir to his title and estate and all that went with it, being in need, not having food or clothing or shelter.

Miles gently squeezed her hand as if he knew what she was thinking, and inquired of the other man, "I assume your initial encounter with the Chubbs was an unpleasant one."

James surged to his feet and began to pace back

and forth in the book-lined study. "Miss Chubb is, at worse, ignorant, and perhaps a little thoughtless of others." He stopped and gazed upon the Canaletto across from the desk. "This has always been one of my favorite paintings: *Venice: A Palazzo, a Gondola and a View from a Bridge.*"

Alyssa smiled at him. "Mine, as well, Uncle."

He gave himself a shake and returned to the subject of Miss Charmel Chubb. "I suppose we all are a little thoughtless at her age. But her mother and father have much to answer for. There is not one drop of the milk of human kindness in Lady Caroline Chubb."

"I do not like Lady Caroline Chubb," Alyssa confessed out loud as she finished her brandy.

"Neither do I," stated Miles. "What will you do with the Chubbs now, Graystone?"

James made a gesture with his hand. "I have been mulling it over since we placed Sir Alfred under the watchful eye of Galsworthy and the lads, who have him locked in a garden shed, I believe."

"I understand from Mrs. Fetchett that Lady Chubb and her maid are nearly finished packing, and that the coach and driver are waiting at the door even as we sit here conversing," Alyssa reported.

James Gray stood a little taller for a moment. "As Earl of Graystone, I will personally escort the Chubbs to their carriage and off my property. I have several things to make clear to them."

"You're not turning them over to the authorities, then?" Miles said, his eyes following the other man as he began to pace again.

Graystone shook his head. "They are to go into exile."

Alyssa wrinkled her brow. "Exile?"

Her uncle smiled. "A small estate in the north, far from London, far from here, far from everything. Sir Alfred has admitted to me that his wife detests the place."

"Grave punishment, indeed," Miles said dryly. "Lady Chubb had visions of joining Society and running with H.R.H. and the Marlborough House Set."

James Gathier Gray chuckled under his breath. "Perhaps I should reconsider. *That* may be even graver punishment." Then he grew serious once more. "I will make it clear to the Chubbs that they are never welcome here in Devon again."

"What of Sir Alfred's claim to be next in line for your title, Uncle?" It was still of some concern to Alyssa.

This time James Gray put his handsome head back and laughed out loud. It was the first time that she had ever heard her uncle laugh. It was a wonderful sound, a glorious sound: His voice was a rich, deep baritone, not unlike her husband's. Alyssa knew then all would be well.

"Something my lady wife has said has amused you," Miles observed. "I often find that to be true, myself."

Eventually the reason for the earl's amusement was revealed. "Sir Alfred didn't do his research thoroughly enough. He overlooked one entire branch of the family tree. I checked with the solicitors yesterday, after my memory had returned. There is an offshoot of the family in Australia. A fourth cousin."

Alyssa clapped her hands together in delight. "I have always wanted to visit Australia."

Miles explained in an aside, "Your niece tells me that she has been nowhere and done nothing. In addition, she has this insatiable curiosity about everything."

It was easy for Miles and James to make jest of her thirst for knowledge. They had both seen much of the world and its people. "I want to travel and see the world."

Miles gazed at her with a look in his eye that she could not interpret. "And so you will, my lady."

She turned her attention back to her uncle. "Does our fourth cousin in Australia have any offspring?"

"As a matter of fact, he does."

"How many children does he have?"

"Eight." James added slyly, "All sons."

There was a general air of merriment in the study when the full implication was realized. Sir Alfred would be rotting in hell before he inherited the ancestral home.

Before she put the Chubbs entirely from her mind, Alyssa had one more question to ask. "What of Charmel Chubb and Sir Hugh?"

James Gray paused and stared out the window toward the east and the first hint of a new day. "The sins of the father and mother." He shook his head. "No. I will not exact a price of Miss Chubb. She isn't responsible for her parents."

"I'm glad." Alyssa rose from the sofa and came to stand beside her uncle. They stood and looked out the window together for some minutes as the gray light of dawn was transformed into a veritable rainbow of colors: pinks and reds, slashes of brilliant yellows and deep purples, lush lavenders and blues. She reached up and slipped her arm through his. "I want to thank you for being my guardian angel these past weeks, for watching over me."

"I wanted to," the long-absent gentleman explained, "even before I understood why I should want to. It was the same feeling that motivated me to attend your wedding to Cork."

Alyssa squeezed his arm. "I'm so happy you were there, Uncle Jamie."

He went still. "I believe you used to call me that when you were a very little girl."

She reached up and brushed a tear away. Her voice was full and betrayed her when Alyssa murmured, "I'm not a little girl any longer."

"Now you are a married lady and the new Marchioness of Cork," he said quietly. "You have chosen well, my dear."

There was a scratch at the door.

Alyssa went to let Tom into the study—he had been celebrating his heroic part in the night's events by consuming a bit of fish and a dish of fresh cream under the approving eye of Cook.

"What will you do now, Graystone?" Alyssa heard her husband inquire of the older man—older by, perhaps, no more than five years, as it turned out.

"Hire a butler?" her uncle answered with what she glimpsed as his usual sense of humor returning. "I understand the abbey has been without one for a number of years."

"Perhaps Blunt could be of some assistance in the matter," Miles suggested. "He might also recommend a gentleman for the position of valet." Here, the marquess paused and cleared his throat. "You might wish to consider having a new cook trained."

"A new cook? What is wrong with the old cook?" inquired Graystone, puzzled.

"Nothing is wrong with Cook. In fact, the woman works miracles in the kitchen. That is why I'm warning you."

"Warning me, Cork?"

"I intend to steal her, Graystone."

The sin of silence.

How did a man tell a woman that he loved her?

It was not enough, Miles St. Aldford decided, to shower her with gifts, no matter how rare or how priceless. Gifts could be given and gifts could taken away again. They were too flimsy, too easily dispensed with, too quickly dismissed, too much of this world.

A man could make promises to a woman. He could keep those promises, or die trying. In this way, a man could tell a woman of his love for her.

A man could make love to a woman with his body. He could kiss her, caress her, lavish her with pleasure, bring her to the brink of mindless ecstasy and share that moment with her before seeking his own moment.

Or he could simply tell her.

He could say the words to her. Not once, not twice, but for a lifetime.

For eternity.

"It is taking an eternity, husband, and I find that I do not have the patience for it," Alyssa fussed and fumed as she stormed into his sitting room, a bright green satin bodice pinned to her undergarments, a half-finished chapeau—its jaunty bright green dyed-to-match ostrich feather somewhat askew—atop her head, one green satin slipper on her foot, the other on the floor behind her, a stunned—and somewhat pale, Miles thought—courturiere poised for flight in the adjoining sitting room, a gaggle of chattering French seamstresses, pins, needles, scissors, and measuring tapes in hand, nipping at his wife's heels.

He held up one large hand. "Halt! *Arrêt!*"

Silence immediately descended on both sitting rooms. Miles enjoyed the momentary peace and quiet.

"My lord," began his lady wife, with a pointed look thrown over her shoulder at the couturiere, "I have been dressed and undressed, pinned, poked, and prodded until I am quite black and blue from it. I don't wish to continue with my fittings. I would rather wear nothing than endure one more minute of this torture." She was on the verge of tears. He could detect the first precious drop on her eyelashes.

"Out!" Miles ordered, waving the fancy designer and her entourage away with a single sweep of his arm. "The marchioness must rest. Come back tomorrow."

"*Demain?*" the couturiere finally spoke.

"*Demain.*"

There was no argument.

Within ten minutes Miles had cleared both rooms and was once more alone with his wife.

"Here, let me help you off with that ridiculous little hat," he said in a soothing tone.

Alyssa reached up and pulled the green feathered chapeau from her head and held it out in front of her. "It does look rather ridiculous on me, doesn't it?"

Quick! He had to think of what to say. "Only because you're standing in the middle of your sitting room wearing nothing but your chemise, one shoe on and one shoe off."

She gave a tired laugh and placed the hat on a nearby table. "James must sometimes wonder what has invaded his home: French seamstresses, a couturiere who could put a dowager duchess to shame when it comes to haughtiness, you, me."

"We could have had your fittings at Cork House with far greater convenience for everyone involved, but your uncle wasn't ready to be alone."

"I know," she acknowledged in a soft voice.

"I know what you need, my lady." Miles reached for her hand and drew her into the Knight's Chambers. He closed the connecting door with a resounding finality. "You need to forget about green satin and white silk, lace trimmings, whether to go *with* feathers or *without,* and all that froufrou."

Sometimes a man could tell a woman he loved her by making her laugh.

Alyssa laughed then—in the back of her throat, the way Miles loved to hear her laugh—as he dispensed with one article of apparel after another on their way to the bedroom. By the time they fell onto the bed in a tangle of arms and legs, clothing was the last thing on their minds.

Miles brought his mouth down on hers in a concentrated kiss as he slipped his arms around her slender body. He rolled over onto his back, taking Alyssa with him.

She looked down at him with smiling eyes. "Sir, it is the middle of the morning."

"Madam, you are forever telling me what an excellent rider you are, how well you sit in the saddle, how much you enjoy a vigorous morning outing," he murmured playfully, his attention—and his hands—going to the pair of lovely breasts before him, their pink tips the very essence of temptation.

Miles did not—indeed, could not—resist temptation. He reached up and pulled her down toward him, taking her between his lips and drawing her into his mouth.

"Husband, what can you be thinking of?" Alyssa remarked somewhat breathlessly, although he noticed she did not pull away.

Miles arched one dark eyebrow. " 'Gather ye rosebuds while ye may.' "

Alyssa laughed with pleasure. She groaned with pleasure. She gave and he took with pleasure.

Sometimes a man could tell a woman he loved her by making her feel desirable, beautiful, irresistible.

As he settled Alyssa astride his hips and moved beneath her, surging up into her, joining their flesh, he whispered to her, "I see only you, my lady."

"I see only you, my lord knight," she whispered back.

"What are you thinking of, my lord?" Alyssa inquired as she nuzzled his neck later. "You have such an expression of serious concern on your face."

How did a man tell a woman he loved her?

Miles frowned. "I was thinking about the masque," he made up on the spur of the moment.

Alyssa laughed at him. "The masque?"

"We will need to do some recasting, I fear, madam," he told her as if it were a matter of some importance.

"I suppose we will, sir. For one thing we no longer have at least two of the three Chubbs."

"We may still have Charmel as Juliet."

"We may."

"Your part must change, of course."

"Why?"

"You do not make a convincing nun," he stated as she lay curled up in the crook of his arm.

"You thought so once," Alyssa teased.

"Only for an instant that first day." Miles took a deep breath. "I wonder if that's when it all started."

"If that's when *what* started?"

"I wonder if that's when I first started to fall in love with you," he murmured, dropping a kiss on the tip of her upturned nose. "I love you, Alyssa."

"I know. And I love you, Miles." Her eyes were shining with the truth of it.

How did a man tell a woman that he loved her?

He simply told her, Miles St. Aldford realized with a contented sigh.

Epilogue

From a "mention" in the *Morning Post,*
London, September 12, 1878

. . . spotted in Venice recently were the Marquess
and Marchioness of Cork, according to a reliable
source. Lord and Lady Cork are on an extended
tour of the Continent following their "Midsummer Night's" wedding, still the talk of Polite
Society.

In addition to Venice, the couple's honeymoon
itinerary is said to include: Milan, Rome, Florence,
Barcelona, Granada, Segovia, Madrid, Lisbon, Nice
and Paris, as well as the more exotic ports of call
of Athens, Istanbul, Alexandria and Cairo. Their
Grand Tour is to conclude with sailing through the
Greek Isles aboard the *Alicia Anne,* the magnificent
yacht belonging to the Duke of Deakin.

The Marquess and Marchioness are reportedly returning to Cork Castle for the holidays, where they
will be joined by Their Graces, the Duke and Duchess of Deakin; the Duke's younger brother, Viscount
Wicke and Lady Wicke; James Gray, Earl of
Graystone, and uncle to the new marchioness; and

the latest sensation of the London Shakespearean Theatre, Mister Hortense Horatio Blunt and his fiancée, Miss Emma Pibble, daughter of the late Captain Ardmore Pibble of the Royal Navy.

A Word About Old Roses

Old Roses bloom but once a season, but they are a true miracle to behold in the garden. The rose dates from ancient times and has long been associated with the concept of romantic love. The earliest known representation of a rose was discovered in Crete sometime around 2000 B.C.

Milady's Tears grows only within the walls of Graystone Abbey in the heart of the Devon countryside. But a hybrid of the original bush—*Milady's Joy*—flourishes in the magnificent rose gardens at Cork Castle.

Milady's Joy is a pale white rose of delicate features, but with a surprising strength of character and a heart of gold.

◆T◆ TOPAZ

PASSION RIDES THE PAST

☐ **TIMELESS by Jasmine Cresswell.** Robyn Delany is a thoroughly modern woman who doesn't believe in the supernatural ... and is beginning to believe that true love is just as much of a fantasy until she is thrust into 18th-century England. (404602—$4.99)

☐ **THE RAVEN'S WISH by Susan King.** Elspeth Fraser was blessed with the magical gift of Sight, but what she saw when she first encountered the mysterious Duncan Macrae filled her with dread, especially when their growing passion for each other ignited—a passion which she knew could only prove fatal. (405455—$4.99)

☐ **NO BRIGHTER DREAM by Katherine Kingsley.** When Andre de Saint-Simon discovers that Ali, the mysterious young woman whose life he has saved while on his travels, is the long-lost daughter of his mentor, he promptly returns her to England. But Ali knows that Andre is her destiny and arranges his marriage—to herself. (405129—$4.99)

☐ **NO SWEETER HEAVEN by Katherine Kingsley.** Pascal LaMartine and Elizabeth Bowes had nothing in common until the day she accidentally landed at his feet, and looked up into the face of a fallen angel. Drawn in to a dangerous battle of intrigue and wits, each discovered how strong passion was ... and how perilous it can be. (403665—$4.99)

*Prices slightly higher in Canada

Buy them at your local bookstore or use this convenient coupon for ordering.

PENGUIN USA
P.O. Box 999 — Dept. #17109
Bergenfield, New Jersey 07621

Please send me the books I have checked above.
I am enclosing $＿＿＿＿＿ (please add $2.00 to cover postage and handling). Send check or money order (no cash or C.O.D.'s) or charge by Mastercard or VISA (with a $15.00 minimum). Prices and numbers are subject to change without notice.

Card #＿＿＿＿＿＿＿＿＿＿ Exp. Date ＿＿＿＿＿＿
Signature＿＿＿＿＿＿＿＿＿＿＿＿＿＿＿＿
Name＿＿＿＿＿＿＿＿＿＿＿＿＿＿＿＿＿
Address＿＿＿＿＿＿＿＿＿＿＿＿＿＿＿＿
City ＿＿＿＿＿＿ State ＿＿＿＿ Zip Code ＿＿＿＿

For faster service when ordering by credit card call **1-800-253-6476**

Allow a minimum of 4-6 weeks for delivery. This offer is subject to change without notice.

⟁ TOPAZ

SEARING ROMANCES

☐ **TEMPTING FATE by Jaclyn Reding.** Beautiful, flame-haired Mara Despenser hated the English under Oliver Cromwell, and she vowed to avenge Ireland and become mistress of Kulhaven Castle again. She would lure the castle's new master, the infamous Hadrian Ross, the bastard Earl of St. Aubyn, into marriage. But even with her lies and lust, Mara was not prepared to find herself wed to a man whose iron will was matched by his irresistible good looks.   (405587—$4.99)

☐ **SPRING'S FURY by Denise Domning.** Nicola of Ashby swore to kill Gilliam Fitz-Henry—murderer of her father, destroyer of her home—the man who would wed her in a forced match. Amid treachery and tragedy, rival knights and the pain of past wounds, Gilliam knew he must win Nicola's respect. Then, with kisses and hot caresses, he intended to win her heart.   (405218—$4.99)

☐ **PIRATE'S ROSE by Janet Lynnford.** The Rozalinde Cavendish, independent daughter of England's richest merchant, was taking an impetuous moonlit walk along the turbulent shore when she encountered Lord Christopher Howard, a legendary pirate. Carried aboard his ship, she entered his storm-tossed world and became intimate with his troubled soul. Could their passion burn away the veil shrouding Christopher's secret past and hidden agenda?   (405978—$4.99)

☐ **DIAMOND IN DISGUISE by Elizabeth Hewitt.** Isobel Leyland knew better than to fall in love with the handsome stranger from America, Adrian Renville. Despite his rugged good looks and his powerful animal magnetism, he was socially inept compared to the polished dandies of English aristocratic society—and a citizen of England's enemy in the War of 1812. How could she trust this man whom she suspected of playing the boor in a mocking masquerade?   (405641—$4.99)

*Prices slightly higher in Canada

Buy them at your local bookstore or use this convenient coupon for ordering.

PENGUIN USA
P.O. Box 999 — Dept. #17109
Bergenfield, New Jersey 07621

Please send me the books I have checked above.
I am enclosing $_____ (please add $2.00 to cover postage and handling). Send check or money order (no cash or C.O.D.'s) or charge by Mastercard or VISA (with a $15.00 minimum). Prices and numbers are subject to change without notice.

Card #_____ Exp. Date _____
Signature_____
Name_____
Address_____
City _____ State _____ Zip Code _____

For faster service when ordering by credit card call **1-800-253-6476**

Allow a minimum of 4-6 weeks for delivery. This offer is subject to change without notice.

〽️ TOPAZ

PASSION'S PROMISES

☐ **THE TOPAZ MAN FAVORITES: SECRETS OF THE HEART Five Stories by Madeline Baker, Jennifer Blake, Georgina Gentry, Shirl Henke, and Patricia Rice.** In this collection of romances, the Topaz Man has gathered together stories from five of his favorite authors—tales which he truly believes capture all the passion and promise of love.
(405528—$4.99)

☐ **DASHING AND DANGEROUS Five Sinfully Seductive Heroes by Mary Balogh, Edith Layton, Melinda McRae, Anita Mills, Mary Jo Putney.** They're shameless, seductive, and steal your heart with a smile. Now these irresistible rogues, rakes, rebels, and renegades are captured in five all new, deliciously sexy stories by America's favorite authors of romantic fiction.
(405315—$4.99)

☐ **BLOSSOMS Five Stories Mary Balogh, Patricia Rice, Margaret Evans Porter, Karen Harper, Patricia Oliver.** Celebrate the arrival of spring with a bouquet of exquisite stories by five acclaimed authors of romantic fiction. Full of passion and promise, scandal and heartache, and rekindled desire, these heartfelt tales prove that spring is a time for new beginnings as well as second chances.
(182499—$4.99)

☐ **THE TOPAZ MAN PRESENTS: A DREAM COME TRUE** Here is a collection of love stories from such authors as Jennifer Blake, Georgina Gentry, Shirl Henke, Anita Mills, and Becky Lee Weyrich. Each story is unique, and each author has a special way of making dreams come true.
(404513—$4.99)

*Prices slightly higher in Canada

Buy them at your local bookstore or use this convenient coupon for ordering.

PENGUIN USA
P.O. Box 999 — Dept. #17109
Bergenfield, New Jersey 07621

Please send me the books I have checked above.
I am enclosing $_____ (please add $2.00 to cover postage and handling). Send check or money order (no cash or C.O.D.'s) or charge by Mastercard or VISA (with a $15.00 minimum). Prices and numbers are subject to change without notice.

Card #_____ Exp. Date _____
Signature_____
Name_____
Address_____
City _____ State _____ Zip Code _____

For faster service when ordering by credit card call **1-800-253-6476**

Allow a minimum of 4-6 weeks for delivery. This offer is subject to change without notice.

◤◢ TOPAZ

WONDERFUL LOVE STORIES

☐ **SECRET NIGHTS by Anita Mills.** Elise Rand had once been humiliated by her father's attempt to arrange a marriage for her with London's most brilliant and ambitious criminal lawyer, Patrick Hamilton. Hamilton wanted her, but as a mistress, not a wife. Now she was committed to a desperate act—giving her body to Hamilton if he would defend her father in a scandalous case of murder.
(404815—$4.99)

☐ **A LIGHT FOR MY LOVE by Alexis Harrington.** Determined to make the beautiful China Sullivan forget the lonely hellion he'd once been, Jake Chastaine must make her see the new man he'd become. But even as love begins to heal the wounds of the past, Jake must battle a new obstacle—a danger that threatens to destroy all they hold dear.
(405013—$4.99)

☐ **THE WARFIELD BRIDE by Bronwyn Williams.** None of the Warfield brothers expected Hannah Ballinger to change their lives; none of them expected the joy she and her new baby would bring to their household. But most of all, Penn never expected to lose his heart to the woman he wanted his brother to marry—a mail order bride. "Delightful, heartwarming, a winner!—Amanda Quick (404556—$4.99)

☐ **GATEWAY TO THE HEART by Barbara Cockrell.** A lyrical and deeply moving novel of an indomitable woman who will win your heart and admiration—and make your spirit soar with the triumph of love in frontier St. Louis. (404998—$4.99)

*Prices slightly higher in Canada

Buy them at your local bookstore or use this convenient coupon for ordering.

PENGUIN USA
P.O. Box 999 — Dept. #17109
Bergenfield, New Jersey 07621

Please send me the books I have checked above.
I am enclosing $_____ (please add $2.00 to cover postage and handling). Send check or money order (no cash or C.O.D.'s) or charge by Mastercard or VISA (with a $15.00 minimum). Prices and numbers are subject to change without notice.

Card #_____ Exp. Date _____
Signature_____
Name_____
Address_____
City _____ State _____ Zip Code _____

For faster service when ordering by credit card call **1-800-253-6476**

Allow a minimum of 4-6 weeks for delivery. This offer is subject to change without notice.

Don't go to bed without Romance...

♥ **150 BOOK REVIEWS AND RATINGS**
> *CONTEMPORARY*
> *HISTORICAL*
> *TIME - TRAVEL*

♥ **AUTHOR PROFILES**

♥ **PUBLISHERS PREVIEWS**

♥ **MARKET NEWS**

♥ **TIPS ON WRITING BESTSELLING ROMANCES**

Read *Romantic Times* Magazine
122 page Monthly Magazine • 6 issues $21
Sample Issue $4.00   (718) 237-1097
Send Order To: Romantic Times
55 Bergen St., Brooklyn, NY 11201

I enclose $_____ in ❑ check ❑ money order

Credit Card#_____ Exp. Date_____

Tel_____

Name_____

Address_____

City_____ State_____ Zip_____